# Five Alarm Fire

Nicole Dixon

Copyright © 2024 Nicole Dixon

Lucky Thirteen Publishing, LLC

All rights reserved.

ISBN: 9798874097004

# ACKNOWLEDGMENTS

Every book that I write has a special place in my heart. They are bits and pieces of me mixed with a story that is only mine to tell.

J. My heart. My inspiration. The man who welcomes countless people that only exist in my brain into our family without question. I love you for always. I will always be down for testing out scenes with you as I write them. *wink*

Mom. My biggest fan. I will never get tired of hearing you brag about how cool your kids are to total strangers. We're only cool because we have cool parents.

Beth. My sounding board. To the woman who calls me on all of my bullshit and does it nicely with a smile. I love you.

Julia. Thank you for pulling me from the depths of a book hangover I couldn't seem to shake. This book wouldn't have happened without you. Love you big.

Kyndall. To the woman who selflessly destroys my books with a red ink pen and does it all in the name of love and family. You will never know how much your help means to me.

Rhonda, my beta readers, and ARC team – you're my found family. Kind of like the characters in these books. I appreciate you more than words can express. And that's saying a lot.

My readers. I can't believe how far we've come together. Thanks for hanging with me from the very beginning, when I was winging it and praying that I didn't fall flat on my face. Who am I kidding? I'm still winging it. You guys are awesome. Let's keep doing this together. It's fun.

*XOXO, Nicole*

Five Alarm Fire

# FIVE ALARM FIRE

*This is not a book about a firefighter.*

*If you're looking for that, this isn't the book for you.*

*This is a scorching hot romance novel that will smoke your panties and light a fire between your thighs.*

*If you're looking for that, you're in the right place.*

XOXO, Nicole

Five Alarm Fire

*Blood Runs Thin*

They say blood is thicker than water, but the betrayal of blood leaves you colder.

Sly like a fox, not an ounce of sincerity.

Fake like a Hollywood movie—no sign of integrity.

Cry like a wolf, squander like a sheep.

Lay your head down at night and wonder why you can't sleep.

Greed is a curse and money is a disease—it separates blood with much ease.

A knife in the back, words hit like a fist. You can't erase the hurt like it never exists.

The one you expect to have your back will help the enemy when you're under attack.

Run and tell, make your story fit.

Manipulate the others, they'll believe you for a bit.

At the end of the day, it's your narrative at stake…we all know you are nothing more than an exhausting fake.

- *Jacob Dixon*

Five Alarm Fire

# PROLOGUE
# TUCK

*Cassandra Elyse Stafford,*

*We have some things to discuss. I'm sorry I had to trash your place to find this. This journal confirmed what I thought all along. I'm not who you assume I am, and yet I am exactly the man you think. Consider this your formal invitation. I'm leaving you my number.*
*You have sixty days.*

*Your dearest brother,*
*Tucker Stafford*

I finish scrolling my name and place the cap back on my fine tip, black ink pen, sliding it into the pocket of my gray slacks with haste.

I quickly scan back over the words I've jotted down in the diary I was finally able to locate, hidden beneath the mattress of her bed. I look around at the complete and utter disaster I've left in her apartment. Maybe I should have started in the bedroom.

My words sound menacing enough to garner her attention.

I don't have time to dwell. I've already been here too long. The ball is in her court. Now, I wait and hope that I've done enough. I shove the diary back beneath the mattress. It's the only item I've left where it originally belonged…whoops.

It had to be done.

I close my eyes briefly and remind myself of all the reasons that I'm doing this. I'm risking everything.

*The rose.*

My father is a man of many secrets. He's made a name for himself as a highly successful real estate investor. Rubbing elbows with the social elite will get you everywhere. Trading dollar signs for souls might give you worldly prestige, but it will also guarantee your spot in Hell.

I'm the youngest, the baby of the Stafford family. One of three.

That's what my father would have the public believe, anyway. It's a farce.

I've been searching for the truth since I was five years old. I know what you're thinking, really Tucker, five years old? Yes. I'm haunted by a woman I've never formally met. Her story changed my life. Since that moment, I've refused to sleep on my relentless journey for the truth. My father must be brought to justice for his actions. His list of indiscretions spans so much further than this single woman.

Unfortunately, events of late have sped up my process of exposing Hilton Stafford as the man he truly is. The man who raised me is not a good man. Greed, infidelity, you name it. He traded his soul to the Devil long before I was born.

He's a narcissist at best. At worst, he's a cold-blooded murderer.

Now, he's running for Senator, and I can't allow that to happen. Simple as that. I'm no fool. I recognize the plot of corruption buried beneath a façade of democracy. Someone has to expose the truth, it's me. I'm someone.

I'm not the person they think I am. I'm an imposter in my own life—a spy. Risking it all for truth and honor. Something my dear ol' dad would know nothing about. I'm a journalist, I write what I see. I seek the truth in a sea of lies that I've been privy to my entire life.

Up until this point, I've worked alone. I thought I could do this by myself. I can't. I've hit a wall. I can admit when I need help.

I need someone with unmatched legal intelligence. I need someone willing to fight for what's right, even if it means taking down an elite empire. I need someone who is not afraid of my father, or his money.

I need someone willing to watch the world burn for vengeance.

I need Cassandra Elyse Stafford—my sister.

# CHAPTER ONE
# TUCKER
*A few-ish months earlier...*

"Hilton Tucker Stafford you have the right to remain silent..." I roll my wrists, and the cold metal bites into my skin.

"No, thanks." I don't look up. I kick small rocks on the cracked asphalt with the heel of my black combat boots.

Catching movement in my periphery, my attention is diverted from the burly cop I'm currently choosing to ignore. This man has clearly eaten one too many donuts in his career and neglects his knowledge of current events. His belly juts out awkwardly between us.

Instead, my eyes are drawn upward to soot-covered blonde hair. The woman standing adjacent to us is what I would describe as petite. The top of her head barely meets my shoulders. Her ponytail sits slightly askew on top of her head. Loose strands fall around her face in messy disarray. Her soft pale skin is tinged with dirt that matches the grime on my exposed forearms.

She shouldn't be dirty or grimy, not under these circumstances. It bothers me. I don't like it. What's worse? I'm not sure why. I have no ties to her or any woman for that matter. I'm here to do a job—nothing more, nothing less.

She's wearing a pair of blue jeans that hug the slight curves of her narrow hips and an oversized t-shirt. In truth, the shirt is probably of standard sizing, but it swallows her small frame and leaves everything above her waistline to the imagination. I've always enjoyed surprises.

*Not why you're here, Tuck. Focus.*

She wasn't supposed to be here tonight. That's a surprise I could have done without.

My plan went to complete shit, and now the file folders I was searching for have no doubt gone up in a plume of smoke. I had one job: find them, confirm the name, verify the date, and get the hell out of town.

Water runs in steady streams along the concrete where we stand. Smoke saturates the air and swirls around us, coating the inside of our lungs with a slow poison that will no doubt leave us both coughing for days. Firefighters continue to battle the blaze that lights up the night sky and casts an eerie glow over what is typically a quaint street. The men in filthy turnout gear all but ignore us as they try to salvage what's left of Hydrangea & Vine, a flower shop in a small town about thirty minutes outside of the city.

"You've got the wrong guy, he's not Hilton Stafford!"

I'm taken aback as a growl rolls effortlessly up from her throat. She's defensive on my behalf, which surprises me because she doesn't have a damn clue as to why I'm here tonight, invading her space and endangering her life.

I try not to react, hearing her say my father's name so callously.

It's comical that she thinks they'd arrest Hilton. A world does not yet exist where Hilton Stafford is cuffed and led to prison. *One day.*

I stare into her blue eyes. They're light blue, like a cloudless sky on a hot summer day. The clarity that I see there speaks volumes about her. She's pure. Ballsy as hell, but pure. "No, I'm not. I'm Tuck. Tucker Stafford." I grunt out the words.

No use trying to hide my identity. I've been in the tabloids enough that I'm easily recognizable. That, and I'm not beyond using any means to get out of the predicament I've found myself in. Using my name is at the top of that list. I don't have time to deal with this tonight. I'm going to have a hard enough time explaining this if and when word gets back to my father.

I might be a grown-ass man, but my age will never matter to Hilton. He demands control of everyone and everything around him. Fall in line or die. There is no in-between. I'm searching for my freedom, but until that day comes, I prefer to live.

The medics try to direct my new acquaintance into a waiting ambulance, but she pulls away, refusing any part of it. I casually prop myself up against the patrol car, handcuffed. I think they've figured out that I'm not a flight risk and, despite the cop's best attempts, the chaos surrounding us continues to intermittently pull his attention away from me.

Slowly, she approaches where I stand. "I'm Daisy. You say your name like it earns you free drinks." She stops about a foot away and sticks out her hand. I lift an eyebrow, as she waits for a handshake that I am currently unable to accommodate in my state of incapacitation.

Realizing her mistake, she quickly drops her hand but doesn't move. A blush creeps up her neck and colors her cheeks. The contrast against her skin is obvious even in the darkness, lit only by the lights of the emergency vehicles surrounding us.

"I know exactly who you are. Go with the medics, Daisy." I nod my chin in the direction of the waiting paramedics. They're looking increasingly more annoyed by the minute. She needs to go. Having her here will only complicate things further.

The cop that cuffed me ducks into the cab of his patrol car to answer an incoming call on his radio. With any luck, I won't be in these cuffs much longer.

Daisy huffs and I follow her eyes to the cop behind me. I see the determination as it settles across her features. She takes a step past me. My hands are tied. I can't do anything to stop the impending trainwreck.

"Daisy," I say her name again as she passes me, this time in warning, but she completely ignores me.

"Excuse me. Excuse me, sir." She walks up directly behind the cop and taps him on the shoulder.

Jesus, does she have no self-preservation skills? Is she trying to get herself thrown into jail tonight? First the fire and now this.

"Step away, ma'am. Hands where I can see them." He turns and she backs up one step, barely giving his enlarged gut enough room between the two of them.

"I'm warning you, ma'am. Take a step back." He reaches for his belt, and I know he's getting ready to apprehend her. From all observations, she's harmless. She's completely unarmed unless you count the mouth she's got on her.

"No, you aren't listening. You've got the wrong guy. You can't just come into my flower shop and arrest the man who saved my life and, quite possibly, my entire future." I watch utterly bewildered as she lifts her hand between them and, using her delicate finger, pokes him directly in the chest.

His eyes follow mine. I think he's stunned.

"This flower shop belongs to Hilton Stafford, miss…?" He looks from her finger, which is still glued to his bullet-proof vest, and back up to her eyes. She doesn't allow him to finish before she's already interrupting him again.

"Chandler. Daisy Mae Chandler. This is my shop. I've worked here my entire life. My aunt owned it before me, and my grandmother before her. With all due respect, you don't know what you're talking about." Her words are clipped with certainty.

I wish she were right. I get the feeling that the truth will break her heart.

Despite what she says, he's not wrong. The flower shop does belong to my father, unfortunately. That's why I'm here, in the middle of the night, on what was a vacant street just an hour ago.

"Daisy. Go with the medics. Now." I repeat.

Pushing off of the patrol vehicle, I maneuver my body into the practically nonexistent space between them. I try to communicate with her using my eyes, but she's not taking my cues.

"I won't stand for this. Fine. Cuff me." She yells at the cop over my shoulder, and I hang my head in defeat. I can strike telepathy from the list of skills on my resume.

She can't obey for one second. I'm equal parts intrigued and fucking pissed. This is the thanks I get for pulling her out of that damn fire.

"Daisy…" I groan under my breath.

"I really don't want to do this, ma'am."

I give up and step out of the way when the cop behind me begins to move. She made her bed. I tried.

I look over just in time to see Daisy lift her hands on her hips. She straightens her spine and gains, eh, maybe a quarter of an inch on her small frame.

"You let him go, or you take the both of us. You're tired, aren't you? I bet you're ready to get off your shift. Hungry? Well, guess what? You arrest me too, and you'll be doing paperwork until lunchtime tomorrow. Sounds fun, huh? I mean, honestly, what did we do? This guy saved my life, and I'm merely a target in a fire that stole everything I had left in this world that mattered. Do you really want to choose to be the bad guy tonight? Officer…" She leans into his space again, completely unphased by his uniform and threats of apprehension. "Officer *Remington*." She reads off.

His chest rises and falls as he stares at her in astonishment that matches my own.

"Dispatch says you're clear to go Mr. Stafford. Please send our apologies to your father."

Slowly, he extricates himself from her imposing finger and steps behind me, uncuffing me. I shake out the cramping in my wrists as he turns back to Daisy.

"Looks like I only have paperwork for one after all." Holding the handcuffs that he just removed from my wrists, Officer Remington dangles them from his finger as he speaks to Daisy.

I should walk down that street, hop on my motorcycle and get the hell out of here. Every second I stand here is one more second that I'll have to answer for later. I don't owe this woman anything. I'm a stranger to her—mostly. She seemed to recognize my father's name, which doesn't necessarily bode well for me from any angle.

I didn't get what I came here for, but it's gone now. It's too late. I need to cut my losses and find another way.

I'm sweating. My shirt is soaked through and sticks to my skin uncomfortably. Heat from the blaze radiates across the street and licks at my skin, the thought of what could have been taunting me in the back of my mind.

I take a step off of the sidewalk.

Fuck it.

The smoke has gotten to me. I've lost my damn mind.

"She's coming with me," I say as I backtrack until I'm once again standing next to Daisy. She holds her wrists out in front of her body, ready and waiting to be cuffed for no reason. Who does that? The only thing she's guilty of is talking too damn much.

"You sure about that?" The cop eyes me skeptically, but his lips tip up into a grin that says he'd rather send her with me than shove her into his vehicle when there's a full-fledged fire behind us threatening to burn down half of Main Street.

"I'll take her home," I reiterate reluctantly.

She looks up at me like she wants to challenge me but, given her options, I'm her best bet at the moment. I cut my eyes in her direction. For once, please, just fucking keep quiet.

"Thank you, Mr. Stafford. Have a good night. We should have a report ready with the cause of the fire within forty-eight hours; we're making this a priority." Officer Remington tips his hat in my direction, a complete one-eighty in his demeanor from the moment he slapped the cuffs on me. Funny how things work when your last name is Stafford.

Taking Daisy's hand in mine, I waste no time tugging her down the street behind me. It feels like days have passed, not just a few hours. This was supposed to be a quick stop.

With each step I take I become more aware of my skin touching hers. I don't drop her hand. I can't risk letting her run back toward the blaze. The hair on my arms prickles with awareness of our proximity.

The shock will wear off and she'll realize that her beloved flower shop is gone. I don't want to have to answer for that. Honestly, I have no answers to give, only suspicions.

"Who do you think you—" She lifts onto the tips of her sneakers and hisses the words as close to my ear as her lack of height will allow. I feel the heat of her breath on my neck. The meaning in her words comes across loud and clear. She's angry with me for saving her ass not once, but twice.

"Shut your mouth, Daisy, before I shut it for you." I lean into her space, cutting her off before she can continue. This isn't the time or place for this discussion.

Her quick intake of breath is audible. It can be heard even amongst the chaos that surrounds us. I lead her down the street, further away from the fire, and turn left down an abandoned alleyway. When we reach my motorcycle, carefully hidden behind a large green dumpster, I drop her hand and snatch up the helmet from the seat.

Her mouth pops open as I shove the helmet onto her head in one swift motion. Gripping her hips in my hands, I lift her onto the seat, forcing her to straddle the bike. Am I being a touch overly aggressive? Maybe. But I'm not taking any chances with this one. She's unpredictable at best, a fucking grenade at worst – and we've only just met.

She scoots back as I make room for myself in front of her. Her thighs grip my hips, and I try not to let my mind wander to places it's not allowed.

"You don't know where I live." She leans over my shoulder as I grip the handlebars with white knuckles.

"I make it my job to know everything."

# CHAPTER TWO
# DAISY

**I** think I'm being kidnapped.

My throat burns from smoke inhalation. My eyes itch. I'm positive I've never looked worse. I didn't expect to see anyone tonight so I chose comfort, not aesthetics. It was supposed to be me and the floral arrangements I was working on for a wedding in the city this weekend. That wedding was my big break. It was supposed to put my tiny flower shop on the map.

*Ugh.* This has been a really fucking long day. The longest.

The wind hits my face as we fly down Main Street. I don't turn around. I can't look back. My life is up in flames. Literally.

Come to think of it, looking at my current situation, being kidnapped by a smoldering man on a motorcycle is better than the alternative of facing what my reality has become.

This man is smoldering in both the figurative and literal sense of the word. I kind of love that for him. Or I would, if I didn't have so many questions.

None of which I can ask, as my words are silenced the moment the beast between my thighs roars to life and I'm forced to wrap my arms around the strong, solid torso of a man that shares a name with a man that I detest.

*Stafford.*

Gross.

That man is a total creep, the absolute slimiest of slimy. He's nothing at all like the man that sits between my thighs…at least I hope he's not. Despite my complete and utter exhaustion, tingles light up my belly like fireflies caught in a mason jar as the black denim on his scrumptious-looking ass vibrates against my nether regions. This is the most action I've seen in months…okay, fine, *years.* Yeah, I checked him out while he was handcuffed earlier. Judge me all you want; I do not care in the slightest.

The men I see on a daily basis are either taken, don't swing in my direction or they're big fat jerks. Those are the three options you get in a flower shop.

Speaking of jerks, Hilton Stafford has been coming to my family's shop for years and he is the biggest jerk of them all. My earliest memories of him date back to when my mom was still alive. Every week it was a different order. Every week a different flower. But the absolute worst part about it? With each change in flower came a change in addressee. Aunt Fran swore she'd never seen a man with so many mistresses.

She was always so nice to the old goat. When I finally

got the nerve to ask her about it, her eyes darkened. She turned more serious than I'd ever seen her. She gripped my hands in hers and made me swear that I'd always treat him just like all of our other customers. She made me promise to always be kind and respectful, even though he never said thank you, and not once did he slip money into the tip jar at the register.

And I have. I've always been cordial. I'm not willing to lose that kind of repeat business, even if I can't stand the guy. Do I conveniently forget to put the flower food in with his weekly order? Maybe.

The man drips money, and he can't bother himself to slip a Lincoln into the tip jar on occasion? That tells me everything I need to know about him.

*The tip jar.* Ugh, it's probably gone now too.

I'm not sure what it says about me, but the fact that my livelihood is now a smoking pile of ash barely registers on my Richter scale of bad luck. It's like I've come to expect anything that I love or care about to be completely obliterated at a moment's notice.

My life is so far from perfect it's almost laughable. We could call it...a series of unfortunate events. That'd be putting it lightly.

But I am no pessimist. I refuse to admit defeat. My glass is half full, and I'm chugging a margarita dammit.

Regrettably, alcohol is probably off the table tonight, given the current state of my damaged esophagus. Which brings me back to the entire reason I'm speeding through the night on a death trap on wheels with a potential kidnapper...or arsonist. Why else was he at my shop in the middle of the night at the exact moment a fire broke out in the loading bay?

We turn down the street I grew up on. I've lived here almost my entire life, in this small bungalow that's like my very own security blanket. A few years back, I inherited it from my aunt. If Aunt Fran could see me now…she'd probably give me a high five and hand me a strip of condoms. She was the best kind of aunt; she was my best friend.

After my parents died, it was Aunt Fran who took me in – no questions asked. I was six. My parents were mugged while out on a rare date night in the city. In my dreams I like to imagine that my dad died a hero, defending my mom against their attacker. No one knows for sure, but I'm certain that's how it happened. They were victims of a senseless crime. *Victims*, I hate that word.

Back then, mom and Aunt Fran ran the shop together. When my parents died, there was no one else. My aunt took me in and raised me as her own while single-handedly running the family business. She never married, never had any children. It was the two of us against the world. Until it wasn't anymore. Cancer's a bitch that takes no prisoners.

Now it's just me, against the world…and the world packs a mean fucking punch when your name is Daisy Mae Chandler.

Brown eyes turn back to look at me. The moment they meet mine, I realize we've come to a complete stop. How long have we been sitting here? He smiles, and it's handsome and dangerous. I'm shaken from my thoughts. *Tucker Stafford.*

"Go inside, Daisy." He nods toward my front door, but I don't budge. For whatever reason, I can't seem to get my legs to work. I don't like being ordered around; it irks me.

Cutting the engine on the motorcycle, he lets out a frustrated groan that echoes throughout the empty street. It's still dark out. If I had to guess, it's probably closer to morning than night. I left my phone back in the shop. If I were a betting person, which I'm not, because I'm basically the unluckiest person on the planet, I'd bet it's a goner along with my purse and everything else I had with me. It'll all need to be replaced. That's a problem for tomorrow. Or today. Whichever day it is. Luckily, I keep a spare house key stowed away under one of the flowerpots on my front porch.

"Do you ever do as you're told?" His knee brushes my leg and sends a zap of electricity straight up my calf.

He extricates himself from the clutches of my thighs and stands. He waits beside where he's parked the motorcycle next to the curb, and the impatience radiates from him so strongly that I feel like I can actually hear it.

"When it fits my agenda." I shrug and spin my body to one side, lifting my leg up and over the seat but not yet standing. I've got to find some strength from somewhere, but I just can't muster it at the moment.

"You almost got yourself arrested back there." He grabs the bulky helmet that I somehow managed to forget I was wearing and pulls it off of my head with a quick tug. My hair falls into my eyes, the ponytail elastic I was using earlier having finally given up. Maybe that's a sign that I need to give up too.

Maybe I should give up fighting the Universe and admit defeat. Maybe that would be easier than living in this constant battle and never winning.

"Why do you know where I live?" I blurt out the first of many questions that I need immediate answers to.

"We don't need to have a conversation, Daisy. You don't need to know who I am. Forget my name. Forget this night ever happened." He avoids my question altogether. He steps to the side, motioning up the stone path to my front door as if to hurry me along.

"Right, I'll just go inside and snuggle up in my comfy bed. I'll dream about sugar plum fairies and rainbow unicorn farts. Then I'll wake up and go to work and…oh wait, I can't." I cross my arms over my chest, irritated that he thinks he can make all of the rules here. Who does this guy think he is?

Lifting his hand to his chin, he rubs the stubble that peppers his jawline. He thinks before saying, "I'm sorry about that."

Sounds like sincerity, but I'm not buying it. I suspect he's just a really good faker.

"No, you're not." Calling his bluff, I stand from the motorcycle and straighten to my full height. All five feet and two inches. This guy's got a full twelve inches on me, but I've got news for him, my blonde hair doesn't come from a bottle, and I have blue eyes that'll swindle a car salesman with a single wink. He doesn't intimidate me.

After everything I've gone through in my life? Honey, please. Not much intimidates me anymore.

I live for the motto…*how much worse can it get?*

Try me.

"What, you think it was me? You think I set the fire to your beloved flower shop?" He dares to look surprised at my suspicions. If it quacks like a duck...it's a duck.

*Waddle, waddle.*

"Why else were you out in the middle of the night snooping around my shop?" Finally, I ask the question that's been driving me crazy. I need answers. This complete stranger swooped in out of thin air and carried me out of the flames as I fought a losing battle, but...why? Why was he there?

I don't make enough money to employ anyone. There's too much to do and not enough time to do it. I do my best work in the middle of the night. I can think when everything's quiet, and there's no one to interrupt me. It's so much harder to focus in the middle of the day when customers are constantly coming in and out of the shop.

"I've already told you. We shouldn't be having this conversation." His words are clipped and rigid, and it bothers me that he continues to dismiss my questions so easily. If he didn't want to have this conversation, he should have just let Officer Remington take me in.

"Then stop talking!" I throw my hands up and push past him, stomping up the path to my front porch.

I fully expect to hear his motorcycle tear out in the distance after my little outburst, but for a moment, it's deceptively quiet.

"Wait!" He yells after me. His voice is so loud that I fear he's woken every person on the entire block.

This is a safe neighborhood. I am the vice president of the Neighborhood Crime Watch group. How would it look if I were caught out gallivanting in the middle of the night with a potential arsonist?

Sure, I almost got myself arrested defending this man less than an hour ago, but that was brazen Daisy in the heat of the moment protecting my savior. That was noble. Now that I'm home and we're back on my street and this man might actually be an arsonist, I can't risk being seen like this. Especially when he continues to evade my questions.

Why? I'm thinking of a six-letter word that starts with the letter *g* (u-i-l-t-y).

I spin on the toes of my sneakers, losing my balance and nearly toppling over my gerbera daisies. I just planted these flowerbeds last week. My breath catches in my lungs. That was a close call.

"For what?" I whisper-shout back at him as I attempt to regain my footing. For someone who swears he doesn't want to talk to me, I can't seem to get this man to leave.

Slipping his hands into the front pockets of his jeans and rocking back on the heels of his boots, he stands in front of his motorcycle. His brows pinch together in thought, but he says nothing.

"Spit it out." I reiterate, irritation coloring my voice the longer he stares at me. I don't know how much more I can handle tonight. I'm maxed out.

"I need a favor," he releases a loud sigh. Like he can't believe he's asking me for anything. Shock me silly. I'm almost as surprised as he is. I pop my hip out, shifting my weight to one leg. Look who's got the upper hand now.

"Why should I help you? You're a criminal." I smirk

with all of the sass that I can garner given my limited capacity for dealing with bullshit at the moment.

His eyes narrow. In two strides he's standing in front of me again. The tips of his boots touch my sneakers. I have to look up to meet his eyes. Welp, there he goes. He's smoldering again, and it's melting my insides. Sheesh, I have got to get out more.

"You've got it all wrong, Daisy Mae. I saved *you*. You owe *me*."

I think back to the fire. I was in the middle of a particularly intricate arrangement. My personal workstation is closer to the front of the shop so that I can simultaneously work and watch for customers during the day. Tonight though, it was empty. I was hyper-focused. The baby's breath accents the bride requested were really giving me a run for my money.

I didn't smell the smoke until it was too late. The fire was coming from the loading bay, quickly engulfing my supply room. Immediately I dropped everything and ran to the front door. It was locked. I couldn't see, I couldn't breathe. Panic raced through my veins. Every survival lesson taught to me in grade school went out the window with the billowing smoke. I couldn't find my keys, and the enraged flames were coming closer by the second.

Out of nowhere, a man appeared. Without a word, he pulled me into his arms and ran straight through the flames. Everything after that happened so fast. This is a small town. A single patrol car drives up and down Main Street at all hours of the night. It's one of the reasons I felt safe enough to work in the shop by myself at night.

This stranger…he ran, carrying me until we burst

from the back door out onto the asphalt. Our feet barely hit the sidewalk and sirens wailed in the distance. Police and fire rescue were called from neighboring towns.

Next thing I know, the man who saved me is being handcuffed by cops I don't recognize, and paramedics are trying to shove me into an ambulance.

So, maybe he's not wrong. He did save me. But why? And where did he come from if he wasn't the person who started the fire to begin with? He wants favors but won't give me any answers. How do I know I can trust him? What if I'm wrong and he is exactly like his creepy old man?

The answer is…I can't. I can't trust him.

"Excuse me? Say that again. One more time, for my cute little delicate ears." I bring my hand up to my ear, cupping it and leaning further into his space. The smell of burning wood, smoke and ash invades my senses and makes me woozy.

"You. Owe. Me. Daisy Mae." His words are a demand.

I'm slapped in the face by the audacity of this man. If he thinks that he can bully me into helping him with whatever it is that he needs help with, he's got another thing coming. I drop my hand and place it right back on my hip. I need the additional support for the rebuttal I am fully prepared to bring to this situation.

"Whew, for a minute there I thought you said I owed you something for burning my flower shop down…"

My words are stolen straight from my mouth. I don't have time to react. I'm yanked off balance. His large hand wraps around the back of my head and pulls me to him.

His fingers tangle in the mess that is my hair. The moment his lips touch mine, I sink into him. My body betrays me. His lips are warm and so much softer than I would have expected from someone so…grouchy and irritating.

My spine tingles, and I feel myself lift up onto my toes reaching higher, searching for more.

His tongue swipes at my lips, and I open for him, allowing him just a second to explore before I come to my ever-loving senses and realize that I'm kissing a vagabond right here in front of the dandelions. Who am I?

I push at his chest, and the moment is broken as he pulls away slowly. His lips tip up into a knowing grin, and that grin alone is exactly why I refuse to be indebted to this man.

"You didn't ask me if you could kiss me." I feign indignation or at the very least try to. I want to sound offended, disgusted even. But that's not how the words leave my lips. My voice betrays me. My words sound breathy, and I hate to even admit it, but…lustful.

I'm shocked by him. He's crass and bold when he shouldn't be, that's all. That coupled with the mixture of tonight's events is too much.

"You didn't ask me to save your ass tonight. Both things happened. I'm not mad about either of them. Now, about that favor. I need you to help me retrieve some records that I hope to God you have backed up on a drive somewhere."

My head spins like it's on a swivel, as I struggle to catch up. *Records?*

"Pretentious much? I mean, you say *records* like an old man with an expensive cigar habit. What gives? What the heck kind of records and backups are you looking for anyway? I don't have anything that belongs to you."

"On the contrary, I don't know what you're talking about, Daisy. I don't have an accent. This is the way I speak. Forgive me for having an education. It's the only damn thing my father gave me worth anything. Listen, you have files that I need to see. Information only you have access to."

"You've lost me, Tucker." I blow out a breath before continuing. "I'm trying, but I'm tired. You're making me work too hard to understand what the heck it is that you think you need from me. Can this not wait until I've slept at least an hour or ten?"

I give up. I surrender.

He makes a noncommittal sound in the back of his throat and takes a step back. "I'll swing by tomorrow around noon. I'll accompany you to assess the damage at the shop, and then we can discuss that favor."

I don't need his help, and I sure as hell don't need him to *accompany* me anywhere. Who says that? *Accompany*…like this is 1927.

"What if I don't want you to pick me up at noon? Did you consider that? Or were you too busy assaulting me with your tongue?" I fire back at him, but my words lack the intended heat. I'm tapped out.

Ignoring my continued protests, he walks back to his motorcycle and slides onto the seat.

"Noon, Daisy. Goodnight." He calls back over his shoulder before the engine of his motorcycle roars to life, and then he's gone.

I'm left standing alone. I have to wonder if this is all just a really bad nightmare. I lift my fingertips to my lips, where they still tingle from the remnants of the kiss I never asked for, but don't think I'll be able to quickly forget.

Can a single kiss from a stranger ruin a person? No reason, just asking for a friend.

# CHAPTER THREE
# TUCKER

"Tucker."

I quickly minimize the document I've been working on and look up to meet a pair of brown eyes that match my own. I wish they didn't. The color is the same, but I hope that mine never look as empty and lifeless as his.

I close my laptop and clasp my hands together, placing them on top, where they can easily be seen. I know the drill. I've been doing this my entire life. "Father," I answer assertively because there is no other choice when you're talking to the Devil.

I live alone in an open, loft-style apartment in the city; I have for years. That doesn't stop the man who stands before me from intruding whenever he deems it necessary to do so. Which usually corresponds with something I've done to displease him.

I studied mass communication and journalism at one of the most prestigious universities in the United States.

I graduated at the top of my class. What does that mean exactly? Absolutely nothing if I can't manage to publish something worthwhile to the masses. And it sure as fuck means nothing to the man standing in front of me, who thinks my choice of profession is a waste of my genetically inherited *assets*.

I guess, according to Daisy, if I got nothing from furthering my education and growing up among the elite, at least I have my...what did she call it...*pretentious* accent.

Writing is my passion. I chose passion over practicality. I chose passion over the family business. Do I regret my decision? No. Did that choice bite me in the ass when I had to step out into the real world? Absolutely.

When I refused to move back in with my parents after college, my dad made me an offer that I should have refused. I didn't. I couldn't. It didn't make practical sense. Trying to make it on the streets selling commissioned work for pennies wasn't going to help me accomplish my end goal.

I've found myself in a unique situation. I need to maintain a relationship with Hilton in order to continue working on this project. I can't blow our family to hell and back until I have enough dynamite to do so, and the moment I become completely estranged, I may as well be dead. And all of the work I've done to expose my father for the man he truly is? It would have all been for nothing.

Hilton owns a property he is willing to allow me to live in while I continue to work. Don't let the kind gesture fool you. I have no delusions of privacy. My living here is merely a tactic that allows him to maintain control over my life. Which, much to my dismay, he exercises whenever he damn well pleases.

I knew this moment was coming, it was just a matter of when.

"Care to explain why I was awoken in the middle of the night last night?" He subtly adjusts his suit jacket and stares out of the expansive floor-to-ceiling windows that look out over the city below. I live in a newly revitalized area. I love the vibe here, he hates it.

My shoulders stiffen. I know he's responsible for the fire, and I don't think it's a coincidence that I was there. I'm not sure who tipped him off or how much he knows, but the fact that he slept peacefully through the night while someone's livelihood burnt to the ground, not to mention his own son was on the premises, speaks volumes.

"I don't know. Care to explain why Hydrangea & Vine was lit up like a birthday candle at a sweet sixteen party last night?" My hands tighten, and my knuckles press together firmly against the top of my laptop. I toe the line between what I truly want to say to him and what I know I can get away with.

"All good things must come to an end." He rolls his shoulders with annoyance—no remorse. No sign of concern. Not a flinch of surprise.

I can feel my temper building.

"There was a woman inside, Dad." My voice rises, and I'm unable to control it.

"Right, the flower shop girl? Yes, well, she's never been very bright, that one. It all comes down to breeding, honestly. The bloodline of that family isn't very strong, Tucker." He continues to stare out the window.

How well does he know Daisy and her family? I know he owns the building that the flower shop is located in and that he's been placing weekly orders there for years, but I wasn't aware he was invested in that family enough nor did he care enough to know anything about their family dynamics.

"I pulled her out. She would have died if I hadn't been there." I confess. It's true. She wasn't supposed to be there.

In and out. That was the plan.

"Unfortunate, really. Survival of the fittest, son, isn't that what I've always taught you? Which brings me back to my original question. Why were you there, Tucker? What business did you have there? Is it the little flower girl? Pretty young thing, but well below your social status."

My insides roll at his insinuation that Daisy is somehow below me. If anything, I don't deserve a woman of her caliber. I barely know her, but I saw enough last night to know that she's too good for me. Even at her worst, she's better than what I deserve. My life is too dangerous. I'm no good in pairs. I'm alone for a reason. The fact that he knows of her existence and has watched her is enough to put her in danger. Last night is merely further proof of that.

How did this man raise me? How is it that his blood runs through my veins?

"I can't believe you." My words are laced with disgust. My knee bounces beneath my desk as I try and fail to keep my emotions in check.

"What? Do you have something you want to say, son?" He finally turns back to face me, a look of nonchalance effortlessly maintained on his face.

"No, nothing." I bite my tongue. *Shut up, Tucker.*

This will all be for a greater purpose. I have to remind myself.

He approaches my desk in his neatly pressed suit and Italian leather loafers. The cost of his cufflinks alone could feed an entire underprivileged village for a year. He looks down at me, tapping the finished mahogany wood with his stubby fingertip two times. The diamond ring on his left finger represents everything wrong with the façade of monogamy in our culture. Relationships are built upon lies and deception. Humans are innately selfish, which makes it impossible to truly trust anyone. Period.

"That's what I thought. Pack up here. We need to meet with the Fire Marshal regarding the cause of the…accident." He straightens his jacket over his shoulders and heads toward the door clearly expecting me to follow without further protest.

The way he so easily calls what he's done an *accident* crawls beneath my skin like a fucking flesh-eating disease.

"Accident? That's what you're calling it?" I push back from my desk and stand, glancing down at my watch. The well-worn leather band is the complete opposite of the gold Rolex adorning my father's wrist. Further representing just how very different we are.

I won't be following him anywhere today. I have somewhere else I need to be.

"Yes, faulty wiring. I have a feeling that is what the report will find. Truly unfortunate." He stops at my door and pauses with his hand on the doorknob.

If he says the word unfortunate one more time I swear to God. My hands clench into fists at my side.

"I can't." I exhale the anger that I've allowed to build up inside of me with nowhere to go, and instead focus on what I know I must do next.

"Excuse me?" Irritation and disbelief drip from his words. He narrows his eyes as he watches me carefully over his shoulder.

"I said, I can't." I reiterate, this time with more conviction than before. "I have a meeting at noon that I can't miss." I pick up my leather bag from beside the desk and grab my laptop, shoving it inside. I clasp the brass buckles and situate the bag over my chest.

Just a few more housekeeping items, and I'll be on my way.

"Fine. I expect you will forward a copy of the report over to my office. From what I have been briefed on, the entire ordeal last night got messy. You know how I feel about messy." He turns the doorknob and takes one step into the hallway before continuing.

"Handle your business, but stay away from that Daffodil girl. She's truly an embarrassment. My campaign for Senate has only just begun. I can't have you stooping to that level for a piece of ass." He closes the door and I'm left standing in his wake of hatefulness and disfavor.

Pot meet kettle. Fucking asshole.

"I'd hate to tarnish your image, Father," I say the words to myself, with more resolve than ever to see this through.

I'm not much of a rule follower. Who knows? The fire-breathing florist just might be what I've been missing.

-o-

Daisy Mae Chandler.

Her name almost feels too pretty for my tongue. The same tongue that slid down her throat last night without permission. I don't know what came over me.

Despite all outward appearances, I'm not a presumptuous asshole. Sure, I know what I like, and I've been known to take what I want, but this was different. This was a sudden infatuation that I had no control over. I needed to shut her up and, for some reason, my automatic reflex was to use my mouth to do so. I almost drove away last night, content to allow Daisy to forget my name.

Instead, I took a gamble, and I'm hoping it will pay off in spades. I need that list, and she's the only one who might still have access to it. All right, and maybe I want just a little bit more time with the smack-talking florist.

I've never had anyone ready and willing to go to jail for me. It's endearing.

I pull up next to the curb, this time in broad daylight. It feels like it's been longer than just a few hours since I was here last, but that could just be my insomnia. I don't sleep. I can't. There are too many words in my brain. I have to get them out or risk losing them forever. So, I write.

Poems. Articles. Novels. Short stories. The list is endless.

Tugging off my helmet, I place it on the seat next to the one I brought for Daisy. Apparently, I'm turning into a considerate bastard. I run my fingers through my dark brown hair and try to make the mess look intentional. A quick glance in the side-view mirror tells me that my attempts at taming my locks are futile.

I turn my attention to her house, it's cute— it fits her. Contrary to what she believes, I didn't stalk her before last night. Sure, I did my research. Part of playing the game is knowing all of the players. She might not realize it, but by managing Hydrangea & Vine, she's become a pawn in my father's game too.

I walk the carefully manicured stone path up to the front porch of her quaint bungalow. The wood siding is painted white with contrasting black shutters. The only pop of color on the exterior of the home is the robin's egg blue front door. That doesn't mean that it lacks her vibrant personality. No, the color comes from the flowers; they're everywhere. Various pots line the porch and steps. They hang from hooks, greenery weaving its way around the stained wooden columns. Intricate, well-thought-out flower beds butt up against the foundation of the home and create a floral map around the neatly cut grass.

Checking my watch once more, I note the time. I'm early, good.

Three steps lead to her front porch. The white-painted wood creaks beneath my feet as I take each step, announcing my arrival before I have the chance to. I can't help but wonder which of Daisy's personalities I'll encounter today. The thought both excites me and makes me nervous. She's so much more unexpected than I thought she would be.

Approaching the door, I turn the nob, finding it unlocked. Slowly, I push the door open and peer inside. The front door opens directly into the living space. The room is dated, but in a way that says what was once in style has gone out and is now back again. The bright colors and shag carpeting have come full circle and, coupled with the arrangements of fresh flowers scattered throughout, make the space feel warm and inviting.

But I don't have an invitation to be here.

Just past the living space is the kitchen and behind that a hallway that leads to the back of the house.

"Go away. You're trespassing." There she is. Out of sight, she calls from a room down the hallway.

She was waiting for me. I can't help but smile to myself. I adjust my brown leather laptop bag across my torso and fully step inside, closing the door behind me.

"It's kind of my M.O., let's go. If we're going to make our reservation, we need to leave now." My smile widens as I wait for her rebuttal in…three…two…

"Reservation? I did not agree to have lunch with you, Tucker. What makes you think you can waltz into my house uninvited and demand we share a meal? Ever heard of knocking?" She storms down the hallway in a flourish of long blonde hair and creamy denim, stopping when she's just a few feet shy of where I stand.

Her ability to both scowl and look stunningly beautiful at the same time is a talent in and of itself. Anger and indignation bounce off of her and ricochet around us in a bubble of undeniable chemistry. Her attitude does not phase me. But the way her hips fill out the denim of her light-washed jeans, and the way she can make a simple white v-neck t-shirt look classy? Those things I can't help but be phased by.

She peers up at me, her nostrils flaring with annoyance and a touch of rage that makes her only that much more appealing. My smile breaks free and stretches my face. "Our reservation is at the 'Flour Sack'."

Her scowl drops ever so slightly. The pinch between her eyes relaxes momentarily. She stares at me in confusion. She doesn't know what to do with me. That makes two of us.

"Come again, potential kidnapping stranger standing in my living room?" she asks, her words hurried and yet curious enough that she doesn't move from within my vicinity.

"I said reservation. I didn't say lunch." I shrug.

Sunlight streams into her living room through the front window panes, illuminating her golden hair. It's so shiny. I have a strange urge to reach up and take a strand between my fingertips. I want to see if it's just as soft as it looks. Last night it was filthy from the fire. She's showered. Today her hair is light and fluffy. It falls around her shoulders in waves of honey. It's alluring and sexy and everything I should stay away from.

"You got us a reservation to have cookies? That place isn't even open to the public yet. They just did their soft opening last week. I know. I was there. They ran out of the extra thick cocoa explosion cookie before I made it to the front of the line."

I grin, smug with my victory. I knew she was a chocolate chip cookie girl.

"Mmmm, and they have cake. Take your pick. I'm more of a cupcake guy, honestly. I like to break it in half and make a sandwich, squishing the icing in between the layers of cake." I lick my lips, imagining delicious cream cheese frosting on a moist, red velvet cupcake, my favorite.

Her outraged gasp catches me off guard and interrupts my delicious daydream. "You're a barbarian! Everyone knows you lick the icing off first and then eat the cake."

"Do you?" I ask, drawing her pretty blue eyes up to meet mine. I don't know why I insist on goading her, but it's an itch I just can't help but scratch. It's easy, and she makes the payoff worth it every single time.

"Do I what?"

Gotcha. She unknowingly walks directly into my setup.

Tilting my chin ever so slightly, I rake my eyes over her delectable body. I shouldn't. It's not why I'm here. But I can't help myself. Like I said, I'm itchy as fuck for this woman. She's contagious.

"Lick the icing before devouring the cake." My voice dips, and I don't bother hiding it, as I imagine her tongue sliding over creamy white icing.

She growls, and the sound elicits a visceral response from somewhere deep inside of me. I can't remember the last time I encountered a woman who intrigued me in this way. I dare say the answer is, never.

"Are you always this infuriating?" She checks me with her shoulder as she brushes past, grabbing her keys and purse from a hook near the front door. Someone should really tell her that's not a safe place to keep her valuables.

"Yes," I answer definitively. "Are you always this argumentative?"

She ignores me. No surprise there. I turn and lead the way back out her front door.

"So, cookies or cupcakes?" I ask as I step out onto the porch.

"I'm not getting on that motorcycle, Tucker." Her words say one thing, and yet I hear her sneakers hit the slats on the front porch behind me.

"Don't forget to lock up. It's dangerous to leave your front door unlocked, Daisy. Anyone could walk in on you at a moment's notice."

# CHAPTER FOUR
# DAISY

I pass people I know on the sidewalk and smile and wave like my shop didn't burn to the ground just one block from here a mere twelve or so hours ago. They all know. There are no secrets in a small town.

I walk next to a man who has no business occupying my time.

*A stranger. A criminal. An arsonist.*

My smile dips. Do I look guilty? People mourning their livelihood don't go out for cookies and cupcakes with strange men driving motorcycles the very next day. My palms sweat.

Maybe this just means I've officially passed the brink of insanity. I've crossed the rainbow bridge into Cookoolandium, successfully arriving next to a hunky bad boy, strike that – man, named Tucker.

What are you doing, Daisy? I am not guilty of

anything.

Well, nothing except living firmly in the land of denial and eating a cookie the size of my head. *That* I am totally guilty of.

I firmly believe that chocolate is the answer to world peace.

The outside of this mouth-watering confectionary masterpiece is browned to golden perfection. The inside is slightly underbaked, just the way I like it. It's all the best parts of batter without the risk of death by salmonella poisoning. The chunky morsels of chocolate melt into ooey-gooey yumminess the moment they hit the warmth of my tongue.

I allow my eyes to flutter closed and tip my head back, basking in the mid-afternoon sun while I slowly chew another bite of cookie and nearly moan when the sugary goodness slides down my throat.

I try to appreciate a moment of escape before I'm forced to face reality. I'm not ready. There aren't enough cookies or margaritas in all of the galaxy to offset the disaster that my life has become.

"Keep that up, and I'll have to find a glass of milk to dunk you in."

Tucker speaks, and I crack one eyelid open to glare at him. I almost forgot he was here annoying me. All sexy in his jeans and button-down shirt with the sleeves rolled up. I've had to actively ignore his arm porn for the last hour. It's been torture.

"Don't make this weird. Let me enjoy my cookie in peace."

We walk side-by-side down a sidewalk I know well.

This is my home. My feet know the way, even with my eyes closed. I know every crack beneath the soles of my sneakers. I grew up racing down these concrete squares on my skateboard. I can't help but smile to myself, remembering how much Aunt Fran hated that thing. I only broke my leg *once*, and it kept me out of her hair after school until I was old enough to start working part-time helping her.

The owners of these businesses are my family. I know their kids and grandchildren. I keep their birthdays marked on my calendar at the shop so that I never miss a special delivery or opportunity to make their day just a little bit brighter.

None of us are out here getting rich, although money would certainly be helpful at this point in my career. It's not easy being a small business owner. Nobody's doing this for the money. Sure, we're making just enough to survive, but that's it. We're barely getting by.

Owning a small business somewhere like this is about community and family. Most of these establishments have been around for decades. Their owners are just like me, they've inherited generations of blood, sweat and tears in the form of a brick-and-mortar building.

Our patrons continue to come back because every time they walk through our doors, we make them *feel* something. That feeling is something we can offer that the big box stores don't have. It's our hopes, dreams and legacy all wrapped into one.

It's a shared dream. It's a kinship that can't be explained. And now, I've lost that.

Tucker walks silently beside me as we turn the corner

onto Main Street. *My street.*

My feet stop moving. My eyes remain closed.

The smell hits me first.

The scent burns my nostrils. It's thick and heavy and, much like the feelings I'm trying so hard to avoid – it's unavoidable. It's a stark reminder that I still have a cough that won't let up from last night. The cookie that I was enjoying just moments ago now sits heavy on my stomach. I hate this. I hate everything about it.

I stand for a second longer, waiting for what, I don't know.

It's now or never.

I slowly open my eyes. It takes a minute for them to fully adjust to the sunlight. When they finally do, I wish they hadn't. I want to close my eyes again and run away.

The bright blue sky only further highlights the destruction laid out in front of me. It's even worse than I thought.

*It's gone.*

I knew it. I knew it was gone. The detective I spoke with this morning told me that it was a total loss, but standing here, in front of the piles of rubble…well, it's another level of grief. Another piece to add to my puzzle of loss.

We stand on the sidewalk, Tucker right next to me, our silence stretching from Main Street all the way back to the big city. For reasons I can't explain, I feel an odd sense of comfort having him stand next to me as I take in my reality for the first time since last night.

I take a deep breath in an attempt to ease the aching in my heart, but it only makes me cough.

Bright yellow tape marks the perimeter of what was once my second home. There is nothing left so I have to assume the tape is there to keep curious onlookers away rather than to protect anything of value. Everything of value lies in the ash that still smokes and smolders.

Tucker's thumb brushes my pinky finger, and my stomach flips.

I swallow, and my throat hurts. My eyes itch. *I won't cry*. Aunt Fran wouldn't have that.

Big girl panties. That's what I need. I need a giant pair of big girl panties with a fishbowl margarita.

"You good?" Tucker finally asks, breaking the stillness surrounding us, even though the thoughts inside of my head are anything but quiet.

I run my fingers haphazardly over the yellow tape in front of us. I wonder how good my insurance for this place was. I never read all of that mumbo jumbo. I just kept signing the papers that were emailed over from the company Aunt Fran set everything up with. I probably should have looked over it at some point, but hindsight is twenty-twenty, and I've always been more about the people than the finances of this venture.

I mend broken hearts. I bring a splash of color when sometimes the world looks pitch black. I create smiles when hope seems like an impossibility.

Taxes. Spreadsheets. Profit and loss statements. They're just not my vibe. More power to the people in charge of those things. I'm just glad it's not me.

*Am I good?* I replay Tucker's question in my mind. I'm always good. I'm a professional at smiling in the face of tragedy. Nobody wants to hire a sad florist. Being *good* is part of my job description. It's ingrained into every fiber of my being. But, am I good? I don't know. I feel weird, and I still haven't decided if it's the good kind of weird or the bad kind.

So, I voice another thought that's been rolling around inside of my head instead of answering his question. "You think we'll get into trouble for being here? This is an open investigation, right?" I cross my arms over my chest, the sun no longer providing the warmth and comfort that it did on our stroll here. I was fooling myself.

"Won't change the outcome." Tucker's morbid answer garners my full attention. What does he mean by that? And why does he sound so certain?

I turn so that my body is facing his. I want him to look at me when he admits that he's responsible for this. I need an explanation.

"Why do you say that? As if you already know, and yet you choose to keep the answer to my question a secret. It's because it was you, wasn't it?"

I wait for him. I watch. The veins in his arms flex. He looks up at the sky. He curses aloud to himself. Then, he turns to me and matches my stance.

"Does it scare you to think it might have been me? That you're standing here with a man who tried to kill you?" His words shove me off kilter. I expected an outright denial. I expected him to give me the run around again.

Is this an admission of guilt? Or is the answer in the question itself?

So, at his request, I take a second to catalog my

feelings before jumping the gun and saying something salty in response. I'm a jumbled mess of big feelings. I'm sad, and I don't know how to process *sad*. I'm still reeling from the shock of what happened last night. I'm nervous about what my life is going to look like moving forward. I am also slightly turned on by Tucker's forearms. But, am I scared of him?

"Oddly, no." I answer with an honesty that surprises even me.

"Well, there's your answer." He smiles arrogantly.

Oof. That grin. That level of confidence. What is it that makes me so attracted to this man? A man that because of his last name alone, I know I should stay far away from.

"So, if you didn't do it, why were you in my shop, Tucker? Why, all of a sudden, have you interjected yourself into my life? Why won't you go away?"

# CHAPTER FIVE
# TUCKER

Her eyes are tired. She's lost everything, and it's not my fault at all, but for some reason, I can't help but feel like it kind of is.

Why did he choose the very night I was planning to break into the flower shop for information to burn it to the ground?

How did he know?

Was he aware that Daisy was in the shop? Did he know I was there? I'm certain of it based on our brief conversation earlier.

I have so many questions that I'll probably never have definitive answers to. I mean, someone had to light the match. That someone wasn't Hilton, that's for damn sure. He makes sure to keep his hands clean of the dirty work. It's part of the reason he's running for a Senate seat and not rotting in a jail cell.

I want to pin the arson on him. I want restitution for Daisy. She doesn't realize it yet, but she's going to need it. The thought that she doesn't even realize the extent of what's been done to her burns my gut.

But, until I verify my facts and track down the person I've spent the past year of my life looking for, we're both shit out of luck.

I can't tell her any of that, because I can't trust her. Sure, she's adorable with her ability to look elegant in only a worn pair of jeans and a white t-shirt. She's obviously intelligent; her quick wit is sexy as fuck. But I know better than anyone how quickly people can put on a mask for others. It's for that very reason that I'm not easily convinced or manipulated. I don't allow it.

My instincts tell me that Daisy's probably a safe bet, but I'm still not willing to share anything more than what is necessary. Because if she's all the things I think she is – if she's loyal and trustworthy and sexy…just knowing me puts her in danger.

That's the crux of why I have to get the information I need and leave her the hell alone.

"I told you; you owe me a favor. I'm here to collect on it."

"And this very moment is the moment that you choose to collect said favor?" She tilts her head to the side and slices open my soul with wide, accusing eyes.

I deserve every cut.

It is wildly insensitive of me to ask anything more of her than her time, but I don't have much room to care. I'm too invested. I'm locked in now, and there is no other option than to get what I came here for.

"Daisy, do you have a computer system?" I ask. I push forward instead of backing down. I lift my hand to my jaw and rub the stubble lining it. I didn't get the chance to shave between last night and this morning.

"You're serious?" I track her eyes as they dart quickly from mine to the smoldering pile of rubble. *There's nothing left*. Hydrangea & Vine as she knew it, is gone.

"I am aware that your aunt, Francis, kept a filing cabinet with past orders ranging for years. Deliveries. Addresses. Did you ever transfer that information from paper? Or were those the only records?"

I watch as she stacks more walls between us the moment I mention her aunt. I know things I shouldn't, and she recognizes that. It makes her uncomfortable, as it should. She doesn't take her personal safety seriously enough.

"That sounds a whole hell of a lot like none of your business." The heated, playful banter from before is gone, and she's back to her default setting of glacial fucking iceberg.

"Look, Daisy. I'm searching for someone. I'm close. I'll know for certain if I can get one final piece of information to confirm my suspicions."

"So, you are creepy? You're stalking someone." She accuses, but her suspicions are wrong.

"I'm thorough. I need to be certain, Daisy. I need to confirm a name and date from over a decade ago. That is all. You can't stalk someone who is already dead."

My work is only as good as the facts I have to back it up. I am fully aware that the FBI has been watching my family for years. Every accusation I make, every truth I write out on paper, has to be one hundred percent factual. I need valid research to support my claims.

I watch her as she visibly swallows.

"I'm not at liberty to disclose that type of information. I'm under oath." She's adamant, but as far as a florist-client privilege, I've never heard of such.

*Liar, liar pants on fire.*

Her long eyelashes flutter as she averts her eyes to me and then back to the rubble, then back again.

"Oath? What type of oath are you under as a florist? That's nonsense."

"I see things, Tucker. I know things." She drawls out the last sentence to drive home her point before continuing. "I know that Chuck Thomley is getting ready to propose to his girlfriend next week, and he won't have a dozen long-stemmed roses when he goes to do so. I know that Coach Fulford down at the high school has bought one too many arrangements in the last six months...Nurse Mandy, the school nurse, might miss her weekly bouquet on Tuesday. I know the name of every baby born within a thirty-mile radius, and I've read more obituaries than I care to remember. These aren't things I share. They're not meant for public viewing. These are people's personal lives, and I take that knowledge seriously. If you're looking for the town gossip, go get a haircut."

"Fair point. However, you just spilled the hypothetical beans on at least five different people in this small town. There are, what? A few thousand people who live within these city limits? Your batting average isn't great on this whole oath-of-floral-secrecy thing. And I'm not asking about Nurse Mandy, although maybe I should. Bet she's not as mean as you are. I need one single name, Daisy. One date. Then, I'll be out of your hair for good."

Her lips turn down and her forehead creases for only a second, and then she recovers. I'm not sure what that's about, and I don't have much time to dwell on it before she jumps to the next subject. She's a fucking ping pong ball today.

"I hate computers." She pinches the bridge of her cute little button nose. *Computers.*

Something in her voice tells me that she's wavering. I hear it. I can feel it.

"What? Clarify for the audience." I ask, needing further explanation. There is no way this woman was operating a business without the use of a computer. Absolutely no fucking way.

"Excel spreadsheets are the spawn of the Devil." Her lips twist into a look of utter repulsion.

My heart sinks to my feet, automatically assuming the worst. Another roadblock.

"Don't say it, Daisy. It's not possible." I shake my head back and forth, not willing to accept the idea that she truly only kept paper files. Files that are now piles of ash behind us.

She sighs, "My senior year of high school I missed curfew by fifteen minutes. It wasn't even my fault! There was a cow in the middle of the road blocking both lanes of traffic. Only, there wasn't any traffic. It was just me and Bessy and a long stretch of highway. It was dark. I had to exit my vehicle and coax Bessy out of the road. Bessy was an ornery old heifer, and she was determined to make me late." She huffs and swats at a piece of hair that falls in her face.

"I will take that story to my grave. Aunt Fran didn't much care. She said if I hadn't cut it so close, I would have still made it home on time. She couldn't ground me like any other normal teenager, though. No. I couldn't be that lucky. Instead, I spent the last semester of my senior year inputting every single paper file the shop ever had into Excel spreadsheets. The punishment was illegal. It was an obvious abuse of power, and honestly one of the most horrifying experiences of my life."

"Thank God for Bessy." I release the breath I was holding in a moment of pure unfiltered relief.

She's got the files. She has to have them. This woman holds the key that will unlock the mystery, confirming my suspicions and putting me one step closer to ending this before it's too late.

"Typical man." She throws her hands up. "Did you hear nothing?" She exclaims, breaking my mental celebration and bringing me right back to the present with a heavy thud. The exasperation in her voice is evident. I need to get to the point quickly or risk losing her interest altogether.

"Can you access those files, Daisy?" I use my manners. I ask nicely. I tried taking without asking first, and that route didn't end well for either of us. I'm hoping karma will appreciate my tact this time around and reward me with access to the information that I need in return.

"Can I, or will I? Those are two very different questions, Tucker."

I take back the manners. I take back my attempt at

being a gentleman. I put the whole damn thing in reverse.

She's a fucking menace.

"Should I remind you again that I saved your life?"

She scoffs. "What? And now I'm stuck with you? No, thanks. I'm a survivor, always have been. I would have found a way." She's completely dismissive.

"This is me asking politely, Daisy," I speak through gritted teeth.

"And this is me, telling you that I don't give a flying horse's butt. No amount of education or etiquette is going to change that." Crossing her arms over her chest, she challenges me. I might be aggravated by her inability to cooperate, but I can't help the way my lips tilt up at her very *colorful* choice of words.

My eyes roam her face. I study the way her nose points more to the sky than anywhere else when she's irritated with me. Her inability to put me in my place is eating her alive. I watch the way her cheeks hollow as she tries to keep this act up without so much as a hint of a smile. It's harder than she'd ever admit.

Her blonde hair falls in soft golden waves against the white cotton material of her t-shirt. I follow the plunging neckline of that t-shirt against her porcelain skin. I unashamedly look at the way her arms, crisscrossed over her ribs, push her ample breasts up into the open V, putting them on display.

"I see." I lick my lips before slowly drawing my eyes back up to meet hers. "So, this flying horse…does he have a name? Does he by chance know Bessy the cow?"

She drops her hands balled into fists at her side and growls at me. Just like she growled last night. A growl that is so ferociously cute that, I know, off in the distance, forest creatures run and hide from fear of her wrath. It starts low in her belly and crawls up her diaphragm until finally escaping simultaneously from her mouth and nose.

Note to self: Daisy resorts to growling in moments of intense frustration. *I like it.*

"I'm not crazy, you know. I might be different from the women you usually *deal* with. I'm sure they fall at your feet with one look at that adorable smug grin. I'm not most women, Tucker. It will behoove you in the future to remember that." I swear I can see the steam billowing from her ears.

She's so angry with me, but I can't think of anything except the way my heart thunders in my chest because my brain stopped working the second she began telling me how adorable I am.

"You think my grin is adorable, Daisy Mae?" I hesitantly take a step closer to her and risk finding out if her bite is truly worse than her bark.

"Seriously? We're done here. Thanks for the cookie." She turns away, tossing her long hair over her shoulder, and flashing a quick grin that says she isn't done at all.

Her eyes gleam mischievously, and that damn smile, it's so fake it's almost cute how confident she is that she's getting away so easily. Against my better judgment, I reach forward and wrap my fingers around her wrist. I yank her to me until our bodies crash together. Her toes touch my toes. Her hips touch my hips.

I don't take time to think about the repercussions of what's happening between us. I don't have to; she won't let me. Her wit is quick, but her lips are quicker.

## Five Alarm Fire

Anything I was prepared to say to her dies in an instant. My world spins and, in a matter of seconds, I'm so dizzy I don't know if the sky is up. She pops up on the tips of her toes and weaves her deceivingly delicate hand around the base of my neck. Her fingers twist in my hair as she yanks me down to her level, foregoing all grace and elegance. Not that she's ever claimed to be either.

Her lips slant over mine and, having the self-control of a thirteen-year-old boy, I groan loudly into her mouth. Instinctively my hand wraps around her hip. I touch and I feel. I hook a finger through the belt loop on her jeans and pull her closer. Her lips burn hotter than the smoldering ash behind us. Her tongue lashes out against my lips, and I suck it into my mouth, much the same way that I did last night.

Only this time it's her demanding entrance; last night when it was me unable to resist her. She's so much better at this game than I gave her credit for.

She takes the heat that sparked between us last night and cranks it up to ten, unapologetically. My dick swells in my pants.

I feed into her kiss. I allow her the control her lips demand, since she's the one that initiated it, and by God does this woman demand everything from me. In one breath she hates me, and in the next, she swallows my oxygen like without it she won't survive.

Just when I begin to debate the consequences of an arrest for public indecency on the very same street I was almost arrested for arson twelve or so hours ago, she pushes me away.

I stare at her madly, panting for the air that she stole

from me, as I watch her turn to leave. I want to chase after her. I want to demand answers just like the ones she's been trying to demand from me. The questions I've avoided for her own protection. But shit, I'm starting to think I might need my own protection from her.

I can't move. I'm fucking stunned.

She glances at me over her shoulder, a playful smile toying on her lips. "Turnabout is fair play, Tuck," she says coyly. The way my name snaps off of her tongue causes the blood in my dick to thrum harder. My need for this woman is further solidified. A woman I can't need. *I can't.*

"Wait!" Against my better judgment, I call out to her, but my feet remain planted on the cracked cement sidewalk. "How will you get home?" I barely recognize the urgency in my voice.

I glance quickly down the street as she walks in the opposite direction of where we parked my motorcycle when we arrived in town.

"I'm walking! It's barely a mile. Do not follow me, Tucker Stafford!" She yells and, for once, I don't fight her. I think we've both been pushed far enough today. Any more pushing and I might do something we both regret.

I rock back on my heels and I let her walk away. She's got the information I need. It's only a matter of time, and I know her weakness. Chocolate and sexy grins. If only I could pinpoint what amalgamation of those two things would produce the winning combination.

# CHAPTER SIX
# DAISY

**W**ho am I?

This is one of those times that I really wish I had a girlfriend. A best friend. A dog. Pet ferret? Anyone I could sit down with and talk through what in the absolute frick is going on. Because it is very clear that I've lost my ever-loving mind.

I kissed Tucker Stafford. I kissed him in front of the whole entire town.

I kissed a man that isn't interested in me for anything other than buttering me up to get some sort of archaic information out of me.

What's worse than that, though? Walking away from him on the street where I left my heart open and bleeding in the wake of one of the more traumatic losses in my life was more difficult than it should have been.

I didn't plan for it to happen. I didn't go into today prepared to plant my lips on the mouth of a total stranger.

I sure as heck didn't think by doing so, I was unknowingly sparking to life feelings inside of myself that I never knew existed. *Need. Want. Lust. Hunger.* All feelings that I realize are totally and completely misplaced.

I was trying to prove a point and, instead, I dug myself in deeper, only feeding my own delusions. This has to be some sort of delayed traumatic brain response.

I throw myself down onto my bed and stare up at the ceiling. I didn't make my bed this morning, and I'm kind of thankful for that right now as the duvet comforter folds in around me and creates a cocoon of fluffy bliss. I make my bed every morning. It's one of those things that's been ingrained in me since I was a little girl. *Make your bed, Daisy, and, at the very least, you begin your day with an accomplishment.*

The logic is solid. There have been many days when making my bed was, in fact, my one and only accomplishment. But tonight, I need comfort, not accomplishments.

Truth be told? Tucker is feeling less and less like a stranger with each passing hour.

I watch the ceiling fan spin around and around and wonder if it will magically hypnotize me and…I don't know…set my world back upright?

Because everything feels upside down right now.

I spoke to my insurance adjuster after I got home from my outing with Tucker.

I'm covered for the contents of the shop.

And only the contents.

Aunt Fran sold the building the year after my parents died. I can't know for sure, but I have to assume it was my fault. She was a single woman running a business alone. She went from a partnership to being a full-time single parent and sole proprietor. She was my age. I can't fathom the pressure of that kind of responsibility. She was thrust into adulthood, and so...she sold the one thing that was most important to her to ease the burden I put on her.

It gets worse. Hydrangea & Vine is owned by none other than real estate mogul and multi-gazillionaire...you guessed it...Hilton Stafford.

All this time. Every week. He'd come in and out of the shop. It was his.

That explains Aunt Fran's weird behavior around him. It explains why she was so adamant that I kept my sass turned off when he was in the building. Still doesn't excuse his lack of tipping though.

I've requested a copy of the contract, but I can't imagine it's going to do me much good. I'm sure that Hilton's expensive lawyers wouldn't so much as forget to cross a single t when it comes to something like property acquisition. Heck, I probably have a copy of the contract somewhere around here, but I wouldn't know what it was if it appeared on my doorstep with the Sunday morning paper. I'm a creative mind. Now, I get to suffer the consequences of my apathy when it comes to the business side of the shop.

This is too much responsibility. I don't want to be a grown-up anymore. I groan and lift my arm to cover my face.

Why couldn't I be one of those girl boss types? You know the ones—they can run a multi-million-dollar business while writing a novel, while also raising a family, and always remembering to feed the dog.

This is why I don't have a dog. Or a ferret. They'd probably die. I couldn't live with that kind of guilt on my conscience. I'm a romantic – a lover not a…animal murderer.

I can barely keep myself alive.

But, flowers? Plants? Those are things I'm good at. But it's not enough. Just like the measly coverage for contents policy isn't going to be enough. I'll be lucky if I have enough to pay off my current invoices with my suppliers.

I need an idea. I need something…ughhhh. I scrub my hand down my face.

What do I need? How do I move forward when I've been plopped right back at the beginning? I need to start over.

I need to find Tucker, and it has absolutely nothing to do with the should-be-illegal veins in his arms, or his soft pillow-like lips, or the way pop rocks ignite in my stomach when he sucks my tongue into his mouth. *Nope.* That's not it at all.

Actually, I have a sneaking suspicion I'm in an excellent position to negotiate. One thing I did learn from Aunt Fran about business…*you gotta know when to hold em' and when to fold em'*. I'm pretty sure some geriatric country singer wrote the lyrics she liked to claim as her own, but it stuck…after hearing her sing it off-key in the shop a time or twenty.

What I'd give to have her here, singing country oldies and sounding like a screeching fiddle. She'd have the answers. She's not here though, and the silence in this house is killing me. I can't sit here and feel sorry for myself. I won't.

I hold all the cards, and I sure as heck don't plan on foldin' anytime soon.

I take one last look up at the ceiling.

*"You didn't raise a quitter did you, Frannie?"*

I sit upright on the bed. Like a gift from an angel above, an idea begins to take shape in my mind. The more I consider the possibilities, the more I begin to convince myself that this could actually work.

Climbing from the bed, I toss pillows and blankets out of my way as I go. Wearing nothing but an old t-shirt and boy shorts, I snatch up my laptop from my nightstand, ready to get my ideas jotted down before I forget them. Excitement begins to replace the feelings of despair I've been drowning in for the last twenty-four hours.

Finally, I feel like I have some sense of direction.

This calls for a celebration. To the margarita mix!

# CHAPTER SEVEN
# TUCKER

Sitting on the brown leather sofa in the open space of my living room, I do one final scroll through what has to be one of the most mind-numbing articles that I've ever written. I'm submitting a publication to a national magazine on the impact of artificial intelligence on journalism. It's not riveting news, but it pays, and money is what I need if I'm going to continue to give my own projects priority over going out and getting an actual job.

I gently set my tablet down on the arm of the sofa and pick up the glass of bourbon I've been sipping for the better part of an hour. What was at one time two fingers of smooth liquor is now watered down, at best. Lifting it to my lips, I finish it off and groan when the burn doesn't hit with the intensity I'd hoped for. What a waste.

I drop my head back and stare at the exposed ceiling.

*"Tucker, where are you? Dammit, Tucker, why are you never*

*here when I am looking for you, boy."*

In an instant, I'm a child again, hiding in my closet, journaling my thoughts and ideas and then stowing them away in a shoebox behind fancy clothing I never wanted to wear. I hated what those clothes represented. The pomp and circumstance were all a façade.

*"Tucker!"* His voice is louder, harsher. He demands to be heard. His footsteps come closer, and I quickly shove my work back where it belongs, away where no one will find it.

How long has it been? Hours? Minutes? I was writing and got lost in my mind.

I stand barefoot in my pajamas. Pajamas that I slept in last night. I missed my etiquette class. I'm in trouble.

Gripping the sleeves of my button-down sleep shirt I stand in the doorway and wait, he's coming. The door swings open, and my heart races, tears burn my eyes, but I don't allow him to see my emotions. I take the consequences he hands down like a man facing a bookie he couldn't pay and not an eight-year-old boy. Crying will mean I'm weak, it'll only make it worse. Eight-year-old boys don't cry. Crying is for girls and babies.

*Fuck.*

I can't breathe. The memories assault me from every angle. I'm too close. Part of writing is feeling. It's emotion. How do you numb the pain when it bleeds from your every pore? How do you make it stop, without stifling the creativity in the process? It's both a blessing and a curse.

For so long, I was able to compartmentalize. Why am I suddenly drowning?

I could barely hold a pencil when I first started journaling my thoughts, ideas, and my…feelings. Maybe that sounds childish. *Tucker, you're a man, you're not supposed to feel.* Bullshit. Those people can go play with a Tonka truck in the backyard and see if that makes their trauma go away. Let me know how that goes for you.

For so long, I didn't know what it meant to feel so strongly. I still don't know how to deal with my emotions. I tend to shove them down until they force their way out through my writing. It's often times the only path I have to feeling any relief.

The same thing that suffocates me, gives me life.

There are so many expectations. I've always fallen short.

The never-ceasing pressure. The inability to release pain, because dammit it fucking hurts to feel sometimes. This is why some men choose death.

For me? The pressure began early. I don't have many happy memories of my childhood. You'd be surprised by the amount of stress a kindergartner is under, especially when their father is Hilton Stafford. At that time, I thought my dad was a king. I revered him. I wanted to be him.

The thought is nauseating now.

I was five the first time he told me what a disappointment I was to him in front of his colleagues, and eight the first time his hand made contact with my face. The sting never went away. I wish the abuse had stopped there. It didn't. Verbal, physical, it didn't matter.

*"Take it like a man, Tucker."*

I was never good enough. My writing is and always

has been a joke to him. I am a failure. In the eyes of the man whose opinion I valued most; I was weak, still am.

Those feelings—the burning need to prove him wrong – that's what drives me toward the truth every fucking day. That, and the weight of knowing so many of the terrible things he's done in his lifetime. Things he feels absolutely no remorse for. How does he not feel? I will never understand.

I'll publish my memoir in conjunction with his arrest. I'll take everything he ever valued, just like he's stolen from me my entire life. Bit by bit, day by day, he's tried to break me.

He thinks he's succeeded. I let him continue to think he's got the upper hand, all while knowing every damn day that *he's wrong*.

I will get justice for each and every life he's ruined in the process, starting with the one that I remember so vividly.

The woman that changed everything. The woman with the—

*Knock. Knock.*

I'm jerked from the downward spiral of my thoughts. I'm not expecting anyone. Fuck my life, if Hilton is here again, I swear.

I am not in the right headspace to deal with him today.

I glance down at my wrinkled grey t-shirt and worn jeans. I went to the gym this morning and threw on whatever was clean in my laundry room when I got home. I'm a runner. I find inspiration on the treadmill. It might sound strange, but it works. It's one of the only places I can go and *not* think. The one place I can hear the words so clearly through the silence. Sounds contradictory, doesn't it? I run to clear my head so that I can think clearly enough to hear my inner monologue. It's where I organize my thoughts and find my inspiration. The moment I get home, I shower and change as quickly as possible and get to work. Today was no different.

I'm not dressed well enough for company, but this will have to do. I've never lived up to Hilton's standards anyway. Why the fuck should I start trying today?

I pad on bare feet to the door and look through the peephole. Today isn't the day I get shot by one of *Daddy's* minions. I'm always prepared for the unexpected.

Or at least I thought I was...

Because fuck me if long tresses of golden, blonde hair standing in the hallway of my building don't surprise the hell out of me. It's been nearly two weeks since Daisy used her lips to shut me up. It worked.

It's been two weeks of silence, both on her end and mine. Two weeks of her pretty blonde hair and sassy mouth haunting my dreams at night. Two weeks my questions have remained unanswered, my suspicions unconfirmed.

I can't help but stare at her, standing there, completely oblivious to my watchful eyes. She mumbles to herself nervously. She fidgets with the bag she's thrown over her shoulder and then looks to the ceiling. Is she praying? Who is she talking to?

Her long eyelashes flutter as, finally, she looks back at the door, a look of determination brimming from her blue eyes. She knocks once more, this time louder, before I hear her not-so-sweet voice. "Open the door, Tucker, I know you're in there. I have a credit card and bobby-pin in my purse, and I am not afraid to use them."

# CHAPTER EIGHT
# TUCKER

**S**liding the brass chain at the top of the door and flipping the bolt, I can't help but chuckle to myself at the conundrum she presents just by being here. She begs me to leave her alone, and yet here she stands, at my door, demanding entrance.

I turn the knob, swinging the door open and spreading my arm wide, motioning for her to come inside.

Her big eyes snap to mine, but she doesn't gift me with her pretty smile. Instead, she smirks and waltzes into my apartment like she pays rent. There's something different about her today. She's professional and put together in a way that suits her, but doesn't quite fit her vibe. She's wearing fitted black slacks that follow the line of her hips until they taper off delicately at her ankle, with a cute little bow at the bottom for detail. She's deceivingly adorable.

Her blonde hair falls in soft waves around her shoulders and down the back of her light pink blazer. The heels of her black pumps click against the polished concrete floors as she sashays into my living space without further invitation and places her bag down on my coffee table before finally turning to face me.

I rake my teeth over my bottom lip. I make a show of my eyes wandering over her legs and the added height her shoes give her. *So* damn beautiful.

The outfit alone should be a red flag. The fact that she's here, in my home, unannounced, should be a flashing neon sign. *It's not.* I'm oblivious to the warnings. I'm too blinded by her air of confidence. She commands any room she walks into. The taste of bourbon lingering on my tongue and dulling my judgment isn't helping my situation.

"How do you know where I live, Daisy?" I ask, breaking our stare down.

She shifts her weight to one leg. Her hip swings out, and her arms cross defensively over her chest, in a stance that is quickly becoming her tell. Her default setting has been dialed back to glacial sass today and, as frustrating as it is, I'm becoming quite fond of it.

"What, so you're the only one who can do a little investigative research?" She smarts, and the familiarity of her back talking warms my soul in a way it shouldn't, but it does, nonetheless. This is familiar. This is Daisy, even when her clothes tell me otherwise.

I am truly surprised she found me here. This apartment isn't in my name at all, it's in Hilton's. That worries me. The thought that she'd be anywhere near him

– that she would even utter his name – bothers me.

Walking into the kitchen, I grab two clean glasses from an open shelf. I need water. I'm not prepared to acknowledge her feisty attitude with an immediate response. Without asking her if she wants anything, I make myself busy getting ice and filling both glasses. Opening the refrigerator, I pull out fresh-cut lemons from a produce container, dropping a slice into each glass before placing them on the countertop.

"Come. Sit down, Daisy." I nod my head to one of the leather barstools across from where I stand in the kitchen.

"What's the magic word?" She sings songs. Her blue eyes sparkle with trouble, and the sly smile on her lips assures me that she is most definitely up to no good.

She's toying with me. The fact that she's begun flirting so openly with me tells me that she's becoming more comfortable around me. I'm not sure if that is good or bad.

These aren't my rules, but somehow she's flipped the script on me.

"Please." I let the word roll off my tongue slowly. I could play with her a little longer, but I'm impatient, and my curiosity is beginning to get the better of me.

"Well, look who can be a gentleman when he feels like it. There's no going back, Tucker. I've seen your true colors now. You've been keeping secrets, and secrets don't make friends. First cookies, then there's the fancy thing you do with your words, and now water with fruit." She gasps suddenly. "Wait, are you gay, Tucker? Did we just become best friends?"

"Daisy..." I growl.

"What? A girl can dream." She grumbles as she click-clacks in her heels, making the short trek from my living space to my kitchen. I don't have a ton of space here, don't need it. I live alone and have very few visitors.

"You know, Tucker, every florist needs a gay best friend, it's an unwritten rule of the trade. That is the absolute worst part of living in the middle of nowhere. Pickings are slim." She lifts her hand to her face and studies her nails for a beat before adding, "I got my hopes up there for a second."

Her hips sway as she walks, and I watch her hungrily. She's so far off base that it's comical. She knows that and so do I, but Daisy's got jokes today.

"I am not even going to warrant that with a response, woman. Tell me. Why are you here being hostile to me in *my* kitchen?"

Delicately, she sits down on the barstool, crossing one leg over the other. She places her hands on the butcher's block countertop, clasped firmly together, and completely ignores the water I've prepared for her.

Her spine stiffens and she straightens her shoulders before glancing up and locking her eyes onto mine seriously. "I've decided to give you what you need."

Huh, this is a trap if I've ever seen one. I watch her skeptically. "Why the sudden change of heart?" I tip my chin up.

"Your father owned my building." Hilton...again. I don't like it.

"I know," I confirm her answer and wait for her to make the next move. She came here with intention; I want to know what it is, and what it has to do with my father.

She draws in a deep breath and lets out a sigh before continuing. "I thought Officer Remington was confused. The night of the fire, I thought for sure he didn't know what he was talking about. I'm mature enough to admit when I'm wrong. I feel embarrassed now, admitting this out loud, especially since I guess you knew all along, but he was right. The investigation. The insurance. Sure, we're covered for the contents under our *renter's* insurance, but I'm never getting my shop back. Not in the way it once was."

Taking a sip of water just to give my hands something to do, I set the glass down on the counter between us. I watch her curiously as her demeanor shifts. Vulnerability casts a shadow over the strength that she walked in here with tonight.

She's so different than anyone I've ever met, and I think that's why she intrigues me so much.

She faces life as if it's only rays of sunshine. I think she thinks that if she doesn't acknowledge the rain, it won't come. But what she doesn't realize is that sometimes the storm has to blow through to get the rainbow.

I hate that I knew. I hate that her family ever got mixed up with mine to begin with. Why that flower shop? Why that town? These are questions I've laid in bed over the last few weeks trying to sort through and continue to come up empty-handed.

"All these years...my entire life, I thought that shop was our legacy. I was wrong. Aunt Fran signed an agreement with your father when I was just a little girl. I've never reviewed that paperwork. It's not something I ever even considered. Sure, my lawyer and accountant send paperwork over every year, and every year I blindly sign my name on the dotted line, content to let someone else deal with the spreadsheets and legalities." Her voice catches, and I don't miss the water pooling in her blue eyes as they start to turn glassy.

This isn't her fault. The contract. The fire. She surrounded herself with people she trusted. She assumed the narrative she'd known her entire life was true. The truth about assumptions is that they're always going to bite you in the ass, it's literally spelled out in the name.

I can't stand here and watch her implode in front of me.

Without thinking, I make my way around the counter. I don't stop until I'm filling her space. I nudge her until she's forced to turn and look at me, and when her body moves, I move too. I place my legs on either side of hers, where she still crosses one leg over the other like the proper lady I know she isn't. She says I'm the pretentious one. I have to choke back my laughter because this isn't the time, but nothing about Daisy Mae is pretentious, except maybe her name.

I place my knuckle under her chin and force her eyes up to meet mine, and I don't speak until I'm certain I have her full attention.

"It's not your fault, Daisy." I draw the words out. I don't just want her to hear them, I want her to actually feel them.

"But it is...you're not listening... I..." She

immediately tries to come at me with a rebuttal. This isn't a topic I'm willing to fight her on.

The pad of my thumb meets her chin, and I press hard enough to garner her attention again.

"No. We're not doing that today. Daisy, listen to me for once, dammit. This is not your fault. None of it is. Not the decisions of your aunt. Not the fire. None of this is your fault." My voice rises with intensity as I try to convince her of something I already know to be true.

Unfortunately, this is a feeling I'm all too familiar with. I've had to learn the hard way that blaming yourself for circumstances outside of your control is a lonely road to fucking nowhere.

She hiccups through her words, "You know, it confuses me when you play nice using your grumpy voice."

She shifts and her knee slides along the zipper of my jeans. Singularly, the movement was an accident, I know that. But, coupled with the meaning behind the things that she says and the way my blood is already heating in my veins with her proximity, I'm immediately rock hard. Zero to sixty in an instant.

"What do you mean?" I inch closer into her space, apparently content to make myself even more uncomfortable.

She licks her lips, and I want to bite her tongue before she can pull it back into her mouth. "It makes me think things I shouldn't."

"Like what, Daisy? Say it." I'm close enough that one move, one breath, and my lips will be on hers.

I see the hunger churning in her eyes. I know she's

right there with me. She's fighting it. If she'll just stop pushing me away for one fucking minute, maybe we can both get what we need out of this, and I'm not just talking about business anymore.

Instead, she sighs, and I know in that instant that I'm fighting a losing battle. She blinks, once, twice, and the hunger clears, making way for the wall I'm becoming increasingly familiar with.

Despite the protest currently happening in my pants, I put space between us. I see it in her eyes, she's not ready. Now isn't the time.

"I came here to negotiate an agreement. This is supposed to be about business, Tucker."

"Fine. Pitch. I'm listening, but be careful what you ask for."

"I don't want your money, Tucker." Her words are a slap in the face.

I'm taken aback. I realize that having the last name of Stafford comes with certain connotations, but I don't have a trust fund. I lost all of that the moment I didn't fall in line like a good little boy. I thought Daisy realized that. I thought she knew I wasn't involved with my father in that way anymore. I told her as much. Maybe I wasn't clear enough.

"Good, because there is none," I answer blatantly.

"I want your mind." She says in one rushed breath, her words running together as they leave her mouth.

"As opposed to what? My body?" I can't help the grin that stretches my lips.

"No, crazy, as opposed to your money. Stay on topic." She brings her hand between us and snaps her thumb and finger together in front of my face. She's nothing if not amusing.

Bringing my hand up, I wrap it around hers. I feel the way her body stiffens, but I don't let that deter me. We're both guilty of taking without asking. We're even. Now I get to take her hand in mine if I want to. Especially when she's using it for evil.

"And I told you, Daisy. I do not have a dime to my name. I'm dirt poor, a starving fucking artist."

I lower our joined hands to her thigh and when she doesn't immediately pull away, I take that as a win.

She scoffs, "Says the man that can afford all of this." She glances around the open layout of my apartment. It's small, but it's still in an up-and-coming area of the city. Places like this don't come cheap. I see what she sees, and I know she's making assumptions about me. This only brings us back to the whole topic regarding *ass*umptions.

"It's a rental agreement. Kind of like the one you had with the flower shop. I could say the same about your place. That real estate didn't come cheap." I try to explain in words that I think she can relate to.

She has no idea just how close our parallels run.

She merely nods, and then she's talking again. "Fine. You mentioned computers the other day. I think I've proved that my skills are severely lacking when it comes to the technical side of my business ventures."

I grunt. The fact that she's willing to admit when she needs help is shocking.

Taking my grunt as confirmation her words continue without further pause. "If I'm going to do this, I want to do it right. I have a clean slate to work from now."

Clean slate, my ass. She's got a fucking concrete slab covered in debris and ash to work with, and it's all thanks to one man. Rays of damn sunshine. She doesn't see it for what it is.

"Daisy, let me stop you right there, my father burnt your flower shop to the ground and then took the insurance money. He committed arson and fraud and is going to get away with it. You're calling that a clean slate? Like it's a good thing?"

As I say the words, I realize this is probably the first time I've blatantly confirmed what happened to her shop. My hand tightens around hers. As if the pressure on her fingers is a sudden reminder that we're touching, she pulls her hand from mine, but I leave my palm on her thigh.

"You're bringing me down, Tucker. Do not turn this into a negative." The words rumble from her chest.

"It is a negative, Daisy. You're a victim of a crime."

Is she in denial? Because, from where I'm standing, her situation is dismal, and it's his fault. It's Hilton's fault. Dammit, it's my fault. How can she sit there and be okay with this?

"You don't get to call me that!" She snaps, and the sudden change in her tone makes me pause. I feel a storm brewing.

"What? You don't want to hear the truth?" I cock my head, unsure of which part of what I said set her off, but I'm glad she's finally realizing that this isn't all roses and sunflowers like she's trying to make it out to be.

"You don't get to call me a victim, Tucker. Don't do it." Her jaw clenches, and her eyes fill with a sadness I've never seen from her before. Not when her flower shop was burning to the ground. Not when we stood together on the sidewalk and stared at the ashes. Not even when she told me about the insurance.

This is something else completely, and it changes the entire mood surrounding us. Sure, before we were having a heated discussion, chemistry-filled sparring that I've come to anticipate from every interaction I have with Daisy, sprinkled with a couple of flirtatious comments and touching—enough to keep me hard and grossly unsatisfied when I'm around her.

But now, tears fill her eyes and topple onto her cheeks. My heart aches for reasons I can't put into words. I give up all pretense of giving her space and wrap my arms around her, pulling her into my chest.

The dampness of her tears bleeds through the thin material of my shirt and burns my skin. Every bit of the vulnerability I thought I saw earlier comes tumbling out as the rain falls, and thunder shakes the foundation of whatever this is that's happening between us.

"Whoa, what is it? I didn't mean to make you cry, Daisy. Fuck. I was just trying to play devil's advocate. I was trying to make you see what I see. I didn't mean to hurt you, and now I would really love for it to stop."

"It's okay, it's not your fault. You didn't know." She turns her head so that she's looking away from me, but her cheek remains resting on my chest. Crying makes her feel weak. She's embarrassed. I get that, and it hurts my chest that we have that in common.

"Know what? Want to talk about it?" I've barely asked the question when she tries to pull away again. This time I don't release her so easily. I'm content to hold her until her tears dry from evaporation, however long that might take.

She looks up at me, and my eyes trace the lines that crease her forehead. Lines that are only there because she's overthinking something. "You really don't know, do you?"

"I'm asking, aren't I?"

"You researched me enough to get what you wanted, but you barely scratched the surface. That's on you."

"Daisy, I want to know. But, if you don't tell me, I will continue to stick my foot in my damn mouth, and that's on you."

"You actually care? Like you want to listen to my sob story? Because if you're going to make me feel worse about my situation, I'll leave, Tucker. I can find someone else to help me. I just thought…I thought that we…never mind what I thought. It's dumb."

She tries to fight with her words, but her body remains in my arms.

"You showed up on my doorstep. I want to know if you're willing to tell me. Dammit, Daisy. Don't make this hard when it doesn't have to be."

"Fine. You wanna know, I'll tell you." I realize the moment the words leave her lips, I'm wholly unprepared for whatever it is that she's about to tell me.

Going into this, I knew her name. I knew her age. I knew about her history with the shop, and I knew that she was mostly an orphan raised by her aunt, but that's where my research ended. She's not wrong. I had enough information to accomplish my goal. I *thought* I had enough. I get the feeling that was my fucking *ass-*

umption. I might not ever get enough of her.

Her body stiffens in my arms, and the color drains from her cheeks. She's compartmentalizing, I know that feeling. In this moment, she's lost to me.

"My parents were murdered in cold blood when I was a little girl. One day they went out for a date, and the next morning when I woke up, they were gone. They caught the guy that did it. It was a random mugging gone wrong. The guy admitted to killing them, but there weren't many details outside of that. Not ones I remember. The rest was left up to my childhood imagination and the nightmares that, to this day, still won't go away." I tighten my hold on her as she opens a window into the inner workings of the woman behind the constant hostility and mood swings.

She sniffles again, and the sound guts me. "I remember sitting with Aunt Fran as they read the verdict. I was too young to be in a courtroom, but she was shaken up, understandably. She had just been named my court-appointed guardian. She didn't want me out of her sight. The adults in the room kept calling my parents *victims*, over and over again they said that word. I remember thinking that a victim was helpless. A victim didn't fight back. That's not the way I wanted to remember my mom and dad. Accidents don't produce victims. They fought, and they died. They fought for me, Tucker. I know they did."

"I'm so sorry, Daisy. I didn't know." Emotion clogs my throat. I can't help but feel empathy for a woman who is normally the epitome of strength and positivity.

"It's just part of what makes me, *me*. We all have a

story. Mine may have begun as a tragedy, but I'm rewriting the script. Every day, I'm choosing to work on it. I'm content to continue being a work in progress for as long as it takes to get to my happily ever after, whatever that looks like. I shouldn't have freaked out on you. That wasn't fair to you. I don't want to dwell on the bad. Happiness is a choice. Can we pretend like that never happened?"

"Yeah, if that's what you want. Just promise me, if you get writer's block while you're rewriting, you'll let me help. It's kind of my thing."

I'll agree to let her gloss over it tonight, but we will revisit this. This conversation doesn't end here.

"Sure. We can agree on that." She takes a deep breath and the air begins to clear.

"Damn, we finally agreed on something." I chuckle.

"Don't worry, I won't make it a habit. Now, back to the reason why I'm here. I think I have something you need. I thought we could, you know, negotiate an agreement. I help you, you help me."

"Is this not the time to bring up the fact that I saved you from a burning building?" I circle back to her favorite argument. One that's guaranteed to ruffle her feathers, and a sure bet for shaking off any remaining clouds that might still be lingering over us.

"Tucker. Fuck off with that." She pushes at my chest, and my smile broadens even more hearing such a filthy word come from her pretty mouth. Slowly, she's coming back to me. I let my arms drop and settle my hands on her waistline.

"So, you came here to negotiate a business

agreement?" I reiterate, keeping my features as indifferent as possible.

"Yes, I thought that was obvious. I wore a blazer." She brushes her hands down the lapel of her light pink blazer, and I have to admit, she looks beautiful all dressed up. She looks beautiful in jeans and a plain t-shirt. And she looks beautiful in soot-covered sweats. I can't imagine a variation of clothing this woman doesn't look beautiful in. So much for remaining serious.

"Wait. You're telling me that you dressed like this for me?" Hunger thrums in my veins. An unfamiliar feeling of possession takes over my thoughts.

Before I realize what's happening, she hops off of the barstool, sliding her body along mine, only to swivel out of my arms and walk back to my living room, leaving me standing alone with no other choice but to follow her.

# CHAPTER NINE
# DAISY

The *touching*. The way this man causes butterflies to swarm in my stomach with a single swipe of his tongue over his lips.

I can't focus. I came here for a purpose, and damn it if I don't keep getting sidetracked. I was so confident walking in here tonight, but the conversation took a personal turn that I wasn't prepared for. I don't know what it is about Tucker that makes me open my big mouth and share things that I've never been compelled to share with anyone else.

My indecision makes me look flighty and unprepared when I am anything but that.

"Don't make it a big deal. I just wanted you to realize that this isn't a joke to me. I am very serious about this." I try and fail to shake the tingles from my belly as I walk back to where I dropped my bag when I arrived.

I may not be super tech-savvy, but I worked up a draft

proposal last night after hours of market research. If there is one thing I do know, it's my market. I know my customers, and I know how to grow and sell flowers.

I ruffle through the contents of my bag and pull out my laptop and the notebook I've been using to sketch out my ideas over the past few days. Making myself comfortable on Tucker's couch, I pull out various pieces of paper with numbers and drawings, none of which is going to make any sense without a little context from me.

Powering up my laptop, I try to regain a little bit of the professionalism I channeled on my way here. Most of my notes are on the paper scattered around me, let's be real. After I have everything up and running, I finally look up to find Tucker hovering just next to the couch, watching my every move.

His dark eyes are so intense that, if it were anyone else, I might be nervous. It's like he sees things that most people don't. He catalogs things. Almost like he's taking mental notes about anything and everything around him twenty-four-seven. It should be intimidating, but it's not.

Okay, Daisy, let's do this. Show him what you got.

"I'm not going to lie. The shop burning down, and then finding out that it was never mine to begin with was a blow. As you know, I like to think of myself as a positive person, but there was about a twenty-four-hour period there where I lacked direction. I almost got myself arrested. I kissed a stranger…twice."

Reel it in, Daisy, you're saying too much again.

"You liked it." Tucker interrupts, and I feel a blush creep up my neck and flood my cheeks.

*Focus.*

"I digress, my life felt a little wonky."

Tucker walks over to where I sit and begins thumbing through my paperwork and sketches.

"Is *wonky* a technical term?" He asks, picking up a listing for a used ice cream truck, one of a few options I've printed to compare and review.

"Stop interrupting me, and stop touching until I give you permission." I snatch the paper from his hands.

"Well, Daisy…" He plops down beside me on the couch. I know exactly where his mind went as soon as the words left my lips.

"Do not run with that," I interject abruptly, throwing my hand up in front of his face, stopping him before he has a chance to start.

He grabs my fingers, intertwining them with his, and I let him, against my better judgment, because I know the distraction is only going to make it harder for me to get through this.

"I'm going to create a mobile flower truck." I spit the words out. They lack the finesse I practiced in the mirror before coming here, but they're finally out in the open all the same.

"What is that, exactly?" His thumb brushes over my knuckle rhythmically.

"Hydrangea & Vine is taking off on four wheels. Think about it, Tucker. Less overhead. I can make larger arrangements from home if I need to, but I won't have the upkeep and expenses that I had before, which means I won't necessarily need to take the large orders. I can work from anywhere, and I can focus on what truly makes me happy: people, smiles."

Writing this all down was one thing but saying it out loud to someone other than myself and the ghost of my deceased aunt feels like I'm giving it life, no pun intended. The more I tell Tucker about the ideas that I've been working through, and he actually listens, the more it feels like it could become a reality.

"This is brilliant, Daisy." Tucker's voice is infused with sincerity. It's such a contradiction to the bad boy that I almost got arrested for the night of the fire, and the man that insists on verbal warfare every time we're in the same room.

I like sincere Tucker.

"Really? You think so?" I breathe a sigh of relief.

"I do, but I'm not sure where I fit in with all of this."

Right, here it goes. It's not that I can't do this alone. I can totally do this, but…I don't want to. I have something of value to Tucker. So, maybe I can take something of value that he has for myself in return. It's a win-win and, at the end of this, no one is indebted. Everyone gets what they want.

"I told you; I want a fresh start. I don't want to make the same mistakes I made with my brick-and-mortar business. I felt like a fool when I found out about the building and my lack of coverage, and I never want to feel that way again."

Understatement of the century.

"Don't take this the wrong way, but isn't that why you have an accountant and a lawyer?"

*Fool me once, shame on you. Fool me twice…*

I've always had those people in my life, and I still failed. So, maybe the problem isn't with them but with me.

"I don't need either of those things, Tucker. I need a friend. God, this is so embarrassing." I lean back into the lush leather of the couch and pray it swallows me whole. Why did I think this was a good idea, again?

Oh right, because I have a major fucking crush on Tucker Stafford, and I am very clearly willing to embarrass myself to level ten in order to get him to spend time with me. I am a walking, talking cry of desperation. Hello, rock bottom.

"Nope, we're not going there." Using our hands that are still bound together, Tucker pulls me from the recesses of my couch cave, where I would have been content to wallow and die.

"I'm here. I'll be your friend without getting anything in return. Hell, I want to be a lot more than your friend. Actually, I can think of about thirteen things right off the top of my head that aren't very friendly at all…"

"Tucker!" I gasp when his words suggest more than the friendship I'm requesting.

"Fine." He rolls his eyes and acquiesces to my request begrudgingly.

This is it; I need to finish the proposal. I want a friend, but that's not all. I need a business mentor. Everything else he offers because he's a tease, and he knows he can get away with it. That's not important right now, this is.

"I want to understand technology. I want the capability to process mobile orders and payments with the click of a button. I want convenience for myself and for my customers. I want records that don't burn with fire. I'm broke. What did you call yourself earlier? A starving artist? Well, me too. I talked to the bank before coming here. I actually do own my home. Shocking, right? I can take out an equity loan to buy the truck. The money from my renter's insurance will cover my outstanding debt left over from the shop and give me just enough capital to get the business up and running again. I can start with what I know and work from there. I have a plan."

"It sounds like a solid plan, too. This is amazing, Daisy. I'm impressed."

He's all smiles and thumb tickling. He's not getting it. I'm going to have to spell it out for him, and that just means I'm going to have to make myself even more uncomfortable.

"That's where you come in. I'm creative, it's what I do. I think of plans but fail at execution. I'll give you the information you requested, no questions asked. In return, I'm asking for your friendship. And, a to-do list. And possibly a crash course on this laptop because, honestly, I can't even figure out how to restart it. It's constantly giving me warnings about risk and expired security, and I really just want to toss it out the window. What do you say?"

# CHAPTER TEN
# TUCKER

"Okay," I answer without hesitation.

"Shut up. Just like that?" She stares at me, shocked.

"I said, *okay*, Daisy," I repeat myself, making sure that she understands what I mean when I say it this time.

Her mouth pops open, and she closes it just as quickly. "Seriously? I'm not having sex with you, Tucker. This is a purely platonic business arrangement. No friends-with-benefits funny business."

I can't help the laugh that escapes from my lips before I think better of it. I shake my head lightly with her assumption that I'm looking for something more than what she's offering.

*I am.*

She's not wrong, but we don't have to talk about that right now. Baby steps.

"Whatever you say. I'm here. I want to help you. I'm not going anywhere." I shrug.

"Wow. You truly need that information, don't you?" Her eyebrows crest in disbelief. The insinuation behind her words irritates me.

Sure, it will save me a shit ton of time if she'll just let me confirm a couple of details in her records, but that's not the sole reason I'm agreeing to this. I want to help her. Hilton destroyed her life too. I've been on this journey for a long time, and I don't think I realized how lonely I was until Daisy crash-landed in my life.

Now, we have something in common, and she needs someone. I'm curious enough to admit that I could be that person for her, and just desperate enough with this unsated feeling of want when I'm in her presence to say fuck it to any of the reasons currently eating at me and tempting me to stay away.

"Yes, that's true, but I was looking at other avenues. This isn't about that anymore. I'm not a monster, but just like you, life has shaped me into the person I am today. It's the only way I've been able to survive all these years." I let the words fall around us and give them time to sink in before continuing.

"I'm a writer. That means that, in a way, I guess I'm a creative mind too. Sure, I leverage technology to my advantage, using my tablet and my laptop. Technology isn't the enemy you think it is. I'm not out here trying to write with a quill for the hell of it."

"I use a pen, not a quill. That remark was offensive." She interjects, and I just smirk because I can admit that the comment was pointed in order to get a reaction. I hate to waste a good opportunity to rile her up when I see one.

"I understand living in solitude, Daisy. I'll be the first

to admit that I kind of like having you around." I nudge her with my knee, and she looks at where our legs join briefly before bringing her eyes back up to meet mine again.

"So, wait, you're a writer? Like, an author? How did I miss that? Who do you work for? A newspaper? Is that why you need this information? Is it for some story you're doing? I'm not sure I'm okay with sharing personal information if you plan to exploit someone. We've already discussed my stance on this." She fires off questions like bullets from an automatic weapon, one right after the other without so much as taking a breath.

"Slow down, Daisy. First, you've already agreed to give me the information I need in exchange for my daring good looks and swoon-worthy demeanor." I shamelessly flirt with her in the hopes that it will calm the onslaught of questions and lighten the mood that suddenly feels heavy around us again. "Second, do I seem like the kind of guy that is trying to exploit someone for my own personal gain?"

Her shoulders dip with relief. To be so positive about every fucking thing, she's one of the most skeptical people I've ever encountered. I don't have a reason to lie to her. I might not tell her the entirety of my truth, but that's for her protection. I don't need to blatantly lie.

"No, you're right. I'm sorry. I'm dealing with a lot right now, and I have no one to offload on. Ding, ding. You win. But, you already agreed to be my BFF, so you kind of asked for it." She leans over me, reaching for her laptop again. Her scent assaults my senses and makes me question my own morals. She smells sweet, like lavender and honey, when I suspect she's not sweet at all. I want nothing more than to pull her onto my lap and bury my face in her long blonde hair.

Snatching up her computer, she pulls it back just as quickly, placing it on her lap, and bringing the screen back to life. I watch her as she clicks through various Excel sheets, none of them are organized in any obvious manner. If there is a method here, it's not one I can readily see. Screw security and risks. If someone hacks this computer, they won't know where to start to find information of any value.

"Okay, Tucker, tell me what we're looking for, and I will see if I can find it in this thing." She wiggles her shoulders and fingers simultaneously as she waits for my answer.

I lean in a little closer to the screen, squinting my eyes to make sure I'm not seeing things. "Don't take this the wrong way, Daisy, but is one of those files labeled Nacho?"

This is one of the moments where you have to question your sanity even asking a question, because – really?

"Oh, this one?" She points at the file in question. "Those are the N's. I set this up under the phonetic alphabet."

I stare at her blankly. I don't know if I should laugh or weep. The unaffected look on her face tells me that she is completely serious, so I decide laughter might garner physical abuse and decide against it.

"You can't just create your own phonetic alphabet," I explain gently.

"Um, pretty sure I did." She lifts her hand and motions to the screen in front of us, as if to say I'm the one not making sense.

Instead of arguing, because that will only prolong the inevitable, I continue trying to mentally map a way to find the answers I'm looking for in the chaos of spreadsheets on the screen in front of me. There is no order to speak of unless you count the alphabet Daisy created from thin air.

"How are they organized? Date? Last name? What's the system here? Other than, you know, the obvious…Nachos."

"Last name." She says as if the answer should have been obvious. My stomach sinks. "So, where are we starting?" She smiles and her fingers continue to hover over the keyboard, ready and waiting.

I pinch the bridge of my nose between my fingers and pray the pressure eases the headache that's beginning to form behind my eyes. This is going to be more difficult than I anticipated.

I should have known. Different day, same damn roadblock.

"I don't have a last name," I say with more frustration than intended. I'm not frustrated with her. She's finally working with me. If anything, I'm relieved. I'm upset because no matter where I turn, it seems my circumstances remain the same. It's never enough.

She drops her hands and looks over at me in disbelief. "You *what*?"

The last name. If I had her name, I wouldn't be in this situation to begin with. It shouldn't be that hard to find, but for some reason, it's been damn near impossible. I've tried every available resource and continue to come up empty-handed. It's why I resorted to breaking and entering. I don't know what I thought, but…damn. This isn't good.

"I have a first name and a rough guesstimate of a year that I think my father was involved with this person." And I have a flower and the face of a little girl that will forever haunt my memories, but I don't say those things. I don't want to divulge more than is absolutely necessary.

"I'm going to take a wild guess here and say this *person* is a woman. Is this about the flowers?"

My chest tightens. How much does she know already? Hilton is meticulous. He doesn't get his hands dirty. He doesn't slip up. Is it possible she knows more than I could have anticipated? All from running a small flower shop and filling his weekly orders? Have I so grossly underestimated her?

"You know more than you should, Daisy, and you talk too damn much." My frustration from earlier bleeds into irritation and worry. I know before I even finish the sentence that my tone won't be well received.

"The only way this thing between us is going to work, Tucker, is through communication." I love the way she says my name when she's aggravated with me, which is admittedly most of the time. "You've got to give me a little something to work with here. I don't even know which folder to click on. You do realize how much information is in these files, right? There are literally fifty years' worth of orders here. We're talking thousands upon thousands of names and dates. I know we're a small-town flower shop, but we are the *only* flower shop in that town and have been…forever."

I can see in her eyes how much it hurts her to say those words. The realization that the flower shop is no more. The legacy is lost. "I'm sorry, Daisy. Fuck, I feel like I keep having to apologize. I'm so much more articulate on paper. I swear, I'm not purposely being obtuse."

"Don't apologize for being yourself, Tucker. You're authentic, it's one of the things I like about being around you. And for the record, I don't think you're an asshole. I think you're a man that's had to deal with a crappy hand in life, and what's worse is that everyone thinks it's been a privilege for you to do so. Sure, I had my own set of problems growing up, but I had my aunt. My every move wasn't scrutinized by complete strangers. I'm sure growing up as a Stafford put you under a microscope. People watched and judged you based on what they saw from the outside alone. It sounds miserable. And yet, you're here and you're helping me. You're a good guy, Tucker Stafford. I believe that. Bossy as hell, but good." She laughs softly and the sound sends warmth flooding through my veins. I don't remember a time when someone saw me for just me. Not Hilton's son, or *a Stafford*…just Tuck.

"I'm bossy…" I draw the words out and flash a quick grin. I try to deflect from the emotion she makes me feel when she says things like that and instead focus the attention back on her.

"What? I was being nice. Don't test your luck." She reaches over me once more and grabs a notebook and pen. Bringing it back in front of her, she repositions herself, opening it up to a blank page. "Okay, start from the beginning."

She stares at me as if she's waiting for my brain to catch up. When I finally realize what she's asking, I'm not sure I can give her any more information than what I've already told her. Telling her details means putting her in harm's way. It means exposing her to my weaknesses. It means trusting someone besides myself.

But, isn't that why I'm searching to begin with? I'm looking for someone. Someone that I know can help me. And…maybe, in some way, I'm looking for closure from a day that's lived rent-free in my brain for years.

"Come on, Tucker, we don't have all day." My eyes are drawn to where she begins absentmindedly sketching a flower on the edge of a blank page.

"You draw beautifully," I observe the delicate way her hand scrolls various lines and angles with a seemingly standard black ink pen. Further proving this woman isn't standard by any definition, despite what my father has to say about her *questionable lineage.*

"Thanks, it's just a sketch. I have to keep my mind occupied or I get bored. Creative brain, remember?" She taps the pen against her temple before bringing it back down to the paper. "Comes with the territory."

"I don't draw." I counter.

I don't do anything creatively at all with the exception of writing. Writing is my solitary outlet of creativity. Having a strict upbringing meant that anything beyond the standard of excellence was considered a waste of time. Writing was different. I could write in private.

Painting, art, musical instruments, those were all things that I would have easily been caught doing and reprimanded for or publicly embarrassed.

"Don't or can't?" She glances up from where she's been shading.

"What's the difference?" I eye her curiously. What does my ability to draw or lack thereof have to do with anything?

"Can't means the capability isn't within you. Don't means that it's there, but you just haven't found it yet or you've made a choice to ignore it. I think many people have talents that they just haven't discovered yet or aren't utilizing to their full capacity for some reason or another. Then there are the people who die without ever finding their talents at all. It's so sad if you stop to think about it. It's also why I'll try anything once. I don't want to die without having lived my life to the fullest. I almost died the night of the fire, Tucker. There are things I haven't experienced. Things I want to experience. I'm not missing my chances. That's part of the reason I'm here. So, you can trust me with your secrets or..." She allows her voice to trail off, and I take a moment to think about what she's said. It's a totally different perspective, one I never considered.

I have a choice to make. The lines between right and wrong feel blurred. She makes me question things I've never questioned before. I've kept this secret for so long. On the outside, I'm sure I appear indifferent, but on the inside, the battle that rages between what I've always known and what could be feels like a war I just can't win.

What's the right answer? If I tell her, she becomes my

responsibility to protect. If I don't… I kind of already feel like she's mine anyway.

"I was five years old when I saw her for the first time. That was twenty-two years ago, give or take…" I start, but Daisy's quick intake of breath interrupts me before I can even finish the sentence.

"No way, that makes you twenty-seven?" She asks, and the question calms my nerves because I already know exactly why this is relevant to her.

"Yes, and that matters why?" I hide the grin that threatens to lift my cheeks into a knowing smile.

"It's just… I'm twenty-nine. You did your research, right? You knew that." Her pen stops moving, the tip pauses against the notebook in her lap, creating a small smudge on her otherwise flawless sketch.

I merely nod and sink into the couch, content to watch her process this new revelation. Emotions transform her features in minute movements. Shock. *Horror.* Surprise. A hint of lust.

"Oh God, I'm a cougar." The final word bursts from her lips, and I finally release the chuckle I've been holding in. She is, in fact, two years older than me. Not that it matters much; our age stopped being a big deal the moment we both became legal adults.

"Not to sound cliché, but age is just a number, Daisy." I run my finger down the sleeve of her jacket. I can't feel her skin, but I know she feels me.

"I'm turning into Frannie." She sighs and tilts her head up to the ceiling, just like she did when she was standing in my hallway earlier.

"You're laughing, aren't you?" Her eyes narrow at the

exposed ducts above us.

"You talk to her often?" I mimic her stare, looking for what I know I can't see in the same way that she can.

"More than any therapist would probably deem appropriate." Her chin tilts back down as she looks over at me.

"Let me guess. Aunt Fran had a thing for younger men?"

"She did." She confirms with a brief sigh.

"And now you have a thing for me, and you're drawing a correlation between the two." I'm reaching and garnering a solid side-eye as a result.

"Whoa, slow down there, Hemingway. You kiss a man one time and all of a sudden, he thinks you have a *thing* for him. I hate to burst your bubble, but that is just not the case. This is strictly business." She shifts her focus back to her notebook.

"Twice. You kissed me twice, Daisy." I correct. I'd make it three right now if I knew I could get away with it without being stabbed by her pen.

"No, we're one for one. You kissed me. I kissed you – I don't know what the hell I was thinking. Get your facts straight. And speaking of business, we should get back to it. I apologize for interrupting you. Please proceed."

She creates a bullet point on her notepad and writes my age and approximate year she's already mentally calculated down next to it. Instead of goading her further, I continue with a story I've recounted to myself on paper more times than I can remember.

"Alessandra…I don't know her last name. I just know

he called her Alessandra and he referenced roses. I guess that was her designated flower. There's a significance with the flower choice that I've never been able to place. I feel like she must have been important to him for him to choose a rose. I know that she had a daughter. The little girl was with her that day in the office, and I'm certain she is my half-sister."

"You say you're certain?" She asks, and it's a question I've asked myself a hundred times before.

"It was the way he talked to them. I was young. I had never seen my father act out in that way before. Not to someone outside of our family. I was playing with a puzzle in the corner of his office. My nanny wasn't feeling well that day, and somehow, I ended up there with him. I can imagine how inconvenienced he was by that." As I speak, she only writes down facts pertinent to her search, and I appreciate that.

"He was so hateful to her. The way the woman hid the little girl behind her back. The fear and determination in her eyes were so striking. I can't explain it, but I just knew. I wanted to reach out to the little girl; she could have only been a year or two younger than I was at the time. I thought she'd be safe if only she'd come to play with me. It's funny the things that go through your mind at that age, the things your brain chooses to remember. I can barely remember things from last week, but my memories of this day haunt my nightmares with precision and accuracy."

"So, we're looking for roses. The record will be over two decades old. First name Alessandra, last name unknown. Anything else?" She doesn't look up from her notes.

"You haven't asked me why." I stare at her, taking in the way her blonde hair falls over her shoulder as she stares down at her notes.

"Why what?" She asks, finally lifting her head to meet my gaze again.

"You're constantly asking me questions you have no business asking, and yet you're making a list without asking me why I need the information. The only guarantee you have from me is my word that I won't exploit your customers, alive or dead." I explain.

"You'll tell me when you're ready. We're friends now, right?" She answers simply.

"So, that's it?"

"That's it."

# CHAPTER ELEVEN
# DAISY

File number two million three hundred and sixty-five thousand.

Ugh. I internally groan as I stare at my laptop from across the room. I thought I only hated technology. That machine has now become the absolute bane of my existence.

Good news? I have a brand-spanking new subscription to an annually renewable virus protection program that guarantees that my laptop will not get *cyber herpes* anytime soon. I have the skeleton of a legitimate business model, and I am the proud owner of a broken-down ice cream truck, which now occupies the entirety of my driveway.

I'm pretty sure the neighborhood watch group is preparing to impeach me. There is no homeowner's association. It's just me, Dale down the street, and widow

Nelly next door. Last week I was watering my flowers and Dale and Nelly were having tea on her front porch. Sure, they spoke to me, but they looked suspicious. I have never seen that man having tea before. The whole interaction wreaked of impeachment planning.

Tucker assures me that he'll have the truck up and running with a few new belts, a battery, and something that sounds a tad sketchy and expensive involving the transmission. Maybe then I can at least pull it into the garage. The man has proved himself a jack of all trades. Who am I to question his mechanical abilities?

Bad news? It's been three long weeks since I agreed to exchange information with Tucker for his friendship and all-around technical expertise. Life was so much easier back then...three weeks ago.

Sure, my shop was burnt to a crisp and I had exactly zero dollars to my name when the dust settled and the final paperwork had been filed, but I did not have cramps in my fingers from hitting the enter button on my keyboard over and over and over again.

I did not have oil stains on my concrete driveway complimenting my violet tulips in the worst way.

And I most certainly did not have a friendship with a man who flirts incessantly but has not so much as touched his lips to mine one time in exactly twenty-one days.

I know I said friendship. I know I set boundaries after our kiss – times two. Unfortunately, the reasons for my doing so have become increasingly unclear with every passing hour I spend with Tucker Stafford, and that's a lot of hours. Because we've been sorting through Excel spreadsheets every single night until my eyes cross and I inevitably pass out on the couch from exhaustion.

Sometimes my couch.

Sometimes Tucker's.

Most of the time it's mine. Just like tonight, Tucker is coming here.

He says I sleep like a sack of rocks and it's easier to maneuver me to my room when we're at my house versus his – where he maneuvers me to his bed and then proceeds to sleep on the couch, leaving me to sleep alone in his giant bed, smelling his man smell all over the pillows.

No, I think that his story about my sleeping habits is merely a convenient excuse for him to hide behind. I have my suspicions, and I believe that they all stem directly from his complicated relationship with his father.

When this all began, he made a comment about having a rental agreement similar to the one Aunt Fran had with Hilton at the shop. I have to wonder why he's indebted to him, especially since, in every other aspect, it appears as though that relationship has been completely severed. Tucker hates his father and every time the topic comes up in conversation, he abruptly shuts it down—walls up. His eyes turn darker, and I'm not brave enough to ask any more than I already have.

It's not that I don't want to know more, I do. I can see that there are secrets that Tucker holds close. I have to believe that when he's ready, he'll tell me. Or maybe he'll never be ready, and I have to be okay with that too. He owes me nothing in that regard. Our friendship is still very new, even if, strangely enough, I can't help but feel like I've known him forever.

"Daisy, what have I told you about leaving your front door unlocked? Jesus, woman. Anyone could walk in here and murder you in cold blood." My ears perk up, he's only ten minutes later than I expected.

Tucker peeks his head around the doorframe of my open bedroom door, scowling, and I smile. I knew he was coming, he texted me and said as much. I also know how much it bothers him when I don't "take my safety seriously."

I extract myself from my favorite chair and place the book I'd been reading down on the nightstand. It's a boring read anyway. It's some self-help book about running your own company. Tucker recommended it, bless him. I know he means well, but he has no idea what women truly want in a good book.

I'm quickly distracted by a delicious aroma wafting into the room from where Tucker stands, and it's not his usual cedar and *all-man* scent that I've become accustomed to avoiding like the plague.

"Do I smell Chinese food?" I stand and adjust my tank top when I notice Tucker's eyes straying.

That man loves to look, but he sure as hell doesn't touch without asking anymore. Not unless you count the handholding and the brief moments when he'll brush his fingers over my arm...or thigh. If he's not touching for funsies, then he's not looking for freebies.

I walk the short distance to my desk and grab my laptop, tucking it beneath my arm.

His playful smile brightens the room. His dark hair is a windblown mess, which means that he rode his motorcycle over tonight.

I don't know if it's because of the environment he was raised in or purely genetics, but the man can make a pair of worn denim blue jeans and a plain white t-shirt look like something from a Calvin Klein ad with no effort at all. He's wearing his black boots today, and I'm easily transported back to the night of the fire. The emotions surrounding that night still sting, but the sadness fades with every new day. The sun comes up. I forge ahead, making plans for the future. And Tucker Stafford shows up on my doorstep ready to look through another spreadsheet.

As much as I despise those spreadsheets, I think I might be kind of sad when it's over.

"L is for Lo Mein." He pushes off of the doorframe, tapping his knuckles against the solid wood and swaggers back down the hallway toward my kitchen.

"You're never going to let that one go, are you?" I rush to follow him, my stomach rumbling the closer we get to the kitchen and the scrumptious smell completely engulfing my house.

He's so bent out of shape about my files, but I really don't see what the big deal is with my system. Sure, the organization could be better, but give a girl a break. I was a teenager when I started compiling this information. Not to mention, the project was completed under duress.

It seemed like a good idea at the time, and if our process during this search has taught us anything, it's that it still works – just not as quickly as I think he'd hoped. This is taking longer than I think either of us anticipated.

"Nope." He nods his head back and forth and his

shoulders shake. Staring at him from behind, I glare at his back. I can tell he's laughing at me to himself. I might be irritated, but when the muscles in his broad shoulders flex beneath his shirt, my mouth waters for more than Lo Mein and egg rolls. Oh, for the love of dragons, I really hope he got eggrolls.

"On a positive note, we're almost halfway through the files." I shove down the lustful feelings bubbling up inside of me.

I brush past him, my hip barely missing his as I maneuver around his large frame and work my way into my small kitchen. Lifting onto my toes, I reach into an upper cabinet and grab down two plates for our dinner. If it were just me, I'd eat straight from the cartons, but it's not and that's marriage-level sharing, and those aren't the conversations you have over Chinese takeout.

"We are, and I'm feeling lucky tonight." I feel his gaze on the exposed skin of my back, from where my tank top has ridden up from reaching above my head.

I debate leaving that comment alone and going on about my business, I truly do. He's goading me, and I don't yet know why. I shouldn't respond, but before I know it my mouth is open and the words are already on their way out. "Are you now?" I drop back down onto my sock-covered heels and hand him one of the two plates I retrieved.

His smug smile stretches his cheeks and brightens his dark eyes, causing the yellow flecks normally hidden in the recesses of the dark brown to pop and shine through. That smile, the way he smolders without realizing he's doing anything, it does things to me. Dirty, filthy, annoyingly intriguing things. So, instead of lingering for too long, I switch my focus to the two large brown paper bags sitting side by side on the countertop in front of us.

How much Chinese food did he order? There's got to be enough here for ten people. And where did he stash this on that death trap on wheels? The size of those flappy side compartments is deceiving.

He leans his hip against the counter and crosses his arms over his chest, straining the sleeves of his t-shirt against his biceps.

"Yeah, I am, actually. I read my fortune on the way here and it said, and I quote…" He throws up his hands and makes quotations in the air with his fingers. "*Smile for the moon because today is your lucky day.*" He cranks his smile up another ten watts, and suddenly my knees feel weak. "I'm smiling, Daisy Mae, and luck feels like it is on my side tonight."

His tone changes when he uses my middle name. That coupled with all this smiling and gazing and talk about getting lucky, is almost too much for my self-declared friend-zoned libido to handle. Stronger women have fallen for much less. I deserve an award.

I reach behind him, grab one of the unmarked bags and pop the staples at the top to open it. A familiar scent of soy sauce and pan-fried goodness fills the air in a puff of steam.

Slowly I begin pulling the contents from the bag and setting them out on the counter in front of us, like our own little buffet. Realization dawns on me suddenly, as his words catch up to my brain.

"Stop it. You did not read your fortune before you ate

the Chinese food?"

"Uh, yeah, I did. It's like digging into the French fries from a fast-food joint before you get home. Everyone does it."

"First of all. You were driving a motorcycle. That requires two hands, you can't steer a motorcycle with your knees. Second, everyone knows that if you read your fortune before eating Chinese food, your fortune won't come true. That's why they place the paper inside of a cookie. It's dessert. You eat it at the end." Tilting my head, I watch him from my periphery. I grab the final container from the bag in front of me and set it down with more force than is warranted for what I think is beef and broccoli.

His expression is that of pure amusement. "First of all. I opened the cookie and tossed it into my mouth before leaving the parking lot. It was fucking delicious, tasted like what I imagine cardboard tastes like if it were made with sugar. Second, that's not a thing, Daisy. You're making that up." He turns and grabs the other bag and mimics my movements, opening it up and pulling out the containers, lining them up next to mine.

I reach over him into his bag when he doesn't work fast enough for my now ravenous stomach. His hand brushes mine and small tingles trickle down my fingertips.

"Fine, whatever. Believe what you want, but you, sir, are no closer to getting lucky tonight than you were last night. Or the night before that." I pause, egg rolls in hand, completely and utterly mortified with the words leaving my lips. I feel the blood draining from my cheeks as they pale under his searing stare.

My feet remain firmly planted on the linoleum floor. I'm scared to move, out of fear that breaking the silence will make me regret the very day I was born. Or worse, do something that makes me regret my actions tonight when I wake up tomorrow. I have an overwhelming hunch that I'm already gravely in danger of both.

I remain frozen until, finally, Tucker takes the eggrolls from my hand, placing them down on the counter next to his empty plate. Without a word, he carefully maneuvers his body around mine. His chiseled abdomen presses up against my back hard enough that I can acutely feel every breath that he takes.

My heart hammers inside of my chest so loudly that it echoes in my head and thunders in my ears. My hunger for sweet and sour chicken vanishes and is replaced with a whole other feeling of hunger.

I intensely watch the food laid out in front of me like it might reincarnate itself and run for the hills. It's me. I need to run for the hills, but I don't move.

Tucker clears his throat. The sound is warm and rumbly and sends vibrations up my spine. He leans forward, caging me in by placing one hand on the tiled countertop on either side of my body.

*Friends. Friends. Friends.*

I chant the word repeatedly in my mind but my body is having no part in receiving the message. Slick moisture coats my underwear. I feel it on my thighs.

God, I am not prepared. What was I supposed to think? The man hasn't touched me in weeks, that's what I was thinking. I got comfortable. Too comfortable.

I'm wearing a pair of flannel cotton shorts I bought at a thrift store with panties that are probably old enough at this point to be in kindergarten, paired with a basic white tank top. My hair is pulled up off of my shoulders into a loose ponytail because it gets in my way when I'm staring at the computer screen for hours on end.

I feel his breath first. The warm air hits my neck with a woosh, and I press myself further into the wooden cabinets resting against my thighs. The tip of his nose touches the bottom of my earlobe. He runs it slowly, deliberately, around the shell until he reaches the very top. I feel his lips hovering just over my skin. Goosebumps erupt down my neck and arms.

"It's a full moon outside tonight, Daisy Mae." The seductive way the words escape from his mouth is unlawful. The vibrations of his voice caress what feels like every part of my body at once. I want nothing more than to melt into the heat from his chest as he warms my spine. He's driving me mad.

My stomach dips for reasons that I can't understand, and my heart thuds, once… twice…three times. Well, these feelings are foreign and completely unwelcome. These feelings are the kind that make things complicated, and our arrangement can't sustain complication.

I swallow to lubricate my throat and consider my next move.

If I give in to this, where does that leave us? I'm cursed. Tucker's wrong, I'm so far from lucky that it should be funny—if it was, but it's not. I make the best of what I'm working with, but I am not a winning scratch-off ticket, that's for sure. He doesn't need my bad luck in his life.

On the flip side. I've been alone for so long, and now, suddenly, I have a person. I know studies show that talking to flowers helps them grow but, as a human, having someone talk back for once…it's a welcomed change. Will giving in to what my body wants so badly wreck the friendship we've quickly formed? Or was our meeting doomed from the start?

Licking my dry lips, I quickly try to think of anything other than giving in. I got myself into this mess. Why did I pursue him? Why did I try so hard to save him from the cops that night? He was a stranger. And then again, I pursued him under the guise of a business arrangement. Why?

Because…*he saved you*, Daisy. He's still saving you.

"If you're searching for a good luck charm, Tucker, I hate to break it to you, but you're looking in the wrong place."

# CHAPTER TWELVE
# TUCKER

*I* tried.

I tried so fucking hard, but I can't go another day like this. I can't think. She's inhibiting my ability to write. My head is all kinds of screwed up. And, fuck, it's not her fault. She has no idea what she's doing to me. I'm like a schoolboy doodling the name of his crush repeatedly in a blank notebook, unable to draw a single intelligent conclusion.

The touching, the teasing, the verbal sparring that feels a hell of a lot like foreplay. Hearing her talk about achieving her dreams with a passion that is so damn pure. Her ability to face disaster after disaster and come right back up swinging. I've never met anyone like her before. She has a golden light surrounding her like a halo, and I'm hopelessly drawn to her glow.

I'm scared.

I'm scared because a woman has never made me feel

so out of control. I'm scared of who I will become if I give in to whatever *this* is. I've never crossed these lines. I've never let anyone get this close.

I don't want to be like him. I can't allow myself to lose sight of my end goal. I am so close to finishing this. I've spent my entire life working toward one goal.

I'm scared of losing myself in this woman and then ruining what's left of her because I don't know how to do this. Or worse, exposing her to the danger that I know associating with me is going to bring her way. I would never be able to forgive myself.

I take a deep breath and let my lips brush the soft skin of her ear. I cherish the way her body shudders against mine. I try to memorize her sweet scent because, if she rejects me, I might not ever get this close again.

I wasn't lying. It is a full moon outside. Maybe the stars have aligned or something, making it impossible for me to stay away a moment longer.

I gather my thoughts before speaking, I don't want to fuck this up. Her lips part ever so slightly as her breathing picks up. She's panting. Her spine is pressed against my chest, her body molding to mine, a perfect fit already.

Her exquisitely rounded ass puts pressure on the tops of my thighs, and I want nothing more than to reach down and grip her hips in my hands, yanking her to me so that she can feel exactly what she's doing to me. The prison of tightly self-contained desire I've been living in for weeks is on the verge of collapse.

"Daisy, I took what I wanted that first night. We were both running on adrenaline, and I needed you to ground me. Then, you returned the favor. We were even. It was fair." I take a deep breath before I say what I need to say next. "It doesn't feel fucking fair anymore, Daisy. Because every day I wake up, and I think of you. Every night before I close my eyes, I think of you." My voice is raspy. It is barely recognizable, even to me.

"I'm sorry," she whispers, filling the space between us with more questions than answers.

"No, you don't get it. I can't think of anything else. I can't think of anyone else. It's just you, always you. You're consuming me. I want to run my teeth over your neck. I want to suck your skin into my mouth so hard that the world will see what I've done to you. I've never felt that way before, and I don't know what to do with that shit. You're making me lose control, and that's fucking terrifying. Tell me to leave, Daisy. Tell me to leave, and I will walk out of this house and cool down until tomorrow." I beg her, but she doesn't say a damn word.

Instead, she arches her back further. She turns her head to the side, exposing the entirety of her neckline. Her long eyelashes flutter up to look at me with so many unspoken thoughts…but I need words.

I close my lips down over the lobe of her ear, running my tongue around every curve and crevice, exploring as if I were inside her mouth instead. A soft moan escapes her lips, and I know that the sound is just a taste of what I'm certain she'll give me when I'm finally inside of her.

I pull back ever so slightly, "Tell me to leave, Daisy." I plead again.

I need consent. I need one word.

"Stay." A rushed whisper expels from her lips, and it's

the green light I was waiting for. I spin her in my arms and lift her to the countertop in one swift motion. Her legs spread for me with ease and give me ample room to step between them, claiming the space as my own.

Food containers are shoved out of the way, dinner temporarily forgotten in our haste. Lucky for me, I ate a fortune cookie on the way over.

I press my hardened cock into the countertop and pray for strength and mercy.

Reaching up, I grip the sides of her face with both hands. I pull her to me and press my lips to hers. Fresh hunger pumps through my veins. For weeks I have craved the feel of her lips on mine again. She reaches between us and fists my t-shirt in her hands, twisting the material and anchoring me to her.

Our tongues duel for superiority until I pull back, the need to make good on my promises overruling my need to shove my tongue down her throat repeatedly. My teeth rake over her jawline until I finally reach the sensitive skin of her neck. I tilt her head back with my hands. I bite down before she can react. She cries out, but her fists pull me closer. I let up when I feel like I've successfully marked her as my own. I run my tongue along the indentations I know I've left behind. Her screams turn into deep moans as I work to soothe the pain I've caused.

She grips my shirt with enough strength that I start to consider that the cotton material might not withstand her force. I release her face and move my hands to her shoulders where I pull down the straps of her tank top far enough to release her gorgeous breasts. She frees my shirt and plants her hands on the countertop behind her, thrusting her chest forward.

I've dreamt of this exact scenario more times than I can count. Her breasts are lush and full. My dreams didn't do her justice. Everything about her is…more.

That first touch, it's everything. I take her breasts in my hands and massage them, relishing the way they fill my palms. Her skin is so soft. I gently rub her nipple between my thumb and finger until it hardens beneath my touch.

Her head drops back, and she moans again. "Yes, God. Yes, Tucker."

"They're perfect, Daisy. Fuck, you're perfect." I blurt out the first thing that comes to my mind. You can't overthink when you can't think at all.

I dip my head and pull one of her nipples into my mouth, sucking and burying my face in her heated flesh. Her hands move to the back of my head and tangle in my hair where she holds on as I alternate between massaging and sucking her gorgeous tits.

Her hips rock forward as her body begins to move in rhythm with my mouth. Fuck, I could live in this moment for eternity and never so much as come up for air. I believe this woman could sustain me. That thought alone should make me stop. Turn away. Run. Save her.

But I don't. I couldn't if I wanted to. I'm in too deep already, even if I'm not ready to admit it.

I continue to lick and suck, biting down on her nipples when she pulls me into her breasts so hard that I'm now fucking them with my face as she dry humps my chest.

The motions of our movements are wild and tangled. My cock weeps in my pants. I feel the precum as it drips from the tip of my hardened length and coats my briefs.

"Tucker, I swear I'm going to come just like this, bite me harder, Tucker, please." She begs, but I can't give her what she wants, not yet. I need to touch her. I need to be inside of her in some way. I want to feel her when she begins to pulse for the first time. *For me.*

I release one breast and pull my mouth back from the other long enough to mutter two words before descending upon her again, "Not yet."

I continue ravishing her breasts with my mouth while sliding one hand down her soft abdomen until I reach the elastic waistband of her flannel shorts. It takes no effort at all to slide my hand beneath the band. I move her panties to the side and slide my entire palm over her slick folds.

I smile against the skin of her breasts when the warm, wet liquid of her desire hits my skin. She bucks her hips against my hand, looking for pressure I'm not fully giving…yet. Her fingers yank and pull on my hair in desperation. Slowly, so fucking slowly, I slide one finger inside of her slick opening. So tight. Jesus, she's going to kill me.

She's swollen and needy. I can already feel her tightening around my finger before I slide in a second. Pumping them inside of her, I allow her to set the pace with the movement of her hips.

I drag my thumb up, coating it until I find the nub of her clit. Simultaneously, I bite down on her nipple and put pressure on her clit with my thumb.

"*Tucker…*" Suddenly, she screams my name out. Her body vibrates so hard against me that I have to hold her to the counter with my body weight. She squeezes my fingers like a vise.

I release her breast and leave a trail of open-mouth kisses up her chest until I reach the shell of her ear again. Her eyes are closed. Her head remains tossed back in ecstasy as she rides out her orgasm.

"Give me more, baby. Let it go, Daisy." I growl and curl my fingers inside of her, massaging the place that I know will pull her in even further. I don't let up on her clit, and she screams again, this time only animalistic sounds that are the song my soul sings.

Moisture fills my hand and soaks her shorts.

"Good girl, Daisy." I kiss the skin behind her ear and stroke her down from her orgasm until she feels sated and relaxed in my arms.

Retracting my hand, I reach over her and snag a clean dish towel from a basket on the counter. I clean her up as her eyes begin to flutter open. She watches me curiously with hooded, lazy eyes. Strands of blonde hair fall around her face.

"What just happened, Tucker?" She says the words slowly.

I pull her from the countertop into my arms and hold her weight when her legs sway beneath her.

"We ruined dinner." I kiss the top of her head gently and smile.

"No, not the eggrolls!" Her words are languid, but she laughs into my chest and her body shakes in my arms.

Her arms are folded between us, leaving me to be the one to release her. I don't want to.

She props her chin up and tilts her head back to look

me in the eyes. Her long blonde eyelashes flutter open and closed sleepily.

"You wear happiness like a halo, Daisy. You look so beautiful right now." I guess I'm a fucking poet now.

She giggles, "Is that my fortune?"

"No, but it sounded good, didn't it?"

"You know, your fortune was wrong. You didn't get lucky. I owe you. We're no longer even."

My hands intertwine at her lower back and my fingers absently fumble with her shorts. Her tank has ridden up her belly, and I run my thumb across her exposed skin.

"You're wrong about that," I answer even though my balls might beg to differ.

"Don't know that I am." She teases and wiggles against where I'm still very clearly hard for her. My hands move to her ass with lightning speed. I stabilize her movements before she can torment me further. Before she wiggles one time too many and the next thing she knows, we're sprawled on the kitchen floor instead of the countertop.

That's not how I want this to go. She deserves more from me than that.

I debate forgetting our plans for the evening altogether. Instead, I could pull Daisy into the bedroom and show her exactly how lucky she's made me tonight. But, my thoughts are interrupted when a deep rumbling roar rises up from the space between us.

Her eyes widen, and I grin.

"Food. You need to eat." I lift my hand and smack her ass lightly before finally releasing her. I can't have her pass out on me. Her belly says that she's hungry, and I won't be the reason she eats cold noodles tonight.

"I thought you said we ruined dinner?" She twists her mouth to the side and looks over to where we've somehow managed to shove every food container into one large pile in the corner of her L-shaped counter.

"Five-second rule." I rasp. She might be hungry for dinner, but I'm still hungry for something much more satisfying.

I lift my fingers up to my lips and relish the taste of the sweetest elixir to ever grace my tongue.

-o-
## DAISY

My legs are bent, tucked beneath me on the couch. I'm snuggled next to Tucker, where we've been working for the last three hours. I lost feeling in my toes thirty minutes in. I'm hoping that's not a permanent issue.

"Hey, Tuck?" I ask distractedly, opening a brand-new file. We finished the L's earlier and we've just finished the M's, that list was a beast.

"What?" His laptop is open on his lap beside me. The bright screen casts a glow over his handsome features. He cross-references his notes, comparing them to my lists as we sort through the seemingly endless rows of names. Our process ensures we don't miss anyone. Or, that's the intent anyway.

"What's the most aggressive fast-food business?" A smile tugs at my lips. We've finally made it. I've been preparing for this moment for weeks.

"I don't know, enlighten me." His shoulder

accidentally bumps into mine, and a feeling of contentment washes over me.

"*Nacho* business," I scroll through the first section of N's. It's nearing midnight, and I think I'm beginning to turn delirious.

I'm starting to think what happened between Tucker and me earlier in the night was a figment of my imagination.

Empty cardboard containers litter my kitchen. My belly is full, and my eyes are starting to feel heavy. The mess is tomorrow's problem. We've made it through two letters tonight already. We're making good progress, but I'm not sure how much longer I'll make it before my eyes finally give up and close.

"*Nacho Nacho, Man...*" Tucker begins to sing some ridiculous song, and I have absolutely no idea what he's talking about, but his mangled lyrics make me laugh a loud, snorty laugh and lose track of what row we're on.

The way he bobs and weaves his head to the imaginary beat that only he can hear has tears rolling down my cheeks.

"*Every man wants to be a nacho man...*"

His voice trails off. My laughter turns into a long yawn that stretches my face and strains the corners of my mouth. Real cute, Daisy. I'd say it's about time to call it for the evening.

"I'm tired, Tuck. You were wrong, today is *nacho* day." Tossing my head back against the couch, I drop my hands to my sides.

I flex my fingers to keep the blood flowing so that they don't cramp up on me. I can't lose my toes and my fingers all in the same night, that would be a travesty. My knuckles ache. My wrists are sore. I can spend hours on my feet making delicate flower arrangements, but sitting on my couch with a laptop? My hands feel like they've raced a marathon. I don't know how Tucker does this for a living.

"Wait! Hold on," Tucker shifts his laptop to the side and grabs mine from my lap instead. He taps the up arrow until he stops on a line we've just gone over.

"Navarre. Alessandra Navarre." He reads off of the screen, leaning in for a closer look.

I sit up immediately so that we both stare at the same screen together. *Alessandra.* One dozen long-stemmed roses.

"Alessandra Navarre!" He repeats her name, this time louder, excitement coloring his words.

We missed it.

Somehow, I must have inadvertently overlooked it when I lost my placement while Tucker was singing.

My eyes remain fixed on the screen. How did I miss her?

"We found her. We fucking found her, Daisy!" Tucker wraps me in his arms only to release me just as quickly as he jumps up from the couch. His smile is wide, his enthusiasm fills the space around us. He doesn't care that we almost lost the needle in the proverbial haystack. He's unaffected by my error. So, why can't I allow myself to be as thrilled as he is?

He grabs his laptop and shoves it in his leather bag, abruptly packing his things.

Wait? Is this it? Seriously?

He found what he was looking for and now he's what? Just going to leave?

"Where are you going?" I ask, stretching my legs out from beneath me and trying not to sound needy.

My body is all but asleep from the waist down. My toes prickle. If I stand, I'll fall and make a fool of myself, so instead I stay put on the couch as Tucker heads to the door.

"I've got so much work to do. I need to get started now. I can get started tonight. Can you believe it, Daisy? We did it. We found her!" His hand grips the front door, and an abrupt feeling of sadness washes over me.

My lips flatten, and I exhale. "Nope, I can't believe it," I reply, unable to keep the disappointment from bleeding into my voice. This is an exciting time. I should be excited, but that's not what I feel at all.

"See, my fortune was right. Tonight was my lucky night. Get some rest, okay?" He stands with the door open, straddling my entryway.

"Yeah, I will," I answer halfheartedly.

Tucker steps onto the porch and starts to close the door behind him. He pauses, and my heart trips.

"Oh, and Daisy…" He looks back over his shoulder, and I hate the way my stomach dips with a single acknowledgement. I've never been that girl. I don't want to be that girl. The girl whose happiness is reliant on a man. I'm an independent woman, dammit.

"Yeah?" I ask, allowing a spark of hope to fill my voice when it has no business being there.

This is exactly what was always meant to happen. This was our agreement. Everything else in between was a result of proximity. That's it. That or the full moon. The full moon has been known to make people do some crazy things. Right?

"Don't forget to lock the door after I leave."

# CHAPTER THIRTEEN
# DAISY

*Mothertrucker.*

I kick the tire of the truck in my driveway with my sneaker.

"That's for making twelve different sizes of the same belt for the exact same model of truck and none of them fit."

I release a deep sigh. Huh, that felt surprisingly good.

I kick the tire again.

"And that is for the excessive amount of oil in this thing after I already drained every oil pan YouTube says should be in here."

Of course, a stream of oil trickles from somewhere beneath the truck onto the concrete because why wouldn't it? Frustration builds in my chest once more, overshadowing the temporary reprieve.

I decide to give the tire one more swift kick for good measure and all.

"And that is for Tucker Stafford. The jerk that was supposed to do this shirtless and let me watch while bringing him lemonade."

The words are ripped from my chest, more of a growl than a statement. I channel all of my frustration into the cracked and dry-rotted rubber. The pressure on my chest releases, albeit just barely.

Maybe my tire-kicking frenzy wasn't productive, but it made me feel better. Not my toe, but my heart.

I am not crazy.

Frustrated, yes. Absolutely.

Crazy? No.

Okay, fine, that's open to interpretation.

I straighten my shoulders and push my hair out of my face where stray pieces have fallen into my eyes. I don't miss Dale and Nelly's watchful stares as they sit together quietly next door on Nelly's front porch having tea…again.

I can't make out their whispered remarks, but I know without a doubt that they're gossiping about me. If I were braver, I would march right over there and tell them exactly what I think about their impeachment planning stakeouts. These little tea parties are getting excessive. Kick me off the neighborhood watch or don't. Just make a move already, would you?

I glance down at myself, noting what they probably see when they look at me – aside from someone potentially manic. Grease covers my favorite pair of old denim jeans. There are more holes in them than there is fabric left. I'd say, I think that the grease is giving them character, it's fine.

Now my t-shirt? It's gross. It's probably going to have to go in the trash after this. There's not a strong enough stain remover for this slimy black goo, and honestly, I've never been supremely gifted at doing my own laundry. Whites? Colors? Who truly cares? This is America. We're already a melting pot and pink looks good with my blonde hair.

I've been out here in the heat working on this thing for hours, and the stupid ignition is no closer to turning over than it was this morning. I'm so sweaty that my lips taste like salt. My hair is plopped haphazardly on top of my head in a messy bun tied up with a bright red bandana. I'm probably dehydrated. I'm a mess. This truck is a mess. My life is a mess.

I groan and gather up the tools I've been using today, cleaning up as best as I can and shoving it all back into the garage. The sun will be setting soon, and there's not enough light out here to work in the dark. My body hurts. I don't think I could go much longer if I wanted to.

I trudge past the old, battered ice cream truck once more on my way back to the front of the house. I can't help but consider the parallels. That pile of junk is a physical manifestation of the current state of my life.

Deep breaths. This situation is only temporary. My future is looking up.

I limp slightly where I got carried away taking out my frustrations. I'm totally fine.

I hold my head up high. "Beautiful evening, isn't it?" I call out to Dale and Nelly as I ascend my porch, making sure they know I'm keeping my eyes on the two of them. I know their sneaky little plan. They're not fooling anyone.

They merely lift their teacups and smile. Only, it feels like a pity smile. Ugh.

I don't want pity.

I want Tucker to pick up the damn phone and text me. Or call. Or send a smoke signal for God's sake.

It's been a week already, and all I have to show for it is radio silence and a stubbed toe. I haven't seen or heard from him since he left my house in a flurry of excitement, his not mine. Maybe he owes me nothing, but dammit I was invested. At the very least, I'd like to know if he found what he was looking for. Did the information I gave him help? Or is he back at square one?

I muddle through scenarios in my mind, all revolving around Tucker's potential predicament, or lack thereof, because who knows? Did his batshit crazy father finally get to him? Is he locked away somewhere in a tower? That would be an excellent explanation for his absence. The possibilities are endless, and without proof of life, my brain is beginning to run away with me.

I mean, sure, we made plans about fixing up the ice cream truck, and the future of my business. I shared my dreams with him, and he listened. But he never made me promises, not really. My unrealistic expectations revolving around promises he never made to me are my problem, not his. His whereabouts aren't any of my business. Heck, maybe he likes towers.

Besides, I don't need him. I've never needed anyone. I can do this on my own.

Belts and leaky oil aside, this week has been surprisingly successful. I met with a potential investor for my mobile flower shop. The guy was giving off major high-end lawyer vibes. He was extremely sophisticated. He seemed excited to work with me. Me! He's thinking big. We're talking multiple flower trucks, not just the rust heap that's still sitting out on my driveway polluting the earth with every passing day.

The call came out of nowhere. I wasn't looking for an investor. I'd specifically told Tucker I didn't want nor need an outside monetary investment. I don't necessarily like the idea of using someone else's capital. It's not an idea I've given much consideration to in the past. I was prepared to start from zero. I've done it before and I can do it again.

Walsh, Inc. is the name of the investor group. The CEO, Ryan "Mr. Sophistication" Walsh, flew in and personally met with me. Apparently, he knows the president of the bank I use, it's a fairly large national bank. Our local small-town bank sold out a few years ago. I remember when it happened, it was the talk of the town and everyone was against the idea.

After the dust settled, nothing really changed with the exception of the sign out front. The president of our hometown bank is still the same donut-haired, middle-aged guy he has been for at least a decade, and he's a nice guy. He pitched my idea to Mr. Walsh over drinks at a convention. One thing led to another, and now I might actually be starting a company. Not just a single mobile flower unit. A whole entire company, with the help of Walsh, Inc., of course. Me, Daisy Mae Chandler, bad luck extraordinaire, leading an entire fleet of mobile florists.

I wasn't sure what to think at first. I mean, I haven't

exactly proven myself to be the greatest entrepreneur. But, the more I thought about it, the more exciting the opportunity seemed. If your dreams don't scare you, you just aren't dreaming big enough. That's what I want my next fortune cookie to say. The idea is so crazy that it might just work.

Mr. Walsh's assistant sent over contracts and files for me to review yesterday morning. They want to get moving on this quickly. I know I need to look over the paperwork and get everything signed, but I'm dragging my feet already. It's just…I loathe contracts. I sent copies to my attorney, but if I learned anything from the last time it's that I need someone in my corner. Someone I can trust that will tell me the truth, no matter what. That's where Tucker comes in.

I should have gone with a ferret instead of a friend. That's where I messed up.

I'll be the first to admit that I don't have a clue what I'm doing. I'm just out here winging it because again, what's the worst that could happen? There's nowhere to go but up, right? That's what I told Mr. Walsh, anyway, to which he just smiled his multi-million-dollar smile and laughed casually. It was obvious that he thought I was exaggerating. I wasn't.

I googled the man before agreeing to meet with him, stranger danger and all that. Aunt Fran engrained human trafficking into my brain with such an intensity that it is a level-ten fear in my mind daily. I can't park next to an unmarked van without fearing for my life.

From my quick research, his background checked out. He seems to be on the up and up. He did not appear to be involved in a drug cartel using his investment business as a shelter company. Also worth mentioning, holy smokes, the man is gorgeous. So, that didn't hurt his case.

But really, who knows? I'm not the best judge of character, and I would imagine men in drug cartels are probably also insanely good-looking. Bald heads. Tattoos. Muscles for days.

My track record isn't stellar. I thought Tucker was a good guy too, and look at where that got me. Lucky for me, I at least got one completely epic orgasm out of that ordeal. On second thought, maybe that was unlucky. I'll never be able to eat Chinese takeout again without feeling depressed or horny.

I drag myself into the kitchen, completely exhausted, and open the refrigerator. I'm too tired to think, and yet my brain continues to spin. *Investments. Contracts. Drug cartels. Tucker's missing sexy booty.* It's all making my head hurt. I pull out a pitcher of ice-cold water and lift the entire thing up to my lips, not even bothering with a glass. I chug the refreshing liquid, even when it hurts my teeth and threatens to make my brain freeze.

Suddenly, without warning, my front door swings open at my back. Self-preservation skills activated, I spin and toss the remaining water, plastic pitcher and all, in the direction of my potential assailant. What was left in my mouth is spewed the moment my blood-curdling scream rips its way up my throat and out of my mouth.

My heart jolts. The instant my brain recognizes the figure of a man in my doorway, I freeze long enough to come to a quick decision in my mind.

Live or die?

Live.

Easy.

Within seconds my fight or flight response kicks in, and I am all but ready to go to war to defend myself. I'm mid-stride toward my weapon of choice, a knife from the butcher block on my counter, when the angle of the setting sun shifts and shines light over the face of the perpetrator. I pause.

My breathing comes labored, heavy gasps for air as I try to form words and come up empty.

"Really, Daisy? You left the door unlocked again?" Tucker stands with my front door slung wide open and smiles like he didn't just cause my life to flash before my eyes. I mean, I contemplated homicide. He has no idea the number of ways I just imagined murdering him.

I don't know if I should be alarmed or proud of myself for how quickly I jumped into action.

My eyes have trouble focusing on just one thing. Adrenaline continues to make my synapses fire sporadically despite knowing that I'm totally safe. I take in his clothes, all black. A black t-shirt and fitted black jeans. Black combat boots. Dark windswept hair, wild and unruly, much like the man that stands in front of me. There's something dangerous about him today, and I can't place it. It reminds me of the night of the fire. Or it could just be that until about thirty seconds ago, I thought he was a potential assassin.

Where are Dale and Nelly when you need them? They're the ones that need to be kicked off the neighborhood watch. I know they saw a man dressed in all-black approach my door. I'm sure they noticed his motorcycle when he pulled up out front as they were casually sipping on Earl Grey. Lord knows they heard my screams.

Tucker walks in completely when I don't answer his question and closes the door behind him.

My thoughts finally begin to form some sort of coherence. Who does he think he is? He has the nerve to waltz into my house without invitation after completely ignoring me for a week. My fear effortlessly transitions into anger.

"We don't allow solicitors. You can take what you're selling and peddle it somewhere else. Thanks, but no thanks." I cross my arms over my chest and firmly plant my feet on the kitchen floor. I use the countertop separating us as a barrier of defense. The same countertop that pisses me off every single time I walk by it because of what it represents. Because of what we shared here. I guess that only mattered to me though.

"Listen, Daisy, I'm sorry. I promise I can explain." He starts, and I glower, making my annoyance known. He has the nerve to continue, despite my visible warning. "Have you ever been so caught up in your work that you can't eat or sleep? That you can't think of anything else other than the one thing that's consuming you?"

My anger slowly begins to fade into hurt. I do know that feeling he's talking about. I've felt it before in the shop. The shop I don't have anymore. And I've felt it with this man, who stands in front of me and, without saying as much, tells me that he's been consumed with something that wasn't me at all. And dammit that's a selfish thought, but I can't stop the intrusiveness of it once it's already taken root.

"Where have you been, Tucker?" I ask, feeling defeated.

My resolve crumbles.

I don't want to fight. I enjoy our sparring, but it's no fun when I already feel broken. It's been a long day, and I just don't have the energy for it tonight. I want answers, an explanation, and then I want Tucker to turn his fine ass around and leave so that I can soak in a nice long hot bath. Alone.

"I found her."

# CHAPTER FOURTEEN
# TUCKER

"Found who? Alessandra? You told me she was dead, Tucker!" With seemingly renewed aggravation, Daisy yells across the span of her living room, still refusing to come closer to me. Her eyes glitter with fear, anger and something else that I don't want to admit strongly resembles sadness.

I've walked into the den of a viper.

I guess I deserved that. I ghosted her, and that was a dick move on my part, but I didn't have a choice. She is obviously upset with me, but she won't be if I can just explain. I would never hurt her on purpose, she should know that. I need her to know that.

"No, not Alessandra. I found Casey, her daughter. I found my half-sister."

Casey. I found her. My heart is still racing, my pulse sprinting ahead as if I'm still there, in that apartment. I came straight here. I should have gone home. I should have showered. I should have changed clothes. I should have gone anywhere but here. I didn't.

I needed Daisy. That need alone trumped any logical reason I could possibly come up with for not coming here.

"She's alive? Is she okay?"

The more she watches me the more she sees. I know what I must look like. I feel numb and wired with energy all at once. It's a rush of feeling and emotion, and yet I feel like I'm watching my life from the outside through the screen of a movie theater. It's the strangest feeling.

Daisy drops her hands to her sides and takes a step toward me, removing a single brick from the imaginary wall that currently separates us.

"I'm not going to lie to you, Tuck, you've got crazy eyes right now. Let's calm down for a second. Then we can talk about this rationally, and you can tell me what you found. You are okay, right?" She takes another step and then another, approaching me hesitantly. She makes her way forward, and with each step more bricks fall and the wall begins to fall down.

Maybe I'm worse off than I thought.

I try to calm my nerves. I try to silence the blood that rushes in my ears.

I'm a good guy. I'm a good man.

Then why the fuck did I just break into my half-sister's apartment and completely trash the place, leaving nothing behind in my wake except a single note?

*Fuck*. What have I done?

I rake my hand through my hair, tugging on the ends when it gets tangled from my knotted locks.

"Yeah, it's just, dammit, Daisy. I've waited so long to find her—to know she's living and breathing. She's thriving. She's an accomplished attorney. Actually, she didn't go far at all. She was just a few blocks from me for years. This whole time I've been searching for her, and she was right here all along."

Except, she wasn't in her apartment tonight. Not when I took it upon myself to enter without permission.

She wasn't there when I overturned every single fucking inch of her living space in search of affirmative validation that she was exactly who I knew she was.

Something. Anything. And I did, finally. I found it in the form of an old, battered journal stuffed beneath the mattress of her bed.

I needed to confirm she was who I thought she was. I needed to know with absolute certainty before approaching her. I needed to mitigate the risk. So, instead, I took another risk of my own.

In hindsight, I should have started with looking under the mattress, but it seemed like such an obvious choice for a woman of such a high degree. She went to an Ivy League college on scholarship, she's smart as shit. She should know better than to hide her secrets under the mattress.

"What did she say when you contacted her?" Daisy asks, coming to a stop barely a foot in front of where I stand. I haven't risked moving since I walked in and realized I'd put myself in a pickle of a situation. I underestimated how pissed Daisy was going to be regarding my absence over the last few days. It's sweet, just like her. And a little scary, in a murderous and not at all creepy sort of way.

"Well, that's the thing." I run my hand over my neck, apprehensively.

Her eyes score every inch of me. It feels like she can see through to my soul. My intestines twist into knots, and for the first time tonight, guilt swarms me. I swear it's like she already knows. My skin itches to tell her everything. I was right from the start, she's contagious.

And my God, she's so damn pretty it hurts. This has been both the longest and shortest week of my life. I was immersed in my search for Casey after we confirmed Alessandra's last name. I was a madman, consumed with the knowledge that I was on the cusp of a breakthrough that could change everything.

Staying away from Daisy while I searched for and found my sister was harder than I anticipated. I needed to focus, I couldn't afford the distractions, and fuck if Daisy isn't my very favorite person to get lost in.

"What?" She prods me when I get lost in my thoughts and don't complete my explanation.

See? *Distracted.* Just that quickly.

"I haven't exactly contacted her yet." That's open to interpretation. I hedge the truth.

"You're not making sense, Tucker. Did you or did you not find your half-sister?" I hear the frustration edging back into her voice, and I know I have to give her something to go on here, but I'm scared of what that is going to mean for her.

I didn't have a plan to come here.

I always have a plan. If my actions tonight are any indication, my new plan is not having one. I have to tell her.

"Alessandra Navarre." I repeat the name of the woman we found on Daisy's spreadsheets. "The name gave me a starting point, and the date and order information confirmed some of the details I already believed to be true. With a stroke of luck, I found the birth certificate for Cassandra Elyse Stafford, signed by none other than Alessandra Navarre, her mother. The dates aligned. It was her. She was the little girl." I can feel the anvil that's been sitting on my chest since finding this information begin to lift as I tell Daisy the truth.

"She listed your father on the birth certificate?" She stares at me quizzically. As if to say I should have already found that information. If that were the case, I should have, but it's not and I didn't.

"No, that's the thing. She left it blank. But she gave her daughter my last name—my father's last name." I connect the pieces of the puzzle for her in much the same way as I've connected them for myself over the last week.

"So, if she's as wonderful and successful as you say she is, why not reach out to her? What are you waiting on?"

This is where I've been stuck for days. How do you approach a woman you've never met and tell her that you're her half-brother? How do you tell her that you wanted to save her from the monster? Would she remember me? What was her life like? Did she truly need me to save her, or should I have been asking her to save me instead?

The truth is, I still want to save her. I want to save us all from the tyrant of a man who is our father. It's my purpose and mission, and I'm running out of time. His face is posted on billboards. Signs promoting his candidacy for senate litter the city that once felt like home and remind me every day that the clock is ticking.

It's strange to think that I'm starting to feel more at home here with Daisy than I ever have in the cold apartment I rent from Hilton.

Then, the thought that haunts my dreams at night—if Casey is safe and happy, will I endanger her further by bringing her into my life? It's the same fear I have for Daisy.

"You know my father's reputation, Daisy. I can't just call her up and be like *'Hey, so you don't know me, but we have the same asshole narcissistic father, want to be friends? No worries, I don't yet have solid proof that he is a murderer, arsonist or involved in mafia activity. Just a hunch.'*. She knows who he is, Daisy. What if she already hates him and, by default, me? I need to speak with her. Knowing what I know now, I'm certain that she can help me. If she remembers him, if she hates him, I think I'd like to have her on my team, but on my terms." *Team.* Fuck. Did I just say I have a team? Where did that come from? I don't have a team. I've always worked solo.

"Your team?" She tilts her head to the side and raises an eyebrow, not missing a single beat.

I look at her, cataloging the things I know about her. She's smart and ambitious. She is argumentative and so fucking headstrong. She's combative but in a cute way, like a koala bear. She is nothing at all like what I thought she would be, and everything I didn't realize I wanted or needed. I have given her reason after reason to run for the fucking hills.

I broke into her shop. As a result of *my actions*, my father burnt her family's legacy to the ground and left her with nothing. Despite knowing all of that, here she is. Albeit a little pissed, but I see it in her eyes. She's got my back, and I don't deserve it, but I want it anyway. I want Daisy Mae on my fucking team. For the first time since I can remember, I don't want to be solo. The realization nearly brings me to my knees.

"Yeah, I guess I have a team now." I can't help the smile that teases my lips.

"Huh. Must be nice." She scoffs as if my words weren't meant for her when they sure as hell were.

She has a smeared grease stain on her cheek. It's proof that she's been working on the truck without me. The thought of her turning a wrench is sexy, even if I hate that she was out there working on it alone.

I haven't been a very good teammate to her, but I'm ready to make up for that.

"Nice is a relative term in my world. You see, this team, we're on a losing streak. Just a couple of underdogs against the world. But we're scrappy. What we lack in finesse we make up for in perseverance and ingenuity." I reach forward, my heart rate finally having slowed back to a semi-normal thump, thump, thump. Or, as normal as it gets around Daisy. I'm not sure I remember what normal feels like anymore. I loop my finger through the front belt hole of her jeans and tug her body into mine.

She stumbles into me, bracing her hands on my chest. Oxygen catches in my lungs as I inhale her scent deeply upon contact. She smells like outside, like fresh-cut grass and sunshine. Today was dark. I just want to bask in her light for a little while.

"Lame. Sounds like a couple of losers if you ask me." She looks up at me with a smirk that I've missed.

"Losers. Fugitives from the law. It's a wide umbrella." I shrug and lift my hand to her cheek, running my thumb over the grease there.

She flashes a playful grin. "Seriously? I'm harboring a fugitive? Again?"

If she only knew how close to the truth she is. The thought burns my gut, but I push my worry to the side.

Daisy's hands roam over my chest and shoulders until her fingers reach the hair at the base of my neck. She plays with the knotted strands, tugging lightly and sending bolts of electricity down my spine.

"Admit it, Daisy, it turns you on to think that I broke the law. Doesn't it?" Dropping my hand, I reach between us. I grip her hips in my hands, pulling her to me with the intent of not letting go this time. I have too much pent-up energy, and I know exactly what I plan to use it for this time. I *need* her.

"No, I'm a good girl. You said so yourself." Lifting to her toes, she grazes the stubbled line of my jaw with her teeth. My hands tighten and squeeze until my knuckles crack.

"Admit it." My words are rough, they're a desperate plea for more of her. I have never been desperate for a woman, but this woman continues to prove that she's exempt from the rules.

"I'm not admitting anything until you apologize. I want to hear it, Tucker. You owe me an apology."

I lean forward and place my mouth on her neck. "I'm…" I lick the spot that I know from last time has a direct line to her panties and she moans, dropping back on her heels. "Sorry." I growl.

I hold her steady when she wavers from where I stroke her sensitive skin with my mouth. Sweat has made her skin salty to my tongue, and it tastes fucking delicious.

She rasps. "Dammit, Tucker. This bad boy thing is really working for me." At this moment, I am so fucking thankful for that, but the thing is…I'm not a bad guy at all. I'm a decent enough guy who's had to make bad choices for the greater good.

"I know." I nip at her skin with my teeth.

I might be a good guy, but if a bad boy is what Daisy wants…

A small moan escapes from her lips and sends my blood sizzling in my veins. My hands grip and massage her hips. "How do I continue to get myself into these situations?" I feel her throat move against my lips.

A bad boy is exactly what she will get.

"The question you should be asking yourself is how you're going to get out of this?"

Using my hold on her, I lift her lithe body, and in one move, I spin us. I pin her against the wall using my body weight. Her fingers release my hair, and before she can fight back, I reach up, grip her wrists in one hand, and hold them to the wall above her head.

*False imprisonment.* Add it to the list.

"Tucker!" She cries out when my abrupt movements surprise her.

She's not angry anymore. The seductive grin on her

lips and the way her blue eyes sparkle with mischief as they track mine anticipating what's going to happen next, tell me she wants to be anything but a good girl tonight.

"You make me feel fucking crazy, Daisy Mae Chandler, and we both know my crazy genes run deep." I openly admit what we both know is truth.

"I missed you, Tucker. I didn't want to, but I missed your arrogant face and your annoying attitude."

She smiles when I slam my hips into hers. My hand tightens around her wrists. Reaching between us with my free hand I easily release the button on her jeans and slide the zipper down. There is a time for slow and patient, but that is not right now.

"Are you wet for me, Daisy?" I bark the words out.

I don't wait for a response. The question is rhetorical anyway. I already know she is. I slide my hand down the silky skin of her belly and beneath the elastic waistband of her panties. I slip my hand over the soft patch of hair I can't wait to bury my face in later, and I don't stop until my fingertips make contact with her opening.

Fucking soaked.

"God, Tucker, please." She pleads with me, as she bucks her hips up into my hand and tries to force my fingers inside using her own momentum.

I don't draw this out. I can't. I slide in two fingers and pump them once, then twice, before sliding in a third. So, fucking tight. So wet. My cock weeps in my pants. She's going to kill me.

"Look at me, Daisy. You like to get dirty, don't you, baby?" I pump my hand faster as she rocks her hips harder. Her head slams against the wall. Her wrists tremble in my hands as I hold her securely against the wall.

"So much, Tucker. So good. Please, I'm close."

Her pants come faster, heavier.

I smile. Watching her come apart is the sexiest damn thing I think I have ever seen. Her pupils darken and widen, and I curl my fingers until...

"Tucker!" A guttural scream tears from her throat as her pussy clenches down and begins to pulse around my fingers. Her mouth pops open, and her moans fuel the fire racing in my blood.

# CHAPTER FIFTEEN
# DAISY

The world closes in around me. My vision darkens and stars flash in my periphery. The feeling of ecstasy pulsating from my vagina can be described as nothing less than heavenly.

Tucker. Damn him.

Sometimes forgiveness comes in understanding and acceptance. Other times I guess it comes in the form of a bad boy doing very dirty things to me against the living room wall.

Is this an unhealthy relationship habit to form? Quite possibly. But this isn't a relationship, right? So, I'm good. We're good. *It's fine.*

My legs feel like warm Jello on the dessert aisle at the supermarket. Doesn't matter, their use is rendered useless, as Tucker drops my wrists, releasing me, but for only a second. He pulls his hand from my soaked panties and, at the same time, he scoops me into his arms, carrying me toward my bedroom.

If harboring a fugitive in my bedroom is wrong, I don't want to be right.

I tighten my Jello legs around Tucker's waist as much as they'll allow and enjoy the tingles of pleasure that rocket through my body when his belt buckle presses up against my still very sensitive nether regions.

I'm two for two in the orgasm department, and I have yet to see this man with his clothes off. I'm starting to get a complex. I feel his muscles beneath me. I feel…everything.

Tucker storms down the hallway, not stopping until we're in my bedroom. He tosses me down onto the bed so hard that I bounce when my limp body collides with the mattress. Throw pillows fall to the floor.

Tucker's chest lifts and falls with excessive oxygen. His eyes watch me with the same wild intensity that was there when he arrived. He gasps for air and fights a battle internally that I don't think I'm privy to. I'm not so sure what about me makes this so difficult, but this isn't easy for him. It's like…*I scare him.*

"Tell me what you want from me, Daisy, and I will give it to you. I'll give you everything." His voice sounds like rough wood against fine-grained sandpaper. The last sentence hangs in the air between us, feeling heavy and important all at once.

My belly warms. Tucker Stafford might be a bad boy, but he asks permission. He is considerate. He's a vigilante with a laptop instead of guns or knives. Standing over me, foreboding and lacking his usual self-control, I can't help but crave what's to come.

I sit up and pull my dirty, formerly white, t-shirt over my head, dropping it onto the floor somewhere behind me. I grab the waistband of my jeans, and since they're already undone, I shimmy right on out of them, taking my less-than-stellar lingerie choice with me as I go.

I feel icky and gross, and normally that would be a hard red light, but not tonight.

With minimal effort, my sports bra is tossed somewhere into the growing pile of discarded clothes on my bedroom floor.

I don't have to wait long for Tucker to follow suit. Kicking off his boots, he stumbles in his haste to get rid of them. He pulls his black t-shirt off, gripping it at the back and pulling it over his head in one *shouldn't be sexy, but damn it is* movement.

Tucker unbuckles his leather belt. He unbuttons his black denim jeans and then pulls them down his muscled thighs as if we've done this a hundred times before, and this isn't the first time he's been in my room naked. Almost…naked. Oh God, he's so close to being naked, the anticipation just might kill me before he gets there. He's not nervous, or maybe he is and he's hiding it behind a well-built wall of confidence that has been ingrained into the makeup of his DNA since he was a child.

His body is all hard lines and tanned skin. He's not overly muscular. He's a big guy, but his build is like that of an athlete. Not a football player, but maybe a swimmer or runner. When he grips his briefs and pulls them down, I don't hesitate to slip my hand over my clit and touch myself. Somehow, I've gone from the lazy bliss that follows a typical, one-off orgasm to high-strung and needy again in the short time that's passed between the living room to now.

I lie on the bed, completely exposed to this man, but I don't feel vulnerable or embarrassed. Something in the way he watches me gives me strength. I'm in control. I get to make the rules.

Feeling all sorts of brave, I say the three words I want more than anything right now.

"Fuck me, Tucker."

My declaration hangs in the silent space between us. One second feels like an hour. Two feels like infinity. Our heavy breathing sets the tempo. I lean back onto my elbows. My breasts are full, my nipples hardened with need. My feet dangle from the side of the bed, but I pull them up, bending my knees until my legs are spread wide and open for him. I left any form of self-consciousness I had somewhere back against the living room wall.

His erection stands between us, hard and threatening. The velvet skin is darker than the rest of his body. Veins protrude and it curves just barely at an angle that tells me he's going to hit every single wall inside of me with the precision of a skilled bowman. I've always found the male penis kind of weird, honestly. It's an appendage that I truly only want inside of me, tucked deep in my vagina where I don't have to look at it as it brings me immeasurable pleasure. But I'll admit, I'm no expert or anything. My experience is limited to senior prom night and a couple of Tinder hookups that ended in me doing the walk of shame and dousing my troubles in tequila.

But as I study Tucker's penis with lust-colored glasses,

I realize it's beautiful. Which can only mean one thing. I've well and completely lost my mind for this man. I don't dare think of the other word that tickles the back of my throat and begs to be validated.

He has yet to utter a single word, but it is clear he fully understands the assignment.

In one long stride, Tucker's shins hit the bed frame. Instead of leaning over me, he surprises me. He drops to his knees, and taking my ankles in his hands, he yanks me forward.

My hands form fists around the fluffy duvet. Tucker looks up at me with piercing eyes before quirking his lips into a small boyish grin. His broad shoulders make room for themselves, and my legs fall open.

"This wasn't supposed to happen, Daisy."

His warm breath feathers my sensitive skin. His mouth dances just above where my heart beats due south of my belly button.

"Tucker…" I breathe his name and pray he doesn't ruin this for both of us with stipulations or declarations that I'm not prepared to address at the moment. I don't want to think right now, I just want to feel.

"You're irresistible, Daisy. I need you like I need to write the thoughts that storm my mind every day. I need you like I need my next breath. All my life, I've been consumed by finding answers. Solving mysteries. Finding the truth. Those things are still important to me, but now you're here, and I'm so fucking consumed by you that…I think…trying to keep you safe might kill us both."

I try to listen, truly I do, but his words are lost to me when he buries his face between my legs, and his mouth becomes the only consuming factor my brain can focus on. He engulfs me in fire. The heat of his tongue laps at my throbbing clit, and the flames that were just simmering coals are once again ignited.

Stubble scratches my thighs. The contrast of rough versus the soft striations of the movements of his tongue against my slit is the accelerant to the burning desire between us.

The banter. The wit. The late-night discussions. Everything comes at once, building into what is sure to be an explosion. *Fuck*.

I grip the sheets and hold on for dear life as I feel my orgasm preparing to shatter me once more. This time it builds deep inside of me. It's slow and torturous, not lightning-fast and racing like the prior two orgasms this man has given me.

Something about what's happening between us feels *different*—it feels significant. My heart thuds in a rhythm with the blood that flows beneath Tucker's tongue. Tucker's hands reach around my thighs and grip my ass. His fingers make indentations in my skin that will surely result in purple markings tomorrow. I don't care. He pulls me closer to his mouth, so close that my hips are lifted from the bed, and I'm forced to lean back and let my shoulders hold my weight.

He balances me mid-air and devours me until I think I might collapse. Burying his nose in my clit, he ravishes me with his tongue. My body trembles. My head falls back against the duvet as desire coils tightly in my belly. It's overwhelming. It's all too much.

"Oh, God, Tucker. I'm coming." My words are a

rushed realization as sensation pulls me under. With zero time remaining, I try to warn him. I try, but instead of slowing, he bites down on my clit with his teeth and my world detonates in an explosion that rocks my very soul to the core.

I scream out until my throat is dry and hoarse, and my words are indiscernible.

Tucker's tongue slips into my pussy, and I feel my body immediately clamp down around him, looking for something, anything to grab onto. I want him. Jesus, I want him inside of me right now, but I can't say any of that because my words won't work.

Just when I think it's over, when I think there might be some reprieve from the intensity of it all, he surprises me again. Tucker drops my hips back down onto the bed and climbs over my body.

"You're just as sweet as I thought you would be, Daisy." His smile stretches his chiseled jaw. His face glistens with what I know is…*me*.

His hips fill the opening between my legs that his shoulders occupied seconds ago.

My pussy still pulsates. My words still refuse to work.

Placing an elbow on either side of my head, it's like Tucker is floating above me. His hair flops in his face, and I can't help but reach up and move it out of his eyes. My arms feel like they weigh a thousand pounds.

"You're beautiful, Daisy. So damn perfect." He whispers.

I smell myself on his breath, and it surprises me that I want a taste too. Leaning up, I brush my lips to his. His mouth opens, and his tongue taps mine. The stubble that was just raking across my thighs now scratches my jaw as I swallow down the concoction of flavors his saliva offers. It feels taboo and erotic and only further feeds the desire swirling in my belly.

His hardened cock rests against my swollen clit, and I want nothing more than for him to slide it inside of me. I want to feel him. He's right there. So close, if I could just scoot him down ever so slightly.

I run my hands over his chest. I touch. I explore places that I've only ever imagined. Slowly, my strength returns, and with it my need for release…again. Who am I? *Jesus*. The better question is, what is this man doing to me?

With renewed energy, lifting my hips, I force his cock to slide against my folds, so close and yet so far away. Tucker steals the oxygen from my throat and words that I shouldn't say from my mouth, as he kisses me with a passion I didn't realize existed outside of books and movies.

I run my hands down his back, around his defined shoulder blades, and over the concave of his spine. His skin is hot to the touch. Two small indentations, dimples, rest just above his ass. I continue my explorations until my hands firmly grip his ass.

I rock my hips into his and simultaneously pull him against me using what strength I can muster. I feel his knowing smile against my lips. Pulling back slightly, his eyes shine down at me as he stares directly into mine, his nose kissing my nose.

He's playing with me. *Taunting. Teasing.* And that's not a fair game when he is firmly in the control position—*literally*.

"Tucker, I told you what I wanted, and you promised to give it to me. I asked nicely, and you know how difficult that is for me." I speak with broken words, lacking oxygen as my ability to string a sentence together returns and I try to demand more... *now*.

The tip of his cock is so close, if only he'd angle his hips just...

"I know what you want, Daisy." He has the audacity to smile. "I also know the instant I'm inside of you, I'm going to make a fool of myself. I'm trying to preserve my dignity here, woman."

"Fuck your dignity."

His nose remains touching mine. His breath fanning my face and his lips so close to mine that I could reach up and kiss him. If he deserved kisses, which he doesn't. Not while he's holding out on me. Sure, I've had two other orgasms already tonight, but he created this monster, and now I feel entitled to all of the orgasms.

"You know, you've developed quite a potty mouth tonight for such a sweet, small-town florist." His eyes dance with humor that I don't feel. My sexual frustration is not humorous in the least.

"*Tucker...*" I growl. I've turned completely feral. My fingernails dig into the skin of his ass. I nip at his lip with my teeth before yanking him to me once again.

His eyes turn serious as if finally realizing I am in a true predicament here. "Protection." He mutters.

I fall back on the mattress.

"In the nightstand." I groan and tilt my head to my left, toward the small table next to my bed.

He raises an eyebrow curiously. "Seriously?"

"It might be expired." I shrug. It is absolutely expired. "How long?"

"Um…." I hesitate because I honestly don't know the answer. It's been a while. A long, long while.

"Same." He says before I can mentally calculate if I've had sexual intercourse in the last five years. "I'm clean, tested last month at my annual."

Men have an annual? The thought briefly intrudes my hormone-muddled brain before disappearing just as quickly.

"Me too," I answer while still trying to do mental math. "The clean part. I've also got the birth control part covered. I think my annual was…maybe I should make a note to call about that." Finally, it's my turn to tease him. There is no way I'm moving from this spot until we are both totally and completely satisfied. Even then, I don't want to move from the bed. I might scoot over enough to make room for a slumber party, but that's the extent of it.

Mission accomplished. Tucker's jaw hardens and his nostrils flare. "Focus, Daisy. No notes. No post-its. No reminders. You good?"

I have to work to keep my eyes from crossing, staring at his face so close to mine, but if he's referring to whether or not I'm good with his naked cock inside of me, well, I kind of feel like that answer is obvious. If he doesn't hurry up, I'm about to show him how good I am with it.

"I'd be better if you'd lift your hips and slide down just an inch." I angle my hips up so that the tip of his cock teases my throbbing opening.

I've never done this before. I've never trusted anyone with my body like this, but I feel sure with Tucker, and I don't think that's just the hormones talking. Poor Aunt Fran is rolling in her grave.

"Fuck." Tucker releases a heavy breath before swooping in and stealing one final kiss from my lips. His forehead presses against mine. He reaches between us and grabs his length, placing the tip in the exact right spot. *Finally*.

"We're doing this." His words are hushed, and I'm not sure if they're meant for my ears, or if they're just for him, but I answer him all the same, repeating them back to him because I need them for me just as badly.

"We're doing this."

There's no slow inching. No edging. I am already primed and ready for him.

I lift my hips, and Tucker greets me in the way only he can. Liquid fire. A guttural moan tears from his throat as he slams into me, impaling me with his cock and filling me in the most glorious way.

My body spasms. A whimper escapes my lips. My stomach drops out into the abyss, and my eyes threaten to roll back into my head, never to return again. That's a horrible visual, but damn I'm covered in feelings. They're all over me. Inside of me. They're lighting me up from within.

Tucker stills for only a second, long enough for me to feel the fullness of his girth as it stretches me in the absolute best way.

When I'm finally able to open my eyes, I see only him. His wide eyes stare right back at me, and what I see in them takes my breath away. Because I think he feels it too. It's more than just a physical connection. So much more.

Tucker pulls out to the very tip, only to slide right back in. Again and again, until I don't know how much longer I can take it. His hips slam into mine, and I yank harder. With every thrust, the tip of his cock massages a spot deep inside of me that begs for more.

He fucks me hard and fast. He's not easy with me, and I appreciate it. It tells me that he's just as lost to this as I am.

"Daisy, baby, I'm going to need you to get there for me." He grunts, and I think for a second about the fact that he's about to come inside of me, and I want him to fill me up. I want him to release himself in my body. I want that part of him.

"Tucker!" I scream his name one final time before my orgasm takes me under again.

My fingernails steal skin. My mouth finds his jaw and I bite down with my teeth, muffling my screams as my orgasm rocks me to the very core.

"Jesus, Daisy!" Tucker slams into me so hard that the mattress shifts from the frame and my shoulders fall from the edge of the mattress, but I don't care. I can't think about anything other than the fact that I can literally feel his cock pulsing inside of me.

Our moans, our screams, *our pleasure*, they swirl around us and encompass us in a bubble of ecstasy that I never want to leave.

My orgasm is so intense, so long that I lose track of time. I don't know how long it lasts. I'm not sure how long we stay tightly coiled together, dragging out every last ounce of pleasure.

Tucker's heart hammers against mine. It beats so hard that I swear I can feel it. I swear it matches the wild erratic rhythm of my own.

I feel the bed move when he releases the duvet he's fisted in his hands, and I know the moment he opens his eyes because the air shifts and we both know that we've shared something monumental.

"Daisy, baby, open your eyes." His voice is raw and full of things that are scary in the real world, outside of this small bubble we're wrapped up in. I'm not ready. Blood rushes back up into my head, as I lay halfway off of the bed. I try to hold on to this moment for as long as he'll let me.

"Daisy, fuck. Daisy, I need you to look at me." The sound of his voice cuts through my willpower.

Tears sting my eyelids. Why am I crying? I've never had a cry-gasm. Is it considered a cry-gasm if it's after the fact? Is that a technical term?

*Suck it up.* I sniffle and slowly open my eyes.

Tucker grins, wide and beautiful.

"Wanna be on my team, Daisy?" He asks, and I don't know if it's the way he says it or the fact that at the same moment, he wiggles his hips and I realize his cock is still inside of me and already beginning to harden again but I start giggling.

My watery giggles turn into full-blown laughter and then I'm snorting, and snot is on my face, and I know I must look completely hysterical, but I can't stop the madness once it's begun. Tucker barks out a laugh and then we're both gasping for oxygen between loud ugly snorts and giggles. My eyes water, and I swear if I start crying again, I'm going to make an appointment to have myself evaluated for early onset menopause.

Amid our laughter, one of Tucker's hands skims my shoulder, following an imaginary line to my rib cage, where he slowly caresses my skin.

He's so beautiful. So perfectly imperfect.

Would it be so bad if we did this thing together?

# CHAPTER SIXTEEN
# TUCKER

I lie still next to Daisy's warm, supple body. She sleeps so peacefully. Her breathing is slow and even. I pulled a blanket over her naked body when she fell asleep on my chest last night. She was exhausted, but I can't say that I blame her. I spent hours worshiping her body, finally giving in to the tension that's been tormenting our relationship for months.

Last night was...unexpected. It was life-altering.

Daisy flops onto her back in sleep, causing her golden blonde locks to splay out over the pillowcase next to mine. I wonder what that's like? To just...sleep. To fall asleep easily and stay that way until the morning comes. When I close my eyes, I hear so much inside my head. Constant chaos storms my mind.

The sunrise tints the window panes, but her eyes remain closed. She still has a smudge of grease smeared on her cheek. We never made it to the shower, there wasn't enough time. There wasn't a plan, and showering never quite made it to the top of the list. Suddenly, her eyelashes flutter. Her lips turn up ever so slightly. Is she dreaming? Is it me she sees in the sleepy darkness?

A flash of light catches my eye from somewhere on the floor. I'm drawn to the lit screen of my phone lying next to our discarded clothing. I need to get up. I have business to attend to. A familiar name flashes on the screen. I wish it was Casey responding to my note, but it's not. It's my father. Again. Missed calls appear when the call rings out, all him.

I groan internally. I sure as fuck hope he doesn't know anything about what happened yesterday. I'm not ready for him to know that I'm looking for my sister. I don't ever want her on his radar. Same with Daisy. I can't have him sending one of his cronies over here. They'll need more than a damn neighborhood watch brigade if that happens.

"You're thinking real hard about something over there when we could still be sleeping or, you know, *not sleeping.*" Her voice startles me. I glance back at where I swear, she was just dreaming. She speaks, but her breathing remains even as if only her brain is awake and her body is still resting from last night.

I need to go. I need to get out of here and start cleaning up the mess I've made. But I'm not going to bounce anymore without keeping Daisy informed. If last night showed me anything, it's that I'm already in too deep. I thought I could keep her at arm's length, at least until this was all over with. But I can't. I need her.

I quickly squeeze my eyes shut and then open them

again.

"I broke into Casey's apartment and left a note in her deceased mother's journal." I blurt out my confession. I tell her the truth, all of it, and not at all eloquently.

Daisy's eyes fly open, now fully awake. "You what?"

She stares at me in disbelief, and I'm not sure what words there are left to say. I did it. I broke the law, and I'm hoping that asking for forgiveness proves easier than asking for permission would have been.

She leans up and props her head up with her hand, leaving her elbow positioned on the pillow. "Holy hell, Tucker. I was kidding about the whole harboring a fugitive bit. I've already saved your ass from going to jail once." Her mouth remains slightly ajar, her eyes wide.

"I saved yours first." I try not to smile when the duvet falls around her waist and gives me a full view of her beautifully naked breasts. I don't smile, but my eyes sure as fuck wander.

"Don't start." She throws up her hand in front of my face, but I peek around it because her nipples are hardening after being exposed to the cold air in the room, and I don't want to miss that.

"You started it." I swipe her hand out of my face and intertwine our fingers, to which she merely snarls in response.

"So, we're back to *Perpetually Annoyed Daisy* today?" I raise an eyebrow and simultaneously give her hand a quick squeeze.

She flops back down on the bed with a flourish, and I roll to my side, placing our joined hands on the exposed skin of her belly.

Sighing loudly, her stomach lifts and falls with the influx of oxygen. "When you say you broke in…what specifically do you mean by that? Are we talking about like how you broke into my shop and searched for paperwork? Or…" She lets the words hang in the air, but it's so much worse than she thinks. She's an optimist. She wants to think the best of me, but in this case, she's wrong.

"I ransacked the place. I left a note. Then I came here." I don't try to sugarcoat it, I'm brutally honest for both of us.

Her free hand slams against her forehead. "Great, now I'm an accomplice. I hate you, Tucker Stafford." She grumbles, but I know she doesn't mean hate. She means love. I know first-hand that it's easy to confuse the two. On occasion, my parents told me they loved me. They didn't. It was never love. Just like I will never love the man that helped create me. There is only room for hate in my heart when it comes to him.

"That's not what you said last night." Unoffended, I make sure to flash her my most innocent smile. She didn't say she loved me with her words, but her body told me otherwise.

"Why? Why would you do that, Tucker? Dammit, man. I am the president of the neighborhood watch committee, and I am already on very thin ice. Dale and Nelly are sneaking around, making plans to unseat me." She huffs, unwilling to give in to the new lifestyle I've managed to rope us into.

"Dale and Nelly are too busy canoodling next door to worry about what laws you're breaking. I hate to break it to you, Daisy, but your entire watch team is corrupt."

I know what I saw when I pulled up outside last night. The things Dale and Nelly were doing on Nelly's front porch had nothing to do with fighting small-town cul-de-sac crime, unless Dale found it necessary to give Nelly a full-body pat down after tea.

"Canoodling? What are you talking about?" Daisy gasps, almost more shocked by this revelation than the news of my break-in.

"Dale is putting his noodle…" I start and then give her a moment to catch up.

"No! God, stop it, Tucker. Just…no!" She chokes out, throwing her hand over her eyes as if it would shield her from the visual of Dale's flaccid noodle.

"What, *canoodling*? It's a technical term, Daisy." I swing my leg over hers and canoodle her without asking first because I gained permission into her bed, which I believe now gives me full-on canoodling rights if I'm thinking about this correctly. We're teammates now. Bed mates. Fully and completely…mated and canoodling together until death do us part.

"I can't talk about Dale's noodle when your noodle is touching my thigh. I need you to be serious for a second, Tucker. I need you to tell me why you broke into the home of your half-sister. I want to know why you risked everything you've been working toward because you were too scared to face her. The Tucker I know isn't scared of confronting people to find answers. You do realize how dangerous this game you're playing is, don't you? You could go to jail. The police could be actively searching for you right this very instant. Your sister is an attorney for

God's sake!" Her eyes widen even further the more she talks. Fear and concern disguised as anger color her words.

Maintaining hold of her hand, I reach up and pull the other from where she's tangled it up in her bed head in frustration. I sit up fully in the bed and hold onto her. I like to play. She's fun, and making her smile *and* sometimes growl brings me immense joy. However, I need her to know I'm serious about this. There's a time for fun, and then there's a time for facts.

"I *am* serious about this. You're forgetting that it's more complicated than what you're making it out to be. First, I won't go to jail. My last name is Stafford, and as fucking arrogant and entitled as that sounds, it's the truth. Second, the project that I'm working on…it's an exposé on my father. One that will end with him in handcuffs. Risk versus reward. My half-sister is a very successful attorney with a reputation for stripping men of their dignity, and their wallets, in the courtroom. She clearly has a vendetta against men. Is it against Hilton? I can't know that. But the journal that I found in her apartment confirmed that she knew of him. It confirmed that her mother was in love with him. The business card shoved between the worn pages? It had his name and contact information on it. If she hates him as much as I do, I need her help. I need her knowledge and skills. Most of all? I need her anger. Even if it's partially at my expense." I fill in holes that I've previously left open in the hopes that Daisy will understand why I'm doing this. If she's going to be part of this team, she needs to know what we're fighting for.

"That's all fine and dandy, Tucker, but you said it yourself, she hates men. What makes you think she'll want to help you do anything at this point other than walk you to your jail cell after you've completely trashed her apartment and violated her space?"

"I don't. I didn't think that far ahead. I make the next right move, it's what I do, and the process has served me well up until this point. Like I said, I left a note that I'm certain she'll find. If she finds the note, she'll find me. And when she finds me, I can only hope that I'll have some sort of plan together that will manage to convince her to help me finish this once and for all."

"So, you don't have a plan? Oh God, you're going to jail. You know that right?"

"I'm not going to jail, Daisy. You'll see. It will be fine." My words speak of a confidence I don't completely feel, but I have no choice. I have to believe good defeats evil in the end.

"Famous last words." She snaps back quickly. "The FBI is probably already on their way here." She whips her eyes to my naked chest and then back down at her exposed body, barely covered by a sheet at this point. "I'm not dressed to be arrested, God, I'm not dressed at all. We should put clothes on, I don't want to be naked when the cops show up."

I don't move. I keep her hands trapped in mine despite her protests to escape and ruin our small bubble of solitude.

"Listen, you're panicking for no reason. This is going to work out, I'm the good guy. We are the good guys. The good guys always win."

You can't beat someone who won't give up, and I won't give up. Not on proving my father's guilt. Not on Daisy. Not on us.

Leaning down, I kiss her nose lightly, followed by her jaw. I pepper kisses along her collarbone.

"I'm not going to jail for you, Tucker." Her words turn breathy. She says one thing, but the fluttering of her pulse under the delicate skin of her neck tells me otherwise. I feel her heart beating beneath my lips when my mouth touches the vein in her neck.

"What happened to the tough girl from the fire?" I slide my tongue over where she refuses to admit that her heart beats for me.

Instead, she elongates her neck, giving me more room to work. "She got laid, and realized that there is more to life than prison sex."

"Please, enlighten me, Daisy Mae. What is it that you think you know about prison sex?" I ask coyly as I continue to work my tongue on her smooth skin.

She opens her legs beneath the sheet and I roll into the space she makes for me, pressing my already hardened cock against its newfound home.

"You're changing the subject." Her words are a low moan.

Am I? I've lost track of all thoughts that don't end with me inside of Daisy again. It's been too long already. I need more.

"It's an honest question," I murmur when my thoughts return and then promptly vacate the moment I feel her warmth on my skin.

Daisy wraps her long legs around my waist and crosses

her ankles at my back. Like a magnet, the tip of my cock slips inside of her. I enter her slowly, giving her time, because last night was a lot. I don't want to hurt her.

I lift our entangled hands above her head and she whimpers softly, the sound heightening the sense of pleasure of being inside of her.

"Honest answer?" I hear her audibly swallow before she continues speaking. "I know what I've seen on those locked-up shows, and I just really like the kind of sex we did last night, okay? Not that I have anything against a little girl-on-girl action, but…" I slide in until I'm fully seated. Her words trail off the moment I touch the inner walls of her pussy. God, she feels so damn good.

"New fantasy unlocked." I laugh and smack a kiss onto her lips.

"Tucker Stafford." She says my name like I'm in trouble, and it's sexy as fuck.

"What? You went there."

Slowly I begin to slide out and then back in. All the while we manage to carry on a conversation. Our words are littered between small gasps and quick intakes of breath as I penetrate her pussy at an agonizingly slow pace.

"I don't want you to go to prison either, Tucker." She gasps when I jerk my hips forward unexpectedly. "I like this." I'm not sure if she's talking about us or my dick inside of her, but I'll take either right now and hope what she really means is both.

Dropping her hands, I sit up on my knees. Her legs remain wrapped around my waist, her ass sits on my thighs and my hands grip her hips. My hands splay all the way to her lower rib cage. I'm so deep inside of her at this angle. I pause our movements. I have words I need to say. She needs to hear this, and right now she won't fight me and she can't escape.

"I like this too. I like this a lot, which is exactly why I need to end this thing with my father once and for all. I don't want to live in fear. Not for myself, not for you, not for the corrupt business practices that he is involved in that could affect an entire nation if he's given enough power."

I remain still, but my hands stray from her hips over her torso until they reach her breasts. I slowly massage them, watching her nipples as they peak. They're light pink and perfectly round. Her chest is red with heat. Marks of light purple litter her skin from last night. She arches her back, pressing herself further into my hands.

"So, what does that mean for me? What happened last week was unacceptable. I've lost too many people I care about, my parents, my aunt—I can't go through that again. I can't sit around wondering where you are for days on end while you do whatever this master plan is that you're doing. I just can't. I'm sorry if that makes me sound needy or clingy, but this is me. What you see is what you get."

Releasing her breasts, I bring my hands up to cup her face.

"I know you think I abandoned you last week, Daisy. Fuck, I'm sorry. I don't know how to do this. I've always worked alone. Then you came along, and I swear to God I wasn't just using you for information. Sure, it might have been about that at first. But after the night of the fire, everything changed. You shook my world up, and I've been consumed with you ever since. I thought you were a distraction. I couldn't think. I couldn't write. So, I took some space. I understand now how that was the wrong way to handle it. I need you. I've realized that I can't fucking do this alone. And I'm scared. I know you said that I'm not scared of anything, but you're wrong about that. I've done some bad things. I just…dammit, Daisy, it scares me to drag you into this. We joke about Hilton, but the man is fucking dangerous. I don't want him anywhere near you."

"I never asked to be saved, Tucker." She whispers. A lone tear tracks down her cheek and hits the pillowcase.

"What are you saying?" I ask, needing her to say the words. I need her commitment.

"Let me fight the fire beside you. I mean, I'm not the luckiest person, but I'll show up. For you, I'll show up, even when it's hard. Even when we're losing. We don't have to be alone anymore, Tucker. We can do this together. Like you said, teammates."

"What happens if the flames get too hot? What happens when it's too dangerous? What happens then?" I need more. I need assurance. Certainty.

"We stand back and watch it burn. But we'll have each other. That's more than either of us have ever had before so I call it a win, even when we lose."

Now it's my turn for my pulse to hammer in my neck. My chest aches.

"You scare the shit out of me, you know that right?" My throat feels tight, making words hard, but I speak through the strained muscles anyway.

She says I'm not scared of anything, but I am. I am so damn scared of losing her.

"You've said so a time or two." Her lips curl into a smile that makes me weak.

I move my hands back to her hips.

"Look, I meant what I said, Daisy. We're a team. What that means is that I promise not to disappear again. I promise to keep you in the loop. I promise to keep you safe, and I promise to love you like this for as long as you'll let me." *Love.* The word slips from my lips unfiltered, and I can't get it back once it's out there. I don't think I want to take it back. It's true. I've never felt as deeply for someone as I feel for Daisy.

She laughs softly. "So, that's it? We're just a couple losers against the world?" She doesn't return my words of affection, not yet, but I see how she feels in her eyes. I can feel it inside of her body. I know she's right there with me, she just doesn't realize it yet. I'm going to make it my mission to make her see.

"Nah, we're the underdogs. They won't ever see us coming." That's all I say before gripping her hips in my hands and finishing what we started. Only this time, I make love to her, and she loves me back without saying as much. This time I seal my promises between us and know in my heart that I'll do whatever it takes to keep them.

# CHAPTER SEVENTEEN
# TUCKER

*The person you are trying to reach is unavailable...*

Fuck.

I groan and using my thumb I jam the red button on my cell phone with more force than necessary.

He couldn't be bothered to leave a voicemail. Just three ominous missed calls spaced out over four hours. He's been silent for weeks. Yet he was up before the sun, and he was looking for me. Why?

Where are you, Hilton? What do you want? What do you know?

Glancing back over my shoulder, I look at my motorcycle one last time. I can't shake the feeling something is off, and I don't like it one bit. I hope I'm just paranoid. Now that I've let Daisy into my life, I've opened the door to susceptibility and danger and welcomed it right the fuck on in. I've exposed us both, and the thought doesn't sit well with me. I had no choice.

Leave her or risk losing her. Leaving is off the table—last night made that abundantly clear. So, looks like I take the risk and roll out the red carpet for whatever is sending prickles up my fucking spine with every step I take.

I parked in the parking deck of my building instead of on the street like I usually do. I'm exhausted. I don't have plans to leave again before tomorrow. I shove my phone into the pocket of my dirty day-old jeans. Watching it won't make Casey call any faster. The sooner she responds to my letter, the better for everyone.

I guess this is my very own version of the walk of shame. I left Daisy's this morning after sharing a quick breakfast of Lucky Charms. Apparently, it's her favorite. She only ate the marshmallows. Somehow that did not surprise me. I smile to myself imagining her picking out the colorful rainbow portions all the while claiming the brown cardboard pieces were stale. They're not stale—I know because I ate them for her.

We made dinner plans for later. She's coming here, and I'll order takeout for us. She told me this morning that she has some exciting news to share with me regarding Hydrangea & Vine and she'd like me to review some contracts with her tonight.

I'm calling it a date, even though I know she'll probably fight me on it.

I'll send her a text in an hour or so and tell her not to forget her overnight bag. It's strange how life works. One day you're a bachelor living in solitude and, next thing you know, a beautiful blonde florist has uprooted your life and you're planning sleepovers.

I fumble in my pocket for my key fob to the building

elevator but turn when I hear the sound of someone approaching me from behind. But I see nothing.

Then pain. It lasts for only a split second as darkness transcends upon me like a warm blanket. And even though I fight, it's only a heartbeat before sleep pulls me under.

-

Fucking hell, my head hurts. Pain radiates through my skull and bounces around like a marble inside of an empty drum. My first thought is the pain followed by acute awareness of my captivity.

My eyes are open, but I remain in pitch-black. My hands are bound, but my feet are free. I lie still on my side but repetitive bumps jar my body awkwardly. I'm in a moving vehicle, I'm certain. Fuck, it hurts to think.

I want to fight my restraints. I want to run—find a way out. My instincts scream at me to get away from the danger, but logic tells me that my best chance of survival is to remain silent and still.

I'm careful not to make any sudden movements. I don't know where I am or where I'm headed. I'm working from suspicions alone, and my father is at the tip-top of the list of potentially suspicious characters in my life. One of many, but all roads ultimately lead home.

If he's responsible for this, who the hell knows what set him off this time? That'd explain the phone calls and why he didn't answer when I tried to call him back.

Daisy. Fear rattles my brain, sending a fresh wave of nausea rolling through my gut and burning my esophagus as I fight to remain silent. I swear to God if he touched her. For the first time since waking up, I'm scared. Not for me but for her. I'm worried he got to her. One day on the job, and I'm already failing her. Worst-case scenarios begin to play in my mind on a reel of terror, but they're interrupted when I hear voices that sound like they're merely feet from my head.

"You didn't have to put a bag over his head, Aemilia."

Male voice. Middle-age. His dialect is slang, which tells me that he's possibly a gangster or a thug. The name Aemilia isn't familiar to me.

"Don't be a softy, Straton. The fabric is breathable."

Female voice. Irritated as shit. I'm going to infer that this is Aemilia.

The name Straton's not ringing any bells either. She's not wrong about this fabric. I can breathe through whatever the material is that surrounds my head and reduces my visibility to nothing.

Unable to use my vision, my other senses begin to heighten. I hear a blinker, I guess my captors follow the laws of the roadway. Then, I hear what sounds like someone turning in their seat in front of me. I think it's in front of me, I'm still having difficulty with direction.

"What? He can't see us, but he has oxygen. And I only tased him once, I never even pulled my actual weapon."

She tased me? Hell, I don't even remember being tased.

"You hit him in the head, Em, and then tased him after he was already knocked out cold. That's not protocol, and you know it." He grunts.

Protocol? Since when do criminals follow a protocol?

Of what? Is there a bad guy rule book out there? Seems like that'd be a super handy piece of literature to have on hand.

"You're such a fun sucker in your old age, Alex."

Old? These people don't sound old at all. They carry on with a familiarity that sounds like they know each other pretty well.

My imagination conjures up images of a modern-day Bonnie and Clyde. Shit, imagining makes my brain hurt worse. What did she hit me with? I can't tell, I just know it hurts like a bitch.

"I've got something I'll let you suck, Mrs. Straton, and I can assure you that it has never been soft in your presence."

The fuck? My world spins, and I'm only able to make sense of half of what these people are saying. Are they murder for hire? I'm starting to think I'm hallucinating, floating in and out of consciousness.

"Later, right now we've got to get him in before he wakes up, and I have to put a bullet in his leg. I really hate these Stafford men."

My ears perk up.

"You only know one of them, Em."

Are Em and Aemilia one and the same?

"I know, but I really fucking hate that guy. This one has the same name. Same blood. That's enough for me to know I'm not interested in anything he has to say."

"So, why not shoot him and get it over with? Why are we quite literally bringing him in for questioning if you're not interested in anything he has to say?"

My body stiffens, and I'm careful to slow my

breathing to further minimize my movements.

"Am I losing my touch?" The female, Em or Aemilia, whatever her name is, asks her male counterpart.

"What? You can touch me, sugar plum. You can always touch me."

Is he flirting with her while I'm bound in the same vehicle?

"Be serious, Alex. I knew I should have asked Reid to come instead."

Alex. Reid. I catalog names, all of which are still foreign to me. How many of them are there? I have no idea who these people are. My only hope is that they seem to hate my father with a passion that equals my own. Unfortunately, it appears I might be found guilty by association before I'm able to explain myself.

"The fuck you don't, Aemilia. Now, back to the touching." He teases her and something in the way he says it makes them sound like lovers. They're flirting. The fuck?

"Right, I used to be a badass. I think I'm getting soft. I mean, we're told to bring him in for an interrogation, and he's in the backseat. He's not bleeding."

Interrogation. Puzzle pieces click together. The fucking FBI. Daisy was right.

"You put the man to sleep before tasing him, cuffing him, and then shoving a bag over his head…"

Wait, I got knocked out by a woman?

"Should I shoot him in the foot for funsies? I'd settle on a toe. I have a reputation to maintain, ya know?"

Hell no, you should not. Who let this crazy lady have access to a weapon anyway? She sounds insane. I'd expect more from a federal agent of the law.

"No, think of the paperwork, Em. You hate paperwork."

"You're right. I hate it when you're right. I fucking despise paperwork. Fine. We do the interrogation, find out what his deal is, and then I'll decide if the paperwork is worth putting a bullet in his toe."

Thank God. Someone needs to take her weapon away.

"That's my girl." The man, Alex, speaks softly to her before I feel the vehicle roll to a stop.

How long were we driving before I woke?

A door opens. Then another. Finally, a third door opens, and a breeze hits the exposed skin of my arms.

"Hilton Tucker Stafford."

Her tone changes as she says my name with authority, but I remain unmoving.

"You think he's still asleep?" The man asks as he taps my foot with something I can't see, searching for a response from me. I'm not asleep. I'm just not sure what my next move is. I'm cuffed with a bag over my head. I know they're armed, and the woman is clearly trigger-happy. Running isn't really an attractive option for me at the moment. But I highly doubt lying here in silence is going to make them walk away and forget my existence.

"Not a chance, I think our friend is playing possum with us, Alex." Not friends. Not playing games, just scared shitless to get my toe blown off before I see who's wielding the weapon and how many of them I'm up against.

"Yeah?"

"Yeah, watch, I'll shoot him, and we can find out."

She sounds giddy at the thought.

This woman is completely unhinged.

They joke, but I sit up because the longer I lay here, the more I think they're both lunatics with guns, and my head hurts enough as it is. I've been knocked out, allegedly tased, not to mention kidnapped today. I'd rather not add a gunshot wound to that growing list.

"Told ya. Just a little possum." She snickers and yanks the black shield that's been covering my head off in one quick move. I'm left blinded by natural light that burns my retinas and increases the throbbing inside my brain tenfold.

"Who are you?" I grunt the words out. My throat is dry, my words hoarse.

Straightening my shoulders, I wait for my eyesight to adjust. Everything is blurry, and I'm so damn confused.

One woman. One man. Slowly, my vision begins to clear.

She has at least one visible weapon. That's not counting the human assassin that stands next to her. Alex, I'm assuming, is a large man. He's got at least two inches on me, if not more, and I'm not a small guy. I look around and notice for the first time that I'm in the back of an SUV. I'm on the floor—they could have thrown me in the seat at the very least. Assholes.

Alex is bald. Intricately designed tattoos cover his arms and neck. Aemilia is petite, his total opposite. She has long dark hair. She's not American. Italian maybe? Portuguese? Come to think of it, I'm not sure what his nationality is either. Latino? I've never been one to judge, but I've been around associates of my father's enough to know these two fit the mold, despite what they say about hating him.

"I'm your worst nightmare." She smiles wildly.

"Em..." Alex looks down at her petite frame and she merely smirks up at him, totally unphased by his thinly veiled threat.

It's clear who runs this show.

"What? I've always wanted to say that to someone. I couldn't let an opportunity like that pass." She rolls her eyes and reaches into her black leather jacket.

I stare at them both because if they're going to kill me, I want them to do it with me looking them in the eyes while I die.

"Special Agent Emily Straton, FBI. You're wanted for questioning in connection with a recent break-in that we believe may have ties to mafia affiliations." She pulls out a badge and flashes it open in front of me.

I shrink back and thank God that I'm not staring down the barrel of a gun.

"It's so fucking sexy when you do that." Alex reaches behind her and smacks her on the ass. Zero professionalism.

"Special Agent Emily, Em or Aemilia. Which is it?"

"You call me anything other than Emily or ma'am and I will end you. Are we clear?"

I tip my chin up in response, not willing to test my luck with a crazy person with multiple identities. Her partner merely laughs at her outburst.

"And you?" I look from her to him.

"He's my sugar daddy." She grins and winks at the giant tattooed man next to her.

"Special Agent Alex Straton." If he has a badge, he's not worried about showing proof of it. He stands in front of me with his arms crossed over his broad chest. His legs are spread shoulder-width apart, and he dares me with his dark brown eyes to move from my spot until he permits me.

"You her bodyguard?" I lift my chin in the direction of his tiny boss.

They look at each other, and then they laugh. She laughs so hard that she bends at the waist, and I worry she'll somehow set her weapon off and shoot herself in the foot. I wouldn't be so lucky.

Finally, she straightens and catches her breath with a sigh. I love how comical they find my obvious discomfort with this entire situation.

"He wishes. Come on pretty boy, we've got some questions, and you're going to answer them, or I will throw you back in this SUV and take you somewhere no one will ever find your body."

She motions for me to step out of the car with them.

"Is she serious?" I look to the giant for help. I don't have many options here, and although I ask the question, I know for a damn fact that she is one hundred percent not joking.

"I wouldn't fuck with her if I were you."

# CHAPTER EIGHTEEN
# DAISY

**I**t's fine. Totally fine.

I gather up the notes I've scribbled down on various Post-its and scrap paper. I shove everything into my bag, followed by my laptop and ignore the sound of crumpling paper. That's a problem for later.

After Tucker left, I spent the remainder of my afternoon looking over the contract paperwork for the Walsh, Inc. investment. When I say I wanted to gouge my eyes out reading all of that legal jargon, that's an understatement. I didn't want Tucker to think I was tossing this into his lap without doing my own research first. I'm totally capable. I value his opinion, and I don't want to miss anything. Sure, I might end up in this situation again, starting over from scratch, but it will not be from my own doing. Not this time.

I glance over at my cell phone for the twenty-third time since Tucker left but don't touch it. If I touch it, I will text him. If I text him, it will only prove that I didn't believe anything he said to me about our partnership, team, relationship…whatever this is between us.

So I stare at it and hope that his silence has nothing to do with me. I convince myself that I'm totally overthinking this entire thing. He was just here this morning. We shared Lucky Charms. He ate the nasty bits that nobody eats. He swore that's where they hide the wheat. Wait, was it wheat or fiber? I can't remember. Either way, hard pass. I'll pop a Colace before bed if I need extra fiber.

I walk out of my bedroom, down the hallway and through the kitchen but pause when I reach the living room. I stop in front of the mirror near the front door. I glance at my reflection once and then look down at my clothes and wonder for the tenth time if I'm dressed appropriately.

I'm nervous. I've never been nervous around Tucker but last night changed everything.

He told me he loved me. I froze. *Why, Daisy?* Why did you freeze during one of the most monumental moments of your entire life?

I know what it feels like inside, but my brain and heart can't seem to get on the same page. I guess that's why I didn't say it back. Things were just so intense in that moment and people say things they don't mean in moments of…*intensity*. I don't hand out my love like candy. It's not free for the taking. It's special and important, and if I said those words to him, and for some reason, he woke up tomorrow or next week and realized he was speaking with his dick…my heart couldn't handle it. So, my brain said *no* when my heart screamed *yes*. I've lost every person I've ever loved. I can't lose him, not when I've only just found him.

Tucker mentioned staying in tonight, so there's really no need to throw on anything fancy. I don't want to show up overdressed and then look desperate. I've been rocking the thrift store chic look for the majority of the time we've been together and, so far, that seems to be working for me.

I've opted for a pair of black joggers that I have absolutely not run a single mile in and a cream-colored pullover. I paired the outfit with running sneakers—again, no running—and threw my hair up into a ponytail. I tried to make it look effortless, but in reality, I watched at least ten different TikTok videos on how to achieve this look. I'm going for athleisure. I think that's what the cool kids are calling it these days. Whatever. I feel cute and comfy, and this outfit easily transitions to pajamas if I *happen* to fall asleep at his place. Here's to hoping we don't sleep at all.

Once I'm satisfied with my look and have everything I think I need to go over with Tucker regarding the business tonight, I finally snatch up my phone and shove it into my purse before my fingers take on a life of their own and dial him up. They can't be trusted. One touch and they already feel mutinous.

We set a time. We set a place. He'll be there.

I have to trust him.

-o-
## TUCKER

Ten hours.

It's been ten fucking hours from the moment I was assaulted, kidnapped, interrogated and then released to find my way back home on my own.

Alex and Emily Straton are undercover agents of the Federal Bureau of Investigation. If there was a rating system for their professional performance today, I would give them zero out of ten stars. Hell, negative five stars.

Fuck. My head still hurts.

What I gathered from spending hours sitting on a cold-ass metal chair in a gray interrogation room with a two-sided mirror was that Hilton has been on their radar for almost as long as I've been alive. What was more surprising than that, though? They know my half-sister, well, and they want me to stay the fuck away from her.

They've been watching me.

They were ready to lock me up for breaking into her apartment, but apparently, they have a soft spot for Daisy. Her presence in my life threw a wrench in their plans, and now, instead of arresting me outright or worse, killing me, they think they can use me.

Daisy was their bargaining chip, and I'd do just about anything to keep her safe.

So, once again, I opened up about my plans. I have the information that they need. Their case was going stale. They received a hot tip recently that sent them in my direction. Some convicted insurance guy with ties to the mafia was up for a lesser sentence due to good behavior or some shit. He threw out my father's name in exchange for shaving off a few years, and now we're here. My father isn't the guy who gets his hands dirty. He's a money guy, moving it around from point A to point B, unnoticed and untraceable. He's gotten damn good at it over the years. Lucky for me, so have I.

I'm an insider into a world they've watched from the outside for a long time. Finally, years of research are starting to pan out. They trust that, because I value Daisy's life more than my own, the risk of me running and leaving her behind is slim. They're not wrong.

I told them about the exposé I'm writing about my father—my memoir. I was always planning to hand this over to the Feds. I just needed to have my facts straight, and I needed to bargain for my own safety. I gave them enough detail for them to believe I'd be an asset to them. They agreed to protect me. But more than that, they agreed to protect Daisy. In return, I signed my life away until this is done. I no longer work for myself, I'm a liaison to the FBI. If I so much as breathe in the wrong direction, I'll be charged with a laundry list of felonies. But, before that? I am one hundred percent certain the sexy Italian agent with a gun will kill me and bury my body with zero remorse.

Dragging my tired and beaten body to the elevator, I finally scan the key fob over the panel that will allow me access to my apartment floor. Every step I take forward is one step closer to my bed. My phone died hours ago. It feels like decades since I was last here.

I jab the close-door button and impatiently ride the elevator up. Stepping out into the hallway, I'm confronted by the one person that I gave up everything to protect.

*Daisy.* I wasn't sure she'd still be here. I was worried she'd think I left again.

"Tucker," She looks up from where she sits with her back against my front door. She's not mad. It's worse than that. She's hurt, and her feelings are written all over her pretty face.

I walk straight to where she sits with her oversized purse slung over her lap and her laptop sticking out of the top with various files and papers in disarray all over the place.

"Inside. We have to go inside, Daisy." I reach down and scoop her up into my arms, careful not to let anything drop from her bag. I ignore the way my body protests with physical exertion. My muscles ache. My head throbs. Doesn't matter. We can't speak out here. It's too dangerous.

"What's wrong?" She asks as I turn the key in the lock behind her and guide us through the entrance.

Once inside, I release her long enough to turn and lock us right back in. I slide the chain through, but it offers very little security. I'm paranoid.

I flip on a light and walk the perimeter of the apartment. I'm thankful for the open floor plan as I check every possible space for someone, anyone. I barely know the good guys from the bad ones anymore. I sure as fuck would have pinned the two that kidnapped me today as the latter. They're not, at least not while I am useful to them.

Determining the space is clear, I circle back to where

she still stands with her things in her arms near the front door.

"Tucker! What is going on?" Daisy punches my shoulder and demands answers when I'm too slow for her liking.

"Remember when you told me the FBI was coming for us?"

Crossing her arms over her chest, she pops her hip out. "I was kidding, Tucker."

"I'm not. They found me." I release a deep breath.

"What?" Her eyebrows pull to the center of her face in disbelief.

"The FBI. They found me this morning after I left your place." I continue to explain something that, by all accounts, is unexplainable.

"What do you mean they found you? You're doing that thing again where you act weird, Tucker. Your eyes look crazy. Is this going to become a thing?" She pulls her bottom lip into her mouth and begins abusing it with her teeth.

I step into her, take her face in my hands, and force her to release her lip before she draws blood.

"Look at me. Remember last night when I told you that we are a team? Remember the things I said to you about teammates and working together?"

She nods her head but doesn't say a word, and that scares me. What if this is too much for her? What if she doesn't want to be a part of this anymore? She said that part about watching things burn last night, but I'm not sure she was talking about all of this.

The only reason we're both still here living and

breathing is because of her innocence in all of this. She saved me. She saved us.

"You know Hilton is a bad guy. The worst kind of guy. I'm not. I promise you, Daisy, everything you know about me is true. I've never hidden anything from you. I broke into your flower shop. I trashed my half-sister's apartment. All things I did in the name of finding truth. All things I was straight up with you about." I swallow before continuing. "I'm writing an exposé that, once released, will prove to the world who my father truly is, once and for all. I can't allow him to win that Senate seat. I can't allow him to corrupt our government even more than it already is. The power he'd have would mean that no one could ever touch him. His reach would be too great, and the damage would only grow like a nasty vine, latching on to innocent people and slowly killing them. I thought finding my half-sister was the answer. I thought with her legal help and the information I'd already compiled we could take him down together. I never realized she was protected by the Bureau. I didn't know they were watching her. So, this morning I was not-so-politely taken into a long-ass interrogation. They know who you are. They know about Hilton. They have an entire fucking file on him, but I have more. The only reason I'm standing here with you right now instead of in custody until this is all over is because they like you."

"They like me? The FBI? You're serious? How do they know me?" She whispers, her eyes darting around the room as if she'll see them hiding behind the drapes. "I'm just a florist, Tucker. A small-town florist. I pay my taxes…I think. Shit. Should I call my accountant?"

"Focus, Daisy. I'm sure your taxes are in perfect order. That's the IRS—wrong government entity. No, these people let me go because I agreed to liaise with them until their investigation of my father is complete, until they have enough evidence for a conviction. I have evidence. I have the information they need, and I can lead them right to him. But they didn't want me. They don't trust me. They wanted you."

"Well, that's a major mistake on their part. You told them about my luck, right? You told them not to place bets on me, didn't you? Clearly, they weren't thorough enough with their research, or they would have seen the string of bad events that my life is made up of. Including this one. I told you, Tucker. I told you that I'm bad luck." She protests.

"You're so damn wrong about that. You're my lucky charm. Through all of this, you've been nothing but good luck for me." I smile, thinking of her picking out the marshmallows in her cereal. Was that just this morning?

"I told them you're an amazing woman. I told them that you're completely innocent in all of this. They know that. I also told them that I've reached out to Casey. They don't want me anywhere near my half-sister, not unless you're with me."

"So, what? I'm your babysitter now." She scoffs and tries to pull away, but I don't let her.

"No, you're my teammate. Just like we discussed last night. You're my best friend. You're the woman I...the woman I love." I hesitate to say those words again. Not because I don't mean them, but because her rejection is painful. She didn't say it back last night, and I don't expect her to say it today. Doesn't matter. I'll keep trying, even when it hurts. I'll keep telling her and, eventually, she has to hear me.

"Don't say that, Tucker. Don't say that if you don't mean it. Don't say it if you're only saying it because you're afraid of going to jail if I don't help you. Because you know I'll help you anyway. I'm going to say yes, it's just who I am. But don't use that word to get me to do something. Not now, not ever." Her lips tremble, and her eyes turn glassy. The thought that she would even consider I would use her in that way hurts my heart. My throat tightens.

"Daisy Mae Chandler, I love you so fucking hard that I want to write words devoted to only you. You inspire me. You're resilient. You're dedicated and so fucking loyal when you don't have any reason to be. And I don't understand it, because that's not how I'm wired. We're so different, but you're…you're the light. It's the only way I know how to describe it. You're the bright light I want to surround myself with when my entire life my world has been dark. I didn't know this kind of light existed. I didn't know how to find it or where to look. But I guess when you meet someone who shines so brightly, their light becomes the only way you can see anymore…without it, you're blind. I can't live without your light anymore, Daisy. I can't live without you." My hands shake, and I know she can feel them tremble.

A small smile teases her lips and fills me with hope. "Once upon a time, a florist fell in love with a writer."

"That's a story I want to write. What do you say?" My world stills. I wait on bated breath for an answer that I'm not sure will come.

Daisy stares at me without speaking for seconds, maybe minutes. Nervous anticipation swarms me.

"I love you, Tucker. Please don't break my heart." She admits with a shaky voice.

"I'm not much of a romance writer, Daisy. I don't always know the most eloquent words to say, and I'm going to fuck this up more than once. Despite all of that, I promise you that this story we're writing together ends with a happily ever after. If you'll trust me, I'll make certain of it."

# CHAPTER NINETEEN
# DAISY

**I** squeeze Tucker's hand in mine so hard that I'm surprised he has yet to cry out in pain or stomp on my foot in retaliation.

Instead, we walk hand-in-hand down the sidewalk like an ordinary couple on an ordinary Saturday afternoon. We're unsuspecting. We look typical.

Except, we're not. Not at all.

This is the beginning of an adventure. Right? That's what I'm calling it. Investigation is such a harsh word. Adventure sounds fun and less *death-y*.

It's been almost a month since Tucker and I agreed to work side-by-side with the FBI. The freaking Federal Bureau of Investigation. It feels no less weird saying that now than it did a month ago.

Special Agents Alex and Emily Straton are quite literally the scariest people I have ever met. Especially

Emily. She is terrifying. God forbid you call her by her birth name—made that mistake once and I don't intend to do that again. Alex is hot in the mobster, *I might kill you in your sleep, but we'll have fun first*, sort of way. But I do not dare even look at him for a second longer than I have to for actual fear that his wife will end my life with a toothpick and make it look like an accident.

These people are serious. Tucker Stafford better be glad I love him because if I didn't, no man would be worth all of this.

"Stop it, she's going to love you. Everyone loves you. It's me she hates." Tucker leans into me and gently kisses my temple as we approach a small coffee shop.

"What about guilt by association? I'm with you. You're the enemy. That makes me the enemy." I hiss as he slowly pulls his lips away from my skin and reaches for the door.

He pauses just briefly before opening it. "I promise, Daisy, just go in there and be yourself. She'll have no choice but to love you. Trust me. It's kind of impossible not to, I know first-hand." I hate it when he's so adorable. It was easier to argue with him when he was being an arrogant jerk.

"Are you trying to woo me into doing your dirty work, Tucker Stafford?" I frown at him, but my distaste is completely bogus.

"I don't know, is it working?" He smolders me with one look, and he and I both know he's got me. That freakin' smolder.

We step into the small coffee shop, and the fragrant aroma of fresh ground coffee beans and caramel makes me wish this were a date instead of a meeting that was doomed from the start.

Casey, Tucker's half-sister, finally called and agreed to meet with Tucker, but it wasn't for reconciliation, that I'm certain of. Curiosity maybe? Murder? It's a definite possibility.

I'm not sure what her end-game is, but Tucker and our FBI counterparts seem to think that the only way this doesn't end in bloodshed is to use me as a buffer. Lovely, right?

I still don't understand why the FBI wouldn't step in and mediate this situation. Why does everything need to be a secret? Why does Casey's assistance to Tucker have to be something he coordinates instead of them? Sure, I heard the whole spiel about processes and red tape and paperwork, but I'm not buying it. It all seems excessive and unnecessary. Especially the part that requires me to chaperone this entire thing.

"There she is." Tucker nods toward a table in the back, partially hidden from view behind a half wall that offers little privacy for what might well become a very public fiasco of epic proportions.

I study her before she notices us. She's gorgeous. She has long blonde hair, like mine but different. Tattoos peek out from beneath the cuffs of her perfectly pressed blazer. She wears bright red lipstick that compliments her ice-blue eyes. She sits alone, a Styrofoam coffee cup between her hands and a half-eaten donut on the plate discarded in front of her. I wonder how long she's been here.

I press my side against Tucker's. "Oh my God, she

has your nose. Your complexion and jawline are similar too. It's so strange, and yet, oddly interesting at the same time." I whisper as if he's not noticing the same similarities I am.

Tucker motions subtly to a table with a single chair situated just behind her. "Over in the corner, tall guy, ripped, dark skin, that's her fiancé. He's a former D-1 hockey athlete with an apparent anger problem. He's the most sought-after sports attorney in professional sports right now, and as far as I've been able to determine through my research, he's the only man who's ever been able to penetrate her glacial walls. I found a recently published article in Sports National where she vehemently refuted the fact that the two were even together, but the ring on her finger says otherwise."

As if she feels us watching her, her eyes scan the room until they stop on where we stand.

Her lips turn down. Tucker tightens his hand around mine; I think more to keep me from running than anything as he pulls me toward her table with surprising force. My feet don't want to budge. I'm happy to turn and walk briskly in the opposite direction. I'm tired of dealing with irritable females. First the cranky FBI agent and now this. This is not the future I imagined for myself, and yet here I am.

"Cassandra Elyse Stafford?" Tucker stops us just in front of her table and offers his hand. She stands, but instead of taking his hand in hers, she places her hands on her hips defensively. Oh, great. Here we go.

"It's Casey," she cuts in. "First, you should know that I was fully prepared to have you locked up for that little stunt you pulled at my apartment. You're lucky you didn't steal anything. What you did was disrespectful and inconsiderate—not to mention highly illegal. Second, I will have you know that my *person*, Tyler, is sitting just over there," she nods to the same corner Tucker pointed out to me just minutes ago where her muscled counterpart sits and smirks in our direction, "he's here for your protection, not mine. Lastly, the only reason I came here was because I wanted to personally kick you in the balls. Tyler says I can't do that in public, so here we are. I don't like you, Yuck Stafford. I don't like you, not one little bit."

My eyes widen at her outburst. Anger begins to simmer in my blood. Who does she think she is? My mouth opens to speak, but closes again in shock unsure of what to say. Did she just call him Yuck? I'd laugh if I wasn't so damn pissed off. Tucker steps in before I have a chance to gather my thoughts.

Pulling a quarter from his pocket, Tucker drops it on the table that separates us. Her eyes track his movements, but she doesn't ask, yet.

"You've been thinking about me, it's cool, I have that effect on people." He grins at her, and I see the version of Tucker I met the night of the fire. His devil-may-care attitude. I see it for what it is now, a shield he wields like a sword. "The name's Tucker, but you can call me Tuck if you prefer, just don't call me Hilton. First and foremost, I owe you an apology for my actions. I understand now that there was probably a better way to confirm your identity, but I didn't fully think through the consequences of how what I did might affect you, and for that, I am truly sorry. It's just…I've been looking for you for a long time…" Tucker's voice cracks and he coughs to cover it, but I don't miss the emotion he tries to hide before he continues. "I left the note because I need your help. I was only trying to get your attention, and you called, so it worked."

"Help you? Hell no." She motions to the man she claims is only her *person*. Confirming Tucker's research, he smiles for her with undeniable heart eyes when she briefly looks in his direction. "We're going, Tyler, if I can't kick him—which I know is assault, okay, I get it—but if I cannot assault him without you tackling me to the ground, we are leaving."

"Wait just a minute," I release Tucker's hand and take a step forward, pushing a chair out of the way and leaving the small table she was sitting at as the only thing left separating us. My mouth speaks before my brain can formulate a plan. What am I doing? I'm defending my man, that's what.

"Who the fuck are you?" She swings her fiery gaze in my direction, and I ready myself for battle. I can see why this woman is so successful in the courtroom. She might be tiny, but she is fierce. That doesn't mean she can walk right over people without so much as hearing them out first.

Straightening my shoulders, I take a deep breath and try to gather myself before speaking. I do my best to tame some of the volcano of anger that threatens to explode inside of me. She's not the only woman in the room, and I'll be damned if she's going to speak to Tucker like that in front of me, even if he deserves it. I'm the only one allowed to be an asshole to Tucker.

"My name is Daisy Mae Chandler, and this is my *person*." I use her words and look back at Tucker as I angle myself between him and Casey instinctively. "I really don't appreciate your attitude. You didn't hear anything he said, did you? You judged the situation before you ever arrived. I understand that you're mad, I get it. Tucker is a man, and I think you and I can both agree that men don't always think through their actions before doing them. I didn't care much for Tucker the night we met, either. He's an acquired taste. He broke into my shop in the middle of the night and the place burnt to the ground."

"Not helping, Daisy…" Tucker whispers through gritted teeth. He tries to take my hand and pull me back, but I'm not finished here. The satisfied smirk on Casey's face reminds me so much of her brother's arrogance that it's startling.

I steamroll right over anything either of them might have to say that interrupts me before I get the chance to finish. "Tucker saved my life." I know as I say the words that he's never going to let me live this down, especially now that I've admitted it out loud. There are witnesses present. "Tucker pulled me out of a burning building. He kept me out of jail. He's devoted his entire life to making sure that his father, *your father*, is seen by the world as the man he truly is—a terrible human. Tucker is the reason we're all fighting. Tucker Stafford is a good man, and I refuse to stand here and let you paint him as anything else."

Finishing my tirade, I wait anxiously for her response. I cut my eyes to the man who sits in the corner and watches us. He's amused, but he doesn't try to step in.

"You expect me to just take your word for it? I should just forget about the damage this man has already caused in my life and not only forgive him but agree to help him?" She tilts her head to the side curiously. It's impossible to tell what she's thinking. Her poker face is impeccable.

"Please, just hear me out. I don't think you hate Tucker. I think you hate your father. And what's more? I think that's something the two of you have in common. Something besides the blood that runs through your veins." Tucker yanks me from behind and encapsulates me into his chest.

"I love you, Daisy." He whispers into my hair and the intensity I feel in his words isn't lost on me.

She watches us skeptically. "Do you need a lawyer, Daisy? I would be more than happy to represent you if it means I can take this guy down in the process." She smiles for the first time since we arrived.

"Actually, *we* need your help." I press.

"I don't believe it. Blink twice if you're being held against your will." She raises her eyebrows in expectation.

I stare at her blankly. Is she for real?

She sighs, frustrated. "I've already told you, I'm not helping him."

"Then, help me." I challenge her.

"Sure, I'll be happy to represent *you*. As I mentioned earlier, I would love to take this man down. Hell, I'll take any man down for that matter. We'll take everything he has. Everything he never knew he had and all the things he ever hoped to have. It'll be fun." She lifts her shoulder lightly.

She's not getting it.

"Look, we're taking Hilton Stafford down once and for all, with or without your help. I know you didn't come here to reconcile with Tucker. You wanted something out of this. You can hide behind this façade all day long, but in the end, I know the truth. You're here because you want a slice of the pie. You want to take him down just as much as we do. We thought you might want a hand in this. We thought you might have some things you needed to resolve. So here we are, making you an offer to finally rid yourself of those things, whatever they may be. We're all broken. We've all suffered at the hands of this man be that verbally, physically, or emotionally. He spreads poison wherever he goes. You can have closure." I plead our case, ready to walk out of here empty-handed if she doesn't agree.

Tyler clears his throat from behind her, the first true acknowledgment he's given that he is listening to our conversation. She shifts her weight from one foot to the other.

"Fine. I won't work with you, Tucker." She glares over my shoulder. "I won't help you. Not today. Not tomorrow. Not ever. No offense, but it's kind of my unwritten policy." She shrugs, and I worry for half a second that I'll have to punch her. "But I'll work with you, Daisy. I like you. You're ballsy, and I can respect that. Even if your taste in men is atrocious." Her lips tilt up into a sly grin.

"Agree to disagree." I counter.

"Whatever. What do you need from me? What's the

quarter for?" She pulls out her chair and sits back down, picking up the quarter that Tucker dropped on the table when we first arrived. Tucker and I take the seats across from her.

This is it.

Leaning forward, Tucker keeps his words low and quiet. "I hired you. We'll call the quarter my deposit. As such, I'm invoking my attorney-client privilege, so listen up. We're mounting a case against my father, *our* father. He's running for the open senate seat, I'm sure you've noticed. I can't let that happen."

"Oh, I've noticed. Narcissistic asshole." She rolls her eyes dramatically and takes a sip of her cold coffee. "Speaking of assholes that deserve to be fucked, you seriously can't think this quarter covers my deposit?" She twirls the coin between her manicured fingers.

"No, but I thought this might be a good start." Tucker reaches into his pocket and pulls out what looks like a piece of a puzzle. It's orange and green, but the vibrance of the color has long ago faded. The edges are worn cardboard, and the shape is all curves and dips. It's larger than a typical puzzle, almost like a child's learning puzzle.

He places it flat on the table, and I can just make out the corner of a tiger's face on the edge of what kind of looks like the jungle. Casey stares at him as he slides it across the table, leaving it with her to examine.

Her fingers toy with the corner of the puzzle piece. I see the moment recognition flashes in her eyes. Her shoulders soften if only the slightest bit. "The puzzle, it was you. You were the little boy in the corner."

"And just like this puzzle, you've always been the

missing piece, Casey. I need your side of the story. I think your voice deserves to be heard in all of this. Your mother's voice…"

"Keep my mother's name out of your fucking mouth, Stafford." She seethes, dropping the puzzle back to the table as if she were physically burnt by it. Her exterior hardens just as quickly as she seemed to soften to him.

"It's cool. I understand your anger. It's okay to be angry. I'm pissed too, and I'm not going to make light of what happened to you. The thing is, so much is still missing. I need the missing pieces to a puzzle I've spent over a decade assembling, Casey. And I need legal representation when this all explodes because it's going to explode, it's just a matter of when."

I love watching them together. I love seeing the similarities in their mannerisms. The way they both seem perpetually annoyed. They'd never admit to the likeness, but the similarities are there, and now that I see them, they're impossible to miss.

"Alright, Tuck Face. I'll tell your friend, Daisy what I know. When the shit hits the fan, I'll make sure he's locked up for so long they carry him out in a body bag before he ever sees the free world again. Karma's a bitch, and I fully plan to make Hilton Stafford mine. As for your personal representation, if you need it, I know people."

*Tuck Face.* My throat tickles and I try not to giggle at that one. She's kind of funny, under the whole hardened boss babe exterior.

Her hate toward Hilton Stafford is evident in the way she visibly prickles when she speaks of him. I wonder what he did to her. I know why Tucker hates him. I also know why the FBI is investigating him. But why her? What's her story?

"My turn. Let me ask you a question. If you don't work with men? Who is that man back there? Your *person*?" Tucker asks a question we all know that he already knows the answer to. Tyler's been not-so-subtly watching our entire exchange, and yet Casey still refuses to acknowledge there's a man in her life that she actually does have a soft spot for. That would be admitting weakness, and we know that Staffords don't acknowledge weakness.

"That guy? Oh, you know, he's just the Uber driver." She winks before pushing back her chair and standing. I guess this meeting is done.

Without asking, she snags Tucker's puzzle piece from the table and shoves it into her bag before turning to leave. "I'll be in touch." Mr. Tall, Dark and Handsome, *not the Uber driver*, stands just as quickly and follows the petite blonde from the coffee shop without a word to anyone.

# CHAPTER TWENTY
# DAISY

"Tucker, where are we going? Why are we running? That went well, right? It's not like the FBI is chasing us." Tucker yanks me from the coffee shop with a grip of flipping steel.

I try not to trip over my own feet as two steps of his equal four of my own. He's nearly sprinting, and I don't run. I'm not even wearing my non-running sneakers for God's sake. I wore a skirt today. I wanted to look put together and professional for this meeting. I didn't realize there would be a physical test at the end.

"You were amazing, Daisy." Tucker smiles wildly over his shoulder, but he doesn't slow down. I know that look—the crazy eyes. That look means trouble.

"I'm sorry I got worked up, but she's tough, your half-sister. I shouldn't have expected anything less, but I couldn't stand there and let her talk to you like that. I'm sorry if I overstepped." I sputter out a half-excuse for my actions back there. I'm not sorry, not really, but I've also had enough excitement for the day. If apologizing gets me out of running sprints, I'll get on my knees.

"You didn't." It's all he says as we finally come to a stop in front of a stoop less than a block from the coffee shop. I'm winded. Sheesh.

"Well, what's wrong? What's with all of the running?" I ask while simultaneously trying not to hyperventilate and embarrass myself.

Tucker touches the glass door of a lantern that lights the small porch we stand on and reaches inside.

"You're going to burn your hand, what are you doing?"

"It's right here." Tucker grunts and pulls out a key from some hidden spot behind the gas light fixture. Well, that was a fancy trick.

Glancing behind us, Tucker swiftly turns back to the door where he slides the key in and pushes it open with his shoulder when it sticks to the door frame.

"Where are we?"

He pulls me inside behind him quickly, dropping the key onto a nearby table at the entrance and locking the door at our backs.

"This building is abandoned. Nobody uses it anymore. At one point, it was being remodeled but that project fell through, and it's been sitting vacant for years."

I try to look around, but all I see is darkness. The windows are covered with paper, allowing very little natural light from outside. As my eyes begin to adjust, I'm able to make out a few pieces of vacant furniture and random building materials. It smells stale and dusty.

"Why are we here?" I whisper, and I'm not sure why I'm whispering because we're alone. There's no reason to whisper, but given our circumstances, I'm kind of afraid to speak at a normal volume anywhere anymore.

Is this the part of the story where he turns out to truly be a bad guy and I've trusted him all this time and now he's taking me to a creepy abandoned construction site to finally off me? Dammit, that's just my luck, isn't it?

Tucker's words burst through my overactive imagination and shatter my hypothesis. "Because dammit, Daisy, if I had to wait for another second to do this I might combust." Suddenly, he spins me, and I'm lifted off my feet. My back hits the nearest wall, and I'm forced to wrap my legs around Tucker's waist or risk falling.

The herringbone pencil skirt I chose to wear today rides up my thighs and exposes my black thong. Cool air taunts the lace material. In an instant, I'm slick with desire for him. I forget all about spiderwebs in my hair and homicide. Okay, mostly. I *mostly* forget about the spiders and convince myself the tingles on my back are purely of the frisky variety.

Tucker tangles his hands in my hair as he pins my head against the wall and stares into my eyes until I'm able to focus on nothing but him. The unfamiliar vacant space around us disappears. The questions bombarding my brain disintegrate and, in their place, only one thought remains...*Tucker*. And spiders. Okay, fine, two thoughts.

"Fuck, Daisy, the way you defended me back there. I've never had anyone say things like that about me." I feel his chest rising against mine with every word that he speaks. The seriousness in his voice vibrates the space between us and electrifies the air.

"I said it because it's true. I meant everything I said..." My sentence is cut short as his mouth captures mine with a force that is impossible to ignore. His kiss is fueled with passion and an intensity that bruises my lips. He steals the air from my lungs, and I wouldn't dare protest. His tongue slides against mine, and I moan into his mouth. Self-preservation be damned.

He spins us once more, and without breaking our kiss, he carries me through a hallway and into another room with a familiarity that I don't have time to question. Holding onto him as he lowers himself onto a couch, I spread my legs, encasing either side of his lap. Taking advantage of my new position, I grip his head in my hands and roll my hips over where I feel his length pressing against the fabric of his slacks, begging to come out and play.

"Daisy..." He whispers my name between gasps for air, his and mine.

Moving my hands to my shirt, I pull the stretchy material down and expose my breasts for his access. Yanking his belt from its buckle, I tug on the leather until I'm able to reach the button and zipper.

Tucker hurriedly maneuvers my skirt until it sits in a jumbled mess around my waist. He pulls the lace of my thong to the side as I release his hardened cock from his briefs.

I lift myself onto my knees until I'm hovering over his length. Tucker leans back, spreading his arms over the back of the couch and giving me full control. Using one hand to balance myself on Tucker's shoulder and the other to hold his length in place, I line us up together.

I'm so needy for this man. I guide him inside of me with ease.

The head of his cock stretches me, and I slide down, relishing every single inch until I'm fully seated on his lap.

"So good, Daisy. Fuck, you are so damn good at this." Tucker tosses his head back as I begin riding his cock.

I create a rhythm all my own as I lift myself up before slamming back down again. I roll my hips and rock them against him.

"You're so deep, Tuck," I whisper into his ear. I use my tongue to elicit a deep groan from within his chest. His pleasure is one of my favorite sounds.

I grip the back of the couch behind Tucker's head and use it as an anchor that allows me to ride him. I take everything I need and give him exactly what I know he wants in return. I see it in his eyes. I hear it in the way he breathes.

My hips slam down harder, and when the cold metal of his zipper slides across my clit, I nearly come undone. So, I do it again. And again. And when my belly drops out and my orgasm threatens to take over, I give him a warning because I want more and I won't stop. I can't.

"I'm going to come, Tucker. I want you to come inside of me. Fill me up. I want you, all of you." I beg him. I plead. Feeling and emotion take over my every relevant thought and replace them with only need, and hunger.

My thighs still. I feel myself clench down onto his cock as my orgasm finally pulls me under.

When I can no longer move, Tucker drops his arms from the couch and grips my hips. He fucks me when my body is frozen with pleasure. He drags my orgasm out of me in the most delicious, all-encompassing way and doesn't let up when I scream for reprieve.

"Daisy!" When I don't think I can take anymore, he finally yells my name into the empty room. His body jerks, and I feel him as he empties himself inside of me.

I've never felt anything so good, so fulfilling.

Dropping my head into his neck, my body collapses into his. I feel so heavy. Sated.

"I love you, Daisy." He whispers as he lays us down on the couch and pulls me into the warmth of his arms. We lay there together until our eyes will no longer stay open and we both drift off to sleep.

# CHAPTER TWENTY-ONE
# TUCKER

The sound of a door opening jars me awake, and for a moment, I'm disoriented. My brief moment of confusion is quickly replaced by a bone-chilling fear.

Someone's here. That's impossible. This place has been abandoned for nearly a decade.

"Fuck, Daisy, wake up, baby." I run my hand over Daisy's cheek and try to wake her.

"What? What is it, Tucker? I'm sleepy. Go away and let me sleep." She turns in my arms but doesn't open her eyes. Normally, I find her grouchiness cute, but right now she's too fucking loud.

"Daisy, we need to be quiet. Someone's here." I shake her slightly, and she slowly begins to open her eyes.

"Tucker?" She looks around with the same bewilderment I felt moments ago. Her honey-blonde hair falls over my shoulder, and my stomach sinks.

*So fucking stupid.* What was I thinking, bringing her here? I wasn't. That's the problem.

Footsteps echo in the hallway. I listen as they move in the opposite direction, for now. This room was the main office, my office, or it was supposed to be. Once upon a time, back before I was stripped of my trust fund and everything that came with it, this place was supposed to be mine. I was going to have my own publishing house.

I was overseeing the project. I started noticing some discrepancies on the remodeling invoices. Things weren't adding up, literally. The project kept running over, and the roadblocks were never-ending. So, I used what I knew to my advantage. I began tracing the forensic accounting of the project using data analytics and quickly realized the dirty money I found backing the investments was only the beginning. I dug deeper, looking for answers that I wasn't entirely sure I wanted to find. It was a decision that would change my life.

It was never Hilton's intent to invest in my dreams. Looking back now, I should have known better, but I was young and naïve. The entire project was a front. He was planning to use my publishing house as a shell company to launder money. I wasn't fully aware of just how deep Hilton Stafford's evil streak ran. Wouldn't you know it? He's got a direct line to the devil. When I stepped away, I took nothing—including my hopes and dreams for the future. Those I left riding on my writing and the knowledge that, one day, I would get revenge of my own.

"I thought you said this place was abandoned?" She murmurs.

"Come out, come out, wherever you are. He knows

you're in here. Stop running." An unfamiliar voice taunts us through unfinished sheetrock and partly demolished walls.

We're being followed. I can say with ninety-nine percent certainty that it's not the good guys this time. This is certainly Hilton. His *goonies*. These are men with no conscience. Their moral compass points due south. They follow orders blindly for drugs and money. This only means that he's been keeping tabs on me, even more so than usual.

My heart races. My lungs seize and my brain immediately begins trying to figure out an exit strategy that gets us both out of here alive. We haven't come this far to die because my dick couldn't wait until we got home.

The stairs creak and I am thankful for small mercies. He's moving away from us.

This is our window of opportunity. We have to move.

"Shit, it was. We need to get out of here." I stand from the couch and pull Daisy up behind me. She's still sleepy and confused. Her movements are slow and messy. I try my best to stabilize her before she trips and crashes into something, drawing attention to our location.

"On a scale of one to scared for my life, how dire is this situation?" She squints beside me to see better. I watch as her eyes slowly scan the room around us, realization dawning on her.

"Follow me, and I'll get us out of here safely. Do not say a word. Understood?" I can't hide the implication of danger in my voice. So, I don't try. This is exactly what I was afraid of.

Her eyes widen in fear, but she nods her head in understanding. Daisy takes my hand when offered and holds on tight.

I stop in to check on the place from time to time. It's one of the reasons I chose the coffee shop next door for our meeting with Casey. The area is familiar to me, and I'd hoped the familiarity would help me keep my cool when the nerves of meeting my half-sister for the first time threatened to make me lose my composure.

Hilton still owns this building, but the real estate is tied up in a trust fund he has yet to fully dissolve. I don't want it. I don't want anything he has. But I check on this place because my name is on the paperwork, and I want to make sure he's not running a cartel out the back door without my knowledge. I wouldn't get that lucky.

I shuffle her body behind me but don't release her hand when we move forward, careful not to shift our weight too quickly. My heart sprints again when the floors creak above us with movement that I'm certain is a threat to our safety.

Carefully, I maneuver us around the office and back down the hallway. This time I don't head out the front door for fear that he's not alone. I'm not certain of anything at this moment. Instead, we head in the opposite direction. I hold my breath as we pass the staircase.

We cautiously step over sheetrock and lumber, scooting through what was once a kitchen but has long since been used as storage until we find the back door. I turn the lock and pray that the alley on the other side is empty.

I can't be sure how long we were asleep.

I don't know what time it is. Will there be sun? Light? Or will we be shrouded in darkness? There is no time to prepare.

Together, we push into the alleyway. The sun has set, but the moon is out and lights the street. This isn't a bad area of town. I scan the area and see no one.

It's empty.

Daisy makes a weird humming sound from beside me.

"What are you doing?" I mumble as I turn in the opposite direction of the building we just came from, needing to get out of the area as quickly as possible.

She looks at me with wide eyes and makes the noise again. It kind of sounds like she's trying to speak underwater.

"What is it?" I ask again.

"You said not to speak." She argues, finally speaking, and I smile for the first time since we narrowly escaped.

"So you were, what? Humming?" We weave through vacant lots and fences that are falling down; all the while I try to distract Daisy from the danger we leave in our wake.

"If you truly loved me, you would have been able to understand what I was saying. I'm hurt."

"Is that so? Is that an unwritten code? Dammit, do I need to learn a new language?"

"Fine. Jerk. Forget I hummed. I will never hum in your presence again for as long as we both shall live. Are we safe yet?"

I hope to God that we live until we're old and wrinkly. Today took years off my life. Another day like today and we might not survive it.

"Not forgetting that anytime soon. Maybe I'll mention the humming to our FBI friends. They could potentially use it as an alternative to Morse code."

The heaviness in my chest releases in tiny increments with every step away from the danger that we take.

"Tucker. Are. We. Safe?" She repeats the question that I neglected to answer the first time in the hopes she wouldn't notice. Safety is a tricky concept in our world.

Finally, we turn a corner onto a busy street a few blocks away. I flag down a driver, opening the door before he's fully come to a stop and shoving Daisy in first before sliding in behind her and closing the door.

"For now. That was almost too easy. Let's go home."

# CHAPTER TWENTY-TWO
# DAISY

"Is this necessary?" Tucker gripes at Alex...again.

"Testing, one, two. Testing," Alex laughs to himself when Tucker grimaces from the voice loudly echoing in his ear, I can hear it from where I stand with Emily on the other side of the room.

"Really? How old are the two of you?"

Tucker pulls at the tiny speaker Alex has carefully hidden inside his ear. One more sound check and I think he might blow a gasket.

"All clear on the mic," Alex finally confirms with a giggle that doesn't match his tattoo-covered, muscled frame.

Tucker adjusts his cufflinks, irritation coloring his features. "No shit." He mumbles to himself.

Standing in front of Tucker, Alex holds up a sheet of tiny circular black stickers. Without warning, he invades his personal space and begins strategically placing them on Tucker's suit, spouting off instructions as he goes. "Cameras. Don't touch them. Don't bump them. If you decide to bang her in the coat closet just make sure we have a clear view."

Tucker chokes and I feel my face warm.

"He's joking, right?" I whisper to Emily.

Alex smiles slyly when I forget I'm already mic'd up.

"Wouldn't you like to know?" Emily winks at me and, with that, my face transforms from pink to fully flamed in seconds.

Tucker interrupts when Alex releases him. "What I would really like to know is why we're being suited up like we're headed into battle when the two of you are supposed to protect us. That was part of our agreement." He grumbles.

"I don't know, you tell me. The last time we sent the two of you out together unsupervised you almost got yourselves killed in an abandoned building you didn't tell us a fucking thing about. You went rogue for a piece of ass. We can't protect you when you don't follow the plan." Emily smarts as she stands in front of me, mirroring the actions of her counterpart. She adjusts a speaker between the crevices of my breasts and hides an earpiece behind where my hair has already been swept into a sleek ponytail.

"She's got a point, Tuck." I look over at him and try to smile through the nerves when he pretends to pout. Neither one of us is too keen on tonight's mission. This isn't my thing. I'm a florist. I wasn't built for undercover operatives.

Tucker looks so handsome tonight. I wish I could

convince myself to be excited, but I can't because this isn't Tucker taking me to a fancy Gala and showing me off on his arm as his date. It's all fake.

He's wearing a black tux that's been expertly tailored to fit his tall, lean frame. He shaved, leaving just the lightest dusting of hair along his square jawline. His dark hair is styled by a brush, not the wind, which is an entirely different level of handsome I didn't realize existed until about an hour ago. The intricately trimmed bits are styled so that they are combed over and the tips flop down onto his forehead at a perfect angle.

His blacked-out tux matches the black silk of my dress. The sparkle on his cufflinks compliments the shoes Emily's already picked out for me to wear.

"You do not get to side with her." He stalks over to where I stand finishing up with Emily.

I'm hit with the smell of aftershave, and it strikes me that, while I like this version of Tucker, I miss the smell of motor oil from his bike. He might be the most beautiful man I've ever seen, but I like rugged and disheveled. I like combat boots and black denim. Tonight, Tucker is every bit a Stafford, and I want Tuck back. I know in my heart that he's not that man. I know the reasons we're here, but that still doesn't change the longing in my heart for *my* Tucker, not the illusion of the man his father wants him to be.

He brushes his hand over my shoulder, and I lean into him, allowing my eyelids to fall shut for a moment. I give myself permission to bask in his familiar touch. When I reopen them, I choose to focus on our assignment. I can't allow my emotions to overshadow logic and reason.

Tonight isn't about mingling with the elite. Tonight is about espionage.

"Sorry, Tuck. I'll side with whoever has the gun, and it's her. She has a gun. So, we're friends now."

So, what if I embellish the truth a bit? Emily and I aren't exactly friends, but there is no world in which I want to be on this woman's bad side. So, instead of arguing, I offer a truce of friendship. It's not my usual, but none of this is.

"Ballsy assumption, Chandler." She gives me a side-eye but lets it slide. "So, you met Casey?" Emily ignores the weapons talk, because we all know the assumption was regarding our friendship, the fact that she is locked and loaded is merely fact.

She hands me gold rhinestone high heels. They look like they might kill me before anyone else has the chance to tonight. Somehow the thought is comforting. That fact alone should be alarming.

"Yes, I did. We had dinner again last week. She's great."

Surprisingly, after the disaster that was our first meeting, Casey and I hit it off. Once you get past all of the anger and aggression, she's actually quite nice and funny. I finally got her to admit that Tyler, her *personal* driver, is her fiancé. Just don't call him that to her face, it gets her cranky again. That cranky streak is a strong hereditary trait.

"Here we go." Tucker groans and pinches his brow with his thumb and finger.

"What's his deal tonight?" Emily asks, glancing briefly between the two of us.

"Nothing, he's just jealous that his sister likes me better than him."

Snickering under his breath, Alex taps away on a laptop much fancier than mine and checks the cameras we wear. He walks a circle around us until he's satisfied with the angles and then closes the laptop, moving on to another task without pause. They joke and goof off, but it's clear that they take their jobs seriously.

"Jealous? That's the word you're going with?" Tucker challenges.

"Fine, sour. He's a big ol' sour puss." I continue to tease him.

Alex hands Tucker the keys to a car. "She called you a pussy, dude. You just going to stand here and take it?"

"Would you?" Tucker grunts.

"Like the fucking man that I am." Alex slides his arm around Emily's waist. He pulls her to his chest and slants his mouth down over hers. The two make out right there in front of us—they're completely shameless. I have to admit, watching them together is hot. My hips tingle and sparks alight in my blood. I watch, unable to look away, enraptured by the two of them together.

Heck, this is a porn I would pay money to watch. Their chemistry is undeniable.

Tucker clears his throat. "That's what I thought."

Breaking their kiss, Emily comes up for air only to speak as if nothing happened. "Okay, children." Her lips are red and swollen, and the grin on Alex's face says he was ready for so much more than what he was given. Me too, dude. But that's a fantasy better left in my brain. I would never dare say that to either of them.

She continues. "Let's go over this one more time. Tonight is the official fundraiser gala for Hilton Stafford's senate campaign. He called and personally requested your presence." She motions to Tucker. "Politics are all about kissing babies and shaking hands, aside from the corrupt shit that happens in the background. This needs to look like a real campaign and not the sham we all know that it is. That's where you come in. The people like to elect a family man, and you are an unlucky component of that family. Without your attendance, there will be questions from the media. Hilton can't have that. Our intel tells us that this is more than a fundraiser, and that is where we come in. The corrupt shit happening behind the scenes is what we're banking on."

"They're shuffling funds and shaking hands," Tucker concludes.

"Amongst other things," Alex adds, and I have to wonder how deep these people are truly entrenched in the dark parts of the world. This is all so new to me. Most of the things they talk about, I've only ever read about or watched on television. It's equally surreal and frightening.

"Okay, Daisy, you know what tonight means for you?" Alex turns to me and garners my full attention as if he didn't already have it. Sure, he's distracting, but my heart beats for the man standing next to me in a tux.

"Sure thing, I'm bait in a ball gown."

I look down at the most gorgeous dress I've ever worn and allow myself a moment to pretend this is for me. The thin black silk hugs my skin and shows off my body in a sexy, sophisticated way that I never realized I could pull off, until tonight. Two thin straps run the length of my shoulders and crisscross in the back repeatedly over my exposed skin. The fabric dips, creating a cowl over my breasts and a demure illusion, effectively hiding the spy gear shoved between my tits.

Dressing up like this, it's not who I am. I'm thrift store, not designer. These people, they're going to know I don't belong. They're going to see right through me.

"You're Tucker's plus one." Emily smiles wickedly, handing me a clutch that I hope does not contain a weapon of any sort. I'm not trained to shoot at people. That's her job. I'm banking on them hiding in the wings in case this whole thing goes south.

"You can dress up a pig." I groan.

Under any other circumstances, I'd love to attend a fancy gala with Tucker. Just not like this. Not because Tucker was threatened by his father to attend—*or else*. What is *or else*? What does that mean? *Or else*…I kick you out of your apartment? *Or else*…I hire a hitman and end your life? Who knows? The spectrum is wide open.

Not because we know my presence will elicit a reaction from him, and definitely not because our bodies are covered in more technology than I could ever fathom learning how to use for the sole purpose of spying on illegal activity for the federal government through my boob canal.

"Daisy, baby, you look beautiful." Tucker runs his fingers up my spine and goosebumps erupt over my skin.

Alex stops in front of us and stares at me long enough to make my stomach twist into uncomfortable knots, "Bait means you're a target, Daisy. Remember the plan.

Stay with Tucker. We won't let you get hurt. Understood?"

"What has my life become?" I pout.

Tucker's arm slips around my torso, pulling me closer into his side. "Sometimes we have to fight fire with fire."

# CHAPTER TWENTY-THREE
# TUCKER

"Your nervous is making me nervous, Daisy. Take a deep breath, I've got you." I finish helping Daisy out of the car and close the door gently behind her.

I hand keys off to a valet and smile when Alex says something in my ear about cutting a motherfucker if he so much as breathes on it. His black sports car is almost as sweet as my motorcycle, *almost*. I crease my arm and offer it to Daisy. She loops her hand through, and I feel her tremble.

Light flashes in my periphery. Photos are taken of us by the media as we walk the red-carpet-lined staircase to the entrance of one of the largest, boutique hotels located in the heart of the city.

"I look nervous because I am nervous, Tucker." She speaks through her teeth as she smiles at strangers we pass.

It's been a long time since I've been to one of these circus events. I swore I was done with this life. Swore I'd never have to step foot into a ballroom and wear a fake ass smile for hours on end. Now I eat my fucking words and hope it'll be worth it in the end.

"What can I do to help?" We step into the lobby, and I look around but have yet to see my father or the rest of my family for that matter. I've been estranged for years now, only speaking to Hilton when he deemed it necessary, which was more often than I'd like.

"Ask me a question." She says as we step into an elaborately decorated ballroom. Judging from the number of designer suits and gowns I see, it seems as though the upper crust of society is all here, as I would expect them to be. A podium has been placed on a stage in the center of the room. My stomach lurches. I couldn't care less what he has to say.

We mill about the room, ignoring the fact that there are names on tiny cards in front of expensive-looking gold plates at each circular table. The thought of sharing a meal with my family makes me feel physically sick.

"Okay, let's play a game. Ten questions. It's like twenty questions, except ten because I think we'll run out of privacy before we ever make it to twenty. I'll go first since this was kind of your idea."

"We don't have any privacy, Tucker." Daisy runs her fingers through her hair and lightly taps her earpiece. So far, so good. Alex hasn't screamed any profanities in my ear, yet. Just the warning about his car. And Emily hasn't threatened to shoot me. I can deal with that.

"So, did you choose the flowers, or did they choose

you? You know, with the name and all." I ask a question I've been curious about since we met.

Dropping Daisy's arm, I instead place my hand on her back, guiding her to where I see a bar set up against the far wall.

"A little of both. I didn't choose my name, obviously, it was given to me at birth. But sticking with the shop just seemed like the right thing to do after Aunt Fran died. That, and I've found that flowers are easier than people. Don't get me wrong, I love my customers. I love the relationships forged through something as intricately beautiful as a flower. I love their hearts and their stories. But, at the end of the day when I go home alone, flowers don't talk back, and they always smile when the sun shines."

"That's beautiful, Daisy. I can relate to the family business aspect, even if my experience was very different. However, I can't say that I've ever heard of a smiling flower." A smile of my own teases my lips.

"Give a flower a little water and place it in the sun, it will always smile toward the sunshine. Now, your turn. How many of these shindigs have you been to before?"

I feel her body relax the more she talks. We skirt around people in various conversations, smiling but not engaging with anyone in particular.

"When you get to the bar, step to the left. You'll see two men in a heated discussion. Maintain at least three feet of separation but stay put until we tell you otherwise." Emily gives instructions in my earpiece, and I look over at Daisy confirming she heard the same. She nods and we continue walking.

"More than I care to recall. I didn't grow to hate them until my teenage years. After I was old enough to realize what all the schmoozing was about. Surprisingly, I enjoyed coming when I was a kid. Little to no supervision and all-you-can-eat food. That is, when we got to come and weren't shoved into a hotel room with one of the stuffy nannies my parents regularly hired to watch us."

"Sounds miserable."

My fingers toy with the silk material of her dress where it meets her skin just above her ass.

"It was. Next question. The Walsh offer you were telling me about. His investment in Hydrangea & Vine will be substantial, but if anyone deserves it, it's you. Are you going to take the offer? Before you answer, for what it matters, I think you should. The contracts were clean from what I could tell. It seems like it could be a profitable venture for you, and you already know the idea is genius."

We approach the bar and I order two glasses of champagne, handing one to Daisy before we step to our left and allow our federal counterparts to do their thing.

Holding my glass, I don't take a sip. There is no room for alcohol consumption on my part tonight, no matter how badly I feel the need to numb myself for what I know is to come.

"I know, and I agree. I kind of already signed the paperwork." Daisy smiles over the lip of her champagne glass.

Her eyes dance with a secret I didn't realize she was keeping. "You did? You didn't mention it."

She glances at the men beside us and quickly looks

away. "It didn't seem like the right time to celebrate. We've been a little busy lately." I don't recognize either of the men in question, but whatever they're discussing must be significant in some way.

Pulling Daisy's body closer to mine, I lean into her space and speak only for her, even though I know we're not alone. "Don't ever keep important things from me, Daisy. I will always celebrate with you."

"Have I told you lately how much I like it when you get all growly? I especially like it when you're doing it while wearing a penguin suit." She playfully taps the lapel of my jacket as she takes a small sip of her champagne. My eyes follow her tongue as it dips out and licks a lingering drop from her lip.

"The coat closet is sounding more appealing by the second." Spreading my fingers, I allow the span of my open palm to tease her rib cage and distract us both.

"I second that." Emily's voice echoes in my ear, and I'm pulled from my fantasy. "Incoming." She says quietly, but the warning comes too late.

"Tucker," Ice water trickles down my spine, freezing my muscles and spreading through my veins until finally reaching my heart.

Tipping my forehead into Daisy's hair, I take a deep breath and hope it slows the rage that already simmers in my veins. "*Fuck*. We didn't even make it to five, called it." I mumble into her hair. My muscles turn rigid. I extricate myself from the security of Daisy's body just enough to maneuver her behind me, but I won't release her.

"Excuse me, son? Did you have something of

importance to say?" Hilton. He's the only person who can elicit this level of anger from me in so few words. I've been avoiding him for weeks. If our mysterious visitor at the abandoned office revealed anything to me, it's that he's been well aware of my absence. Now he knows why.

Facing him with a practiced smile that almost identically mirrors his own, I say, "Father, I'd like for you to meet someone. Daisy Chandler, this is my father, Hilton Stafford."

# CHAPTER TWENTY-FOUR
# DAISY

Daisy Chandler. It's such a little thing to leave off. My middle name. Why? Why would he do that? It's part of who I am. Daisy Mae, the way he says it is special to me, to us.

I step forward, despite Tucker's best attempts at hiding me behind his large frame. This is my job, it's why I'm here. I'm ready to play my role in all of this. Questions are for later. Right now, I need to keep it together. We didn't come this far to leave empty-handed.

"Mr. Stafford, I believe we've met before. It's an honor to see you again, congratulations on the success of your campaign." Bile burns the back of my throat with the blatant lies I spew to a man I have no respect for.

I force myself to extend my hand, but instead of shaking it, he takes only my fingertips in his, lifting my hand to his lips and kissing my skin.

I want more than anything to yank my hand back, but

I don't.

A sound rumbles from Tucker's chest beside me. He pulls me into his side, so close that our hips kiss.

"Have we met?" Hilton's smile is slick, much like the gunk in his hair. Greasy. Lies ooze from his pores. He releases my hand, and I drop it to my side, resisting the immediate urge to find a sink and a bar of soap and scrub until I have no skin left to disinfect.

"Hydrangea & Vine," I prompt him. He *knows* who I am.

Emily might have done a number on my makeup tonight, but this man has seen me regularly for years. He doesn't remember because my presence has never been of importance to him. But he knows, he just doesn't realize it yet.

Tucker watches me.

Hilton eyes me suspiciously.

I wait for recognition to tingle his brain synapses and the neuron connections his brain has previously formed about me to light up his memory in the worst way.

His eyes flash with condescension. He tries and fails to hide the way his lips twist into a sneer. "Oh, the flower shop clerk, precisely." His attention shifts briefly from me to Tucker, and I get a very distinct feeling that this isn't the first time I've been the topic of conversation between the two of them.

My spine stiffens with his insinuation that I am merely a clerk. "I am the owner of Hydrangea & Vine." I clarify, more for myself, because I know he already knows that. I don't like the way he makes me feel small. I hate everything this man represents.

"Yes, of course." He easily dismisses me, his phony smile returning with ease. "It's a pity what happened to your little store. I heard there was a fire." Disdain drips from his every word even as his lips remain upturned and in place.

"There was." My voice cracks, and I hate myself for exposing any vulnerability to this monster in human flesh.

His lips curl knowingly. "Total loss?"

Oxygen burns my esophagus. This is so much harder than I thought it would be.

"Father…" Tucker starts to interrupt, but I cut him off before he can step in to defend my honor.

*You're stronger than this, Daisy.* I do not need to be rescued. Not this time.

"No, it's been an opportunity," I answer, anger and emotion clogging my voice. "A phoenix rises from the ashes." Clenching my teeth, I speak louder.

Hilton's smile is pure evil, "The results of childhood stories and myths, no?"

"I would be so lucky as to never outgrow believing the prospect of impossibility." Tears sting my eyes, but I will not let this man see my weaknesses.

"Enough." Tucker steps in. "Father, we will see you at dinner." Tucker wraps his arm around my waist and ushers me to move my feet with such force that I believe if I don't start walking, he'll lift me from the ground and carry me away with brute force alone.

"What the hell was that about?" Tucker whispers once we're out of earshot of his father. He doesn't stop dragging me along. We move through the ballroom hastily, and I paste a smile on my face for curious onlookers when I really want to cry. I wasn't prepared. I thought I was ready, but I was wrong.

"Me? Cut the shit. Excuse me with the Daisy Chandler. That's not my name!" I hiss.

"Yes, it is. What are you talking about Daisy?" He looks at me like I've lost my damn mind, and maybe I have. Considering what I've agreed to be a part of tonight, Frannie would probably say I'm two bricks shy of a full load. But that's neither here nor there. I have a bone to pick with a spy in a tuxedo.

"Mae. You left off the Mae. My second name is important to me, Tucker. I thought you knew that."

"I didn't realize it was that special to you. I wasn't aware you had a Southern heritage, *Sue Anne*. Excuse me for not thinking to use your full name while introducing you to a fucking monster." He counters sarcastically.

"I'm not Southern, jerk wad. You can be from a small town without being from the South. And, if you must know, which you already should, it's only special when you say it. You're right. You weren't thinking. Just like bringing us here. God, he's horrible. I know this is important to you, truly I do, Tucker. I thought I could do it, but I'm not sure I'm strong enough. Standing there, looking into brown eyes that look so much like yours. It makes me so angry. He knows what he stole from me. For him to act like he doesn't know who I am is a slap in the face."

Tucker pulls me into an alcove and through a door that is only meant for staff. A discarded tray sits with empty plates and napkins to our right. The light above us short circuits, flashing on and off sporadically. My eye threatens to twitch. I'm overstimulated. I'm over…everything.

"Look at me, Daisy Mae Chandler." Sobering, Tucker's voice turns serious and deep. He cups my face with both hands and pulls my eyes up to meet his.

My lips quiver. "You're supposed to be a mind reader, Tucker. You should have known…"

He steals my words as he kisses me with a passion that balms the raw and exposed pieces inside of me left defenseless from our brief conversation with Hilton.

Pulling away slowly, he doesn't yet release me. "Hilton's a dick. We know that. We knew that coming into this. You are the reason we're here. You're the only reason we've made it this far. You are strong and beautiful. I'm sorry if I made you feel anything less, that was never my intention."

"When I said I'd try anything once, I didn't necessarily mean becoming a spy for the United States government." I hiccup and sniffle.

"Oh, yeah? You weren't agreeing to a life of action and suspense?"

I snort out a laugh, making sure he doesn't miss the heavy roll of my eyes. "Really, Mr. Jones, I wasn't aware I was signing up for the twentieth century live-action filming of the motion picture *Temple of Doom*."

"My bad, I forgot to mention that monkey brains will be on the menu this evening." He plays along, and I try to hide my smile and fail.

"I'm sorry, okay? I shouldn't expect you to read my mind." I grumble.

"It's funny you should mention that. I happen to know what you're thinking right at this very moment."

"You do? What is that?" I ask, eyeing him skeptically.

"You're imagining dropping to your knees and wrapping that fiery mouth of yours around my cock. I see it so vividly I can almost feel it. Fuck. Can you feel it, Daisy?" Tucker presses his body to mine, pushing me against the wall at my back and pinning me with his hips.

"I wasn't, but now that you mention it, it's possible that I could be persuaded." His hardened length fights the zipper on his pressed black pants, pushing against my belly button. He's impossible to ignore.

My heart races. My breath catches. And then I remember.

"You forget we have voyeurs." I pant.

"I don't think they mind." Leaning down, Tucker runs his teeth along the underside of my jaw, careful not to mess up the makeup Emily so carefully applied.

"Affirmative—copy that." Voices echo in my ear, and Tucker snickers against my neck.

"Creeps. I cannot believe the Bureau tolerates the two of you." I push Tucker off of me. He laughs so loud his chest bounces, and I worry we'll be busted in our small hideaway from reality.

"Get it together, you two. We need eyes on the room. If nobody's banging, we need you back out there." Emily speaks, and I exhale deeply.

Tucker's eyes darken with a significance I don't care to acknowledge. "Can you go back out there for me?" His hand wraps around my wrist, and he tugs me back to his chest.

I want to say no, but I can't. He's not wrong. We're so close. This is almost over. *Toughen up, buttercup.*

"Can I have a margarita? The champagne isn't cutting it. Top shelf." He might be abstaining from alcohol tonight, and I appreciate him for that, but I can tolerate exactly zero more of Hilton Stafford's bullshit tonight without a little liquid encouragement.

"I think we can arrange something." He grins.

"I never claimed to be a champagne kind of girl, Tucker." I let my free hand roam up his chest, careful not to bump into any of the cameras Alex meticulously placed on him earlier.

"I never said I wanted you to be." Tucker draws invisible lines over my bare collarbone with his fingertips. The hair on my neck sparks to life beneath his careful touch. "Tequila and whiskey?" He asks.

"Mhmmm…" I allow myself to melt into him and pretend we're anywhere but here. "Preferably not mixed together."

"Only the finest liquor for my queen." His chest bounces with muted laughter.

"Aw, you mean that?"

His hand grazes my arms as he works his way down my skin. "Which part?"

"The part where you said I'm yours." He pulls the hand he holds with my wrist up to his lips. Flipping my hand over, he places a single kiss on my open palm and washes away some of the evil left by his father.

"Daisy Mae, you are mine forever. I told you that I love you. I don't love voluntarily. It's not something that comes easy to me. But loving you is effortless. It's not forced, it just is. You're hooked to me for life, and unfortunately, all that comes with that."

"You make yourself sound like such a catch, Tucker Stafford." I retort.

"I think I'm going to be sick," Alex grumbles in my ear.

"Butt out, Alex. We're having a moment." I smile for Tucker as I speak to the literal pain in my ear.

"This is not what I had in mind when I mentioned coat closets." Emily reiterates.

Tucker sighs and rests his chin on my head. "You two need us to go back out there?" He speaks words into the space between us that I don't want to accept as a viable option.

"Yep. If you're done with the Hallmark shit. I swear, kids nowadays. You're all up in your feelings and emotions." Emily acts like she doesn't feel things when the brute she calls a husband whispers sweet things in her ear when he thinks nobody's looking. She acts cold-hearted when the fact that I know she's birthed children with the scary bald tattooed man tells me she is anything but.

"The table next to yours has some big players sitting at it." Speaking of, Alex's voice cuts in, stern and direct.

"Fuck." Tucker presses his forehead to mine. His nose rubs against mine and makes me wish I could crinkle it up into a twitch and wish us out of here. It's all fun and games until it's not, and there's nothing fun about leaving the safety of this tiny alcove and heading back out into the gala. "Okay. What do you say, baby?"

I flatten my lips. "Go team," I answer with the very

least amount of emotion I can conjure.

Tucker quietly chuckles. "That's the kind of pep talk I can get behind." He kisses my head once more and pulls me back out into the party against my better judgment.

# CHAPTER TWENTY-FIVE
# TUCKER

Daisy and I drive from the gala in silence. Failure permeates the vehicle and threatens to suffocate us before we arrive back at the location where we began our evening.

Dinner was a shitshow. My father's speech was full of lies and deception, and what's worse? Every person in the room was eating that shit up with a silver spoon.

I could spend the remainder of my lifetime apologizing to Daisy, but it still wouldn't be enough. I wouldn't blame her if she walked away for good after this. She's not wrong, this isn't what she signed up for.

We pull back into the parking lot of what from all outward appearances, is just a random vacant warehouse, but it isn't. It's a bomb shelter, a safe space, and possibly houses enough artillery to start and finish a third World War. I cut the ignition and breathe so heavily through my nose that my nostrils flare and my chest concaves. My hands grip the steering wheel and my knuckles whiten. I'm pissed, but the only person to blame is myself.

"That bad?" Daisy pops the buckle on her seatbelt. Her watchful eyes burn the side of my face.

"They've been silent for over an hour. We got nothing. Zilch. Other than exposing you to my family drama, a shit load of dangerous people, and having to listen to Hilton dredge on about a load of complete garbage. I'm so sorry, Daisy."

"Sorry for what exactly? I signed up for this, Tucker." She rests her hand on my back and offers grace that I don't deserve. "Love doesn't come with conditions; it comes with exceptions because true love can't grow if it's confined by limits of what we deem *good enough*. You come from a family of assholes. Well, with the exception of Casey. I mean, I like her, but she's still kind of an asshole. My family is dead. Doesn't change how I feel about you, and I hope it doesn't change the way you feel about me."

Turning my head, I finally look at her. Floodlights from the exterior of the building illuminate her blue eyes and make them sparkle in the darkness. "I don't deserve you. You realize that?"

"Mhmm…the key is you don't forget that. Especially since I warned you a hella long time ago that I've got a suitcase full of bad luck and nobody to share it with but you." She smiles, but it barely eases the vice that grips my lungs.

"Come on, let's go inside and hope we don't get shot for being shitty investigators." She laughs lightly, but we both know that's a real possibility. "Seriously, they're the ones that thought they could disguise a writer and a florist as whatever it is we were supposed to be tonight. That's on them."

Daisy pushes her door open, and I do the same. We step into an empty parking lot in the middle of the night, but even with their continued silence, I know we're not alone. I step around the vehicle and take her arm in mine as we walk together across the street and prepare to face the consequences of our failure. Death or otherwise.

We won't die tonight, but who the hell knows what ripple we've put into motion in the volatile sea that is my life? The tidal wave is coming. It's just a matter of when and how hard the impact's going to be when it hits.

I try once more to exhale the tightness in my chest to no avail. "None of that changes the fact that we went to all this trouble and didn't make any progress on the case. If anything, we're moving backward."

I scan the key fob on the keychain Alex gave me over a panel located in the wall of the exterior of the building, next to a discreetly hidden door. The sound of a lock clicking open makes my heart pound in my chest and undoes all of the breathing I did on the walk over here.

Stepping through the door first, I pause in the entry to hold it open for Daisy.

Standing just on the other side of the entrance, waiting, is the duo of doom, our jury of two. Standing side-by-side, arms crossed over their chests, they stand as a unit and stare us down silently as we enter the building. Their presence alone builds drama and tension in the room. I would expect nothing less from them having worked with them over the weeks leading up to this.

Alex moves first, reaching out and flipping his palm up and open. I drop the keys to his car into his outstretched hand and he smiles, which only puts me that much more on edge.

"Why are you smiling like that?" I ask, unable to wait for them to confirm my suspicions. That they're fucking lunatics.

Emily's lips twitch. "Can I tell him, Alex? I really wanna tell them."

"Do what you want, babe. This is your show." Alex shrugs nonchalantly and slips the keys into the pocket of his black jeans.

"We got the time and location for a drop. We've got a lead." Emily bounces on her toes. She literally bounces. She hops on her toes like a child who's just been told they're getting ice cream for dessert.

"In English for those of us that do not speak murder lingo please," Daisy interjects.

Emily huffs but proceeds to explain anyway. "While the two of you were playing house with the Stafford family, the table behind you was confirming the time and location of a drop we believe ties Hilton Stafford to some pretty serious criminals."

"You think my father is running drugs?" I ask, unable to believe he'd be willing to get his hands dirty at all. In all the research I've done, he's always kept his record clean. It's why he's been so hard to pin down.

"Not exactly," Alex answers. "We spent the last hour running data analytics on an extensive list of every campaign donation made to your father's Senate campaign fund within the last year."

"You think he's laundering money through his campaign." It's not a question, but a statement as realization dawns on me. *This* is something I can believe.

"We know he is; he's eliciting dirty funds through his campaign from the DA's office and funneling that money back around in a pretty little loop that puts illegal drugs on the street and money in the hands of people that already have too much. We bust up this drop, we kill two birds with one stone. We get Hilton and District Attorney Andrew Smithfield. It's a win, win." Emily's smile only broadens with her assessment of a situation I thought was doomed only minutes ago.

"The District Attorney?" *Smithfield.* It's a name I've linked back to my father on more than one occasion, but I've never found solid proof of his involvement in anything that wasn't above board. I thought Smithfield was clean.

He was at the gala tonight, his table neighbored ours. His back was to mine. He was right there, and I didn't have a damn clue.

Emily hums in the back of her throat, obviously satisfied with herself, but I'm not convinced. I still have questions.

"How can you guarantee they'll be there? Doesn't seem like Hilton to put himself out there like that."

"Our intel tells us that this particular transaction will secure his Senate seat. No signature, no seat. He'll be there, and the DA's writing the check. We're confident in our intel." Alex answers with so much self-assurance that he *almost* has me convinced.

"Democracy is such a fucking fallacy." I run my hand

down my face, unable to believe that there might actually be a light at the end of this tunnel.

"You mean to tell me that you got all of that from eavesdropping on a couple of fancy pants conversations using my boobs?" Daisy pulls equipment from between her breasts and draws my eyes south. She peels off cameras and drops them onto a metal table that sits near the wall adjacent to us.

"We got what we needed, that's all you need to know. You did good tonight, but now we're going to need you to get the hell out of here. It's late, and if we don't relieve our babysitters soon, there'll be hell to pay in the morning." Emily ushers us out of the warehouse.

"FBI agents have babysitters?" Daisy looks at me quizzically, but hell if I know. I've never given it much thought.

"We'll get you the information you need regarding the drop." Surprised, my head swings around when Alex speaks.

Cutting me off before the words on my tongue have a chance to leave my lips, Daisy screeches over her shoulder as they continue to crowd us toward the exit. "Why would you need us for that? I think we proved tonight that we are highly underqualified for any future endeavors with the United States government."

"Nah, you see, we've got some high-class thugs to bust, and I'm pretty sure somebody ordered flowers." Emily's smile borders on manic.

This is their life. This is what they thrive on. Maybe that's the trick, maybe you've gotta be a little bit crazy. Is that what I've been missing this whole time?

"Flowers?" Daisy asks, panic rising in her voice. "What are you talking about?"

"If we're going under one more time, we figured, what more poetic way to end this than to use your flower truck?" Daisy stares up at me with wide, terrified eyes. "I love it when a plan comes together. Don't you, Alex?" Emily suggests maniacally.

"I sure do." Alex chuckles.

Daisy sputters. "The truck doesn't run. It leaks oil. It has a rust stain that maybe used to be an ice cream cone on the side of it, maybe not, it's hard to tell. It looks more like a kidnapper van than a legitimate business right now! Not to mention, it's my business. We can't just turn it into a crime scene!"

"Perfect, you'll fit in just fine on the side of town we're heading." Emily and Alex continue pushing us right out the door.

"What part of *'it does not run'* do you not understand?" Daisy yells back at them, her eyes pleading with me for help.

"Tucker will fix it, won't you, Tucker?" Alex adds. His question is a formality, not a request. It's a matter of fact.

I don't have a choice in the matter, and he knows that. What I don't think Daisy fully comprehends is that it's in our best interest to comply with the good guys, for her safety and mine. If they tell us to sell fucking flowers, we're making bouquets.

She could leave. I could give her an out and she could go, but she's not safe anymore after tonight. They've seen her. She's on their radar. Now, the only choice I'm left with is to protect her. Losing her now might just be the thing that finally kills me.

"Fuck, promise me this is it, and we'll do what we have to do." Comply or die.

"Promises are sticky. I make it a habit not to make them." Emily answers defiantly.

"Like I said, we're confident in our intel, Tucker," Alex reassures me when his wife threatens to send me hurdling off the deep end. I'm so ready for this all to be over with.

"Oh, one more thing, Tucker. Call your sister. I have a hunch; she's not going to want to miss this." Emily adds with a smug grin and a wink just before slamming the door at our backs.

# CHAPTER TWENTY-SIX
# DAISY

It's the middle of the night. My leg jumps involuntarily as I sit next to Tucker on what I can only describe as a Vietnam-era military folding cot in the back of my truck. It's dark in here except for the lights that flash silently around us from the multitude of computer monitors that line the bare metal walls of the tin can we're sitting in.

The brakes squeal as we slow to a stop at the entrance of a high-rise apartment complex not far from where Tucker lives. God, the sound is so loud. Why didn't anyone think to lube up the brake pads? The bad guys are going to hear us coming from a mile away.

Alex idles the engine and the truck purrs like a sweet baby kitten. Thank heavens for small blessings. The day after the gala, the FBI towed my delivery truck from my driveway to their warehouse. When the government decides they want something, they take it. Which is strange considering the amount of time it generally takes them to do anything else.

Tucker spent the weekend working with them to reverse the damage I did while I was in my *do-it-yourself era*. The internet makes things look so much easier than they truly are. I can't be held accountable for the things that I did while angry. Hormones of the heart are fickle.

Some people stress eat. Not me; I try to rebuild transmissions with no previous experience. At least my pants still fit. I glance down at my black leggings and sneakers. These shoes still aren't for running, so I hope Tucker was right when he promised me this was merely a stakeout mission, and we would not be leaving the truck. I threw on an old sweatshirt and pulled my hair up into a ponytail before we left. It's late, and I'm tired. I'm secretly hoping this is boring and I can crawl into Tucker's lap and take a nap.

While Tucker worked on the mechanical parts of the truck, Alex spent the weekend converting the back of this thing from a rust bucket on wheels to an intel control center that looks like it's out of a superhero movie, if the movie were also a horror film where people die at the hands of thugs and deviants.

We might be sitting on a cot that predates my birth, but the computers that line these walls are brand new and collectively cost more than I've ever had in my bank account.

I don't dare touch anything for fear of setting off a bomb. Green button, good? Red button, bad? Is it the blue wire that's going to wipe us off of the map? Who knows.

I might be getting an entire fleet of brand-new trucks

for Hydrangea & Vine, but I'm still kind of partial to this one. It's seen me at my worst, and now that it's running properly—if it survives tonight—I think I'll finish out the remodel and call it mine.

Well, after the FBI takes back all of their gadgets and whatnot. It'll be the OG. We've bonded on an emotional level.

This is our final stop before the *big* stop.

Tucker has barely said a word since we left. I think he's secretly scared, but he'll never admit it. *Men.*

I'm not sure which scares him more. Finding the truth and ending this, or not finding anything and having to start over again. So many unspoken questions hang in the air between us. *What if they're wrong? What if Hilton doesn't show?*

A door opens behind me, and I catch a glimpse of Emily Straton hopping out of the passenger seat and stepping onto the sidewalk. This might be my truck, but she called shotgun, and I didn't dare argue.

"Nice ride, Yuck." The back door swings open and lights from the street briefly flood the interior of the truck. Casey climbs into the back wearing a pair of black leather pants and a matching blazer. Her blonde hair is tied up high on her head into a neat, sleek ponytail. Her hair looks put together and flawless, whereas mine just looks…messy. It's okay, I can admire her beauty and not feel like less of a woman. She is related by blood to the sexiest man I know, so, I shouldn't be surprised that I find her attractive. Ya know…in a womanly sort of way.

"What in the hell are you wearing?" Tucker asks, flashing a wide grin that makes my heart smile.

Her presence here is already distracting him from what's to come, and I can appreciate it, even if, judging from his tone, I'm about to have to hear them argue for God knows how long this stakeout lasts.

"This is my surveillance ensemble, you like?" She sashays around the interior of the truck, surveying our control center, but jumps when Emily slams the door closed behind her with unnecessary force. We're all locked in together, and Casey's not as unphased by all of this as she'd like us to believe. She's nervous too.

I look at the two of them and then myself.

A lawyer, a florist and a writer climb into the back of an old run-down ice cream truck never to be seen again.

This is directly out of some crazy horror film.

We're going to die tonight. No more margaritas. This is it.

"You do realize we're not leaving the truck." Tucker says as he scoots close to me, creating space that we don't really have on our makeshift bench. His thigh presses against mine. My need for his touch swirls with nervous anticipation of what's happening.

"Semantics. Always be prepared for hell to break loose, Yucker. Always." She smarts as the truck cranks back up, and I feel us pulling away from the curb.

"Take a seat before you fall down and break something in those ridiculous high heels." Tucker motions to the sliver of empty fabric wrapped around a metal bar next to him. The budget for this mission was clearly spent on technology with no regard for our comfort or safety.

"Don't mind if I do." She motions with her hand,

"Scoot over. I'm sitting next to Daisy, not you. For the record, I'm not doing it because you asked me, I wanted to sit. I'm tired."

"Man-eating becoming a bit too much for you?" Tucker presses her buttons for giggles and I shift in the opposite direction, making myself the ham to their squabbling club sandwich.

Casey sits and leans forward, dropping her elbows onto her knees. She props her chin up on her hand. Even in the darkness her bright red lipstick shimmers. "I was eating a man alright, but he's never more than I can handle."

Tucker makes a disgusting noise beside me, and I elbow him in the ribs for taking the bait. "I think I just threw up in my mouth." He starts, and I elbow him again, a little harder, and this time he grunts.

"You went there, Yuck. Now, man up and stop being such a child." God, it's like they're trying to make up for their teenage years in ten minutes.

Almost climbing into my lap with no regard for personal space, Casey leans behind me, yelling into the front of the truck. "Hey, Em, can we stop for donuts?"

Emily turns in her seat and glowers over her shoulder, unamused.

Completely ignoring Casey's outburst and the daggers Emily shoots at us from the front seat, Tucker continues to argue. "Child? If anyone is a child, it's you. My name is *Tucker*, dammit. As your flesh and blood, I have a right not to have to hear about your sex life. I couldn't care less if we met five minutes ago. That's got to be written in some moldy-ass law book somewhere. You're my sister for God's sake."

We hit a hole in the asphalt of the road, and it sends the three of us bouncing around, bumping into each other. "Your sister? Hardly. We've only just met. Blood means nothing to me, especially when it belongs to the likes of Hilton Stafford." She pushes off of my lap again.

*I know you are, but what am I?*

"Would the three of you shut up? We've got work to do, and we're here." Turning in her seat again, Emily points fingers like we're her children in the back seat of a minivan and not on an undercover stakeout mission for the Federal Bureau of Investigation.

"Three? I'm not in the middle of this." I try to plead my innocence.

Tucker and Casey laugh, and that's when I realize that I am very well stuck in the middle. Dammit. Why am I always guilty by association? *I did not choose my friends wisely, and for that, I am sorry, Aunt Fran.* I stare at the crusty old ceiling above us.

*Beep. Beep.* All eyes in the back of the truck turn at once. A dark green walkie-talkie sits up on the dash and suddenly comes to life with a voice outside of what I thought was a secret mission. "Backup present and confirmed."

"Ten-Four, we'll observe and then advise before taking action." Alex clicks the side of the radio, sending back a brief response.

"No, we won't." Emily snorts and runs her fingers up the tattoos that cover Alex's neck.

"What does she mean by action?" I look between Tucker and Casey.

"If you pop our father tonight, Tucker, I *might* make a tiny exception and agree to represent you during your murder trial."

"What the absolute fuck, Casey?" Tucker barks out the words.

"What? I'm just saying, I've dreamt of doing it, but I'm a lawyer and lawyers don't kill people." She answers nonchalantly like discussing the assassination of their father is standard chit-chat.

"We aren't killing anyone tonight, that's not what this mission is about," Tucker reconfirms, and I hope to God he's right. I didn't sign on for homicide.

"None of you better have a damn weapon in this truck. If I find out one of you is armed, I'll pop you myself." Emily threatens.

"Em, calm down." Alex places his large hand on her thigh and squeezes. "Any of you assholes armed tonight?" He looks back at the three of us, and I shrivel up and die inside a little.

"Nope. Not me. I don't even own a gun." I answer collectively for the group and hope I'm not wrong when Casey and Tucker both keep their mouths suspiciously shut.

We've been sitting still for too long. We're parked, but where? Why? What comes next? If this is a stakeout, what are we watching?

The questions start getting the best of me. When I can't take the silence any longer, I ask. "What exactly are we doing out here anyway?"

"You sat through the briefing, Daisy." Alex stares at me, and I feel like a student who just got caught sleeping in class.

"Not going to lie, I tuned out everything you said when you pulled up that PowerPoint presentation."

"We wait, and we watch." Emily points to the screens surrounding us. "You three sit back and shut up unless you're told otherwise."

Casey stands and walks over to the wall of monitors. What part of sit down was difficult to understand?

Touching a green button, I am certain she is not authorized to touch, I watch as she threatens to blow us to a bazillion pieces. "What are we watching, the screens are black. Do you have WIFI out here?" She taps at the screen with her fingernail.

"Do we have WIFI out here, Em?" Alex chuckles.

Emily pulls a controller out of the backpack she has squeezed between her legs that looks like a fricking video game remote you could easily buy off of the internet and hands it to Alex. "This is my favorite part." Her lips tip up into a mischievous grin that makes me nervous.

Taking the controller from her, he holds it in his large hands and makes it look like a child's toy. "You lie." He counters.

"I know, the shooting is my favorite, but this is a close second. Swear it." Using her hand, she makes a cross over her chest. I don't know what she's swearing on. Her life? Ours?

With the push of a couple of buttons on the game controller, the monitors surrounding us are simultaneously brought to life.

Fifteen screens all show different angles of the darkness in infrared light.

Some show overhead views of a dock. Another shows an empty room. Then there are hallways where people are actively walking.

Oh God, there are people. People with big guns slung over their shoulder. Suddenly, this feels so much more serious than it did when we agreed to it. This type of thing is cooler on television.

Dammit, Daisy, why didn't you listen to the briefing? Undiagnosed ADHD is not your friend. Now I'm going to die all because my brain can't focus on more than one thing at a time.

My heart flutters. My anxiety tries to get the best of me before the men with guns can.

Realizing I'm on the verge of a meltdown of epic proportions, Tucker pulls me into his body and holds me so tight that I can feel his warm breath feathering over my neck. His heart beats in my ear, and I squeeze my eyes shut for a second before opening them again.

"My thoughts are intruding the fuck out of me, Tucker." I rasp, oxygen becoming more difficult to come by with every second we're trapped inside this truck. The walls are closing in.

"I swear to God, Daisy. You're safe." Tucker leans down to catch my eyes. His warmth wraps around me and hugs me in a cocoon where the bad people with big guns in the world cease to exist.

"We're going to die." I voice my most irrational fear. I'm teetering on the edge of sanity as my fear threatens to get the best of me.

"We're not going to die tonight. It's okay to be scared. I'm scared."

Aha, I knew it! He's scared too. We can't both be scared.

*Think happy thoughts. Think happy thoughts.*

I try to muster up bravery from somewhere, anywhere. I'm not cut out for this. I've never claimed to be anything other than a florist. I don't know how to be a spy. I've never trained on how to be cool under pressure. I am not, in fact, cool.

"I'm not scared. Who's scared? Not me. Not even a little bit. Nope." I tug him closer until I'm mostly sitting in his lap.

"You sure? What's with the leg twitch?" Tucker runs his hand down my thigh and quiets my jumping muscles. His touch is innocent and yet equally as seductive as it is calming.

His lips tickle my ear as he whispers words for only me. "Being scared doesn't mean you stop fighting. It means that you fight harder. This is our battle."

I try to allow his words to calm me.

"You know I'd burn the world to the ground for you, Tucker." I prop my chin up on his chest and fain bravery that I don't feel, no matter how hard I try. This will all be over soon.

"You two are so sappy. You could do so much better, Daisy," Casey calls out over her shoulder, and I roll my eyes. Tucker's chest bounces with laughter. He knows Casey can't see my face buried in his chest in the darkness. Her interruption is well-timed and meant to shake up the intensity of our little bubble. I appreciate her for that.

I partially extract myself from Tucker's hold so that I

can look at both of them. "I think it's evident that you two got the rogue gene in the Stafford family. You're more alike than you think." The half-siblings stare at me like I've grown a third head.

"Right. I follow rules. He breaks them. We're nothing alike." Casey argues. I'm certain her defiance is merely a shared personality trait.

"Says the woman that just said she would legally represent me in a homicide case of which I was guilty." Tucker chuckles, and the continued movement of his chest against my arm soothes me.

"Innocent until proven guilty. I'm good at what I do, Yuck. Real good." Casey oozes a confidence that I wish I had. Especially right now.

"The line between right and wrong blurs sometimes. I think you both enjoy toeing it." They're both so blind to their similarities.

Turning her back to us, Casey ignores me and shifts her attention back to the wall of monitors. We weren't given directions, or if we were, I wasn't paying attention.

I have no idea what she's looking for—what we're looking for.

"Hey, Em, Daddy Stafford at two o'clock. Middle screen. Are these numbered? This is what we're watching for, right?" She points her manicured finger at an image of two men standing together on one of the monitors.

That didn't take long.

Every set of eyes in the truck follows the line of Casey's finger. I swear I hear the moment the adrenaline begins thundering through Tucker's veins. It's loud and undeniable.

I look from the screen to the federal agents that I hope are trained to handle whatever is about to happen.

"Aw, fuck." Emily takes a visible breath, appearing more annoyed with our newest development than concerned. "It's go time, babe." She looks to Alex, who only smiles as he runs down a quick checklist on the screen of his phone.

"You three, watch our six." She grabs the walkie-talkie and tosses it at Tucker. "Radio Rico Suave 9-1-1 if we get into a situation that a grenade can't get us out of. We shouldn't, but just in case. I trust the man on the other end of that radio with my life, his," she points to where Alex is strapping up, "and all of yours."

Without another word, Emily and Alex are gone, disappearing into the darkness, and wearing the shadows of the night like a second skin.

# CHAPTER TWENTY-SEVEN
# TUCKER

*Finally.* For the first time in years, maybe ever, I slept without waking with words in my head that demanded to be heard.

I'm not broken. I haven't hit a wall. I will write again, but my brain finally allowed my body to rest.

Hilton was taken into custody last night. Along with the District Attorney. Alex and Emily were right. They got them both, and we were there to witness it.

They didn't need us last night, but the closure I felt the moment my father was handcuffed and led into a waiting SUV, I think they knew it was what I needed.

Watching his demise—it's what we all needed. Somehow, two completely insane Special Agents created a path to healing for a little boy with years of physical and emotional trauma and a little girl who never got to fully realize her only wish.

This isn't over yet. Official charges haven't been

brought against Hilton, yet. Once he is charged, we will have to build a defense. There will be a trial. There is so much more to come. Yet, I feel at peace. Today we will watch the headlines as he withdraws from the Senate race.

Today I will hand the manuscript of my memoir over to my editor. I've signed an NDA, so it won't go to my agent for publication until the trial is over, but this is a step in the right direction. This is true uninhibited progress. At the same time, my notes and years of research will be submitted into evidence. I wasn't sure I would see this day come to fruition. We did it.

I thought I could do it alone. *I was wrong.*

Gently, I run my hand over Daisy's exposed shoulder blade. She fell asleep in my bed wearing a sports bra and a pair of my boxer shorts as pajamas. The green spandex creates a crisscross pattern across her spine, and I allow my fingers to follow the maze it creates.

I sit propped against the headboard with a pillow at my back and just exist. When was the last time I was able to do that?

The cool air hits my bare chest. Our shared white sheet lies draped over my lap, barely hiding my morning erection. Daisy's cheek rests on the mattress next to me. I continue my exploration of her spine, down the slight indentation it makes until I reach the elastic waistband of shorts that don't fit her and trace the letters of a brand I bought for myself.

Slowly, she opens one eye, peeking at me before opening the other. She blinks the sleep away and then smiles lazily. "That was exhilarating."

"What?" I trail my fingers back up and over her

shoulder, brushing her blond hair off of her skin and onto the pillowcase away from her face.

She sighs, unmoving and clearly content, "Stakeouts. Arrests. The freaking FBI. Owning a flower shop has been nothing compared to the level of intensity we experienced last night. We have secret agent friends, Tucker. So cool, right?"

A long slow smile stretches my face. Our memories of last night are obviously very different. "Friends might be a stretch." I counter.

I don't believe Alex and Emily Straton will be inviting us over for family dinner anytime soon. We did our job. They let me live for the disruption I caused in their lives when I crashed into Casey's.

"Emily and I exchanged numbers. She's cool. Last night was fun." Daisy continues, happy to reminisce in retrospect.

"Really? That's not what you said last night when you puked on my shoes in the back of the truck." I raise an accusing eyebrow. My boots might never recover.

"I forgot to eat dinner. Sue me." She giggles. Her excuse is lame, and we both know it.

"You weren't scared?" I tease her, tugging at a stray piece of her hair.

Hiding her face in the mattress, she refuses to look me in the eyes. "Nope."

"Not even when Emily used a bomb to break down that cinder block wall before arresting my father?"

It took Alex and Emily thirteen minutes from the time they exited the vehicle last night to the moment they approached my father. They worked with skilled precision that doesn't come with training alone but with a lifetime of having to learn how to survive on the fly. When a cement wall was the last remaining barrier to their end game, they blew it up.

"Nuh-uh." She mumbles into the sheet.

When the dust settled, four sets of gang bangers held guns pointed directly at them.

They were easily outnumbered.

"How about when his goonies had their guns pointed directly at them? If I recall that moment correctly, I think that's when you were pressing the button on the side of the radio repeatedly screaming 9-1-1."

Frantically, Daisy radioed for help, but we never saw the man they called Rico. Doesn't mean he wasn't there. The fact that the radio remained silent on the other end tells me that it's more likely that our counterpart was otherwise preoccupied with the safety of our agents.

She flips her face back to me, now rosy and red from restricted oxygen.

"I was just trying to be prepared, Tucker. Why have backup if you aren't planning to use them?"

"Mhmm, I see. So, you're considering a career with the Bureau then?" I ask, knowing good and damn well that Daisy Mae Chandler is going nowhere near a crime scene for the remainder of her life if she or I can help it.

"I mean, I'm not, *not* considering it." She shrugs as if she's got a full-fledged offer from them already sitting in her inbox, she doesn't. "But I did sign that contract with Walsh, Inc. and I'd really hate to break the terms of a perfectly good legal agreement. My future career as an agent may have to wait." She allows her words to trail off.

Her eyelashes flutter innocently up at me.

Flipping onto my side, I prop my head up on my hand and lean in close enough to her that my nose kisses hers. I allow the scent of her sweet morning breath to infiltrate my lungs, and I resist the urge to immediately tackle her onto her back. If this entire ordeal has taught me anything, it's that delayed gratification has its merits.

"That's too bad. I think you'd be sexy as hell with a badge." I tease.

Her hands stay shoved beneath the pillow half under her head, half pushed to the side of the bed.

"Oh, really? You do? Tell me more about that fantasy. Do I have handcuffs?" She asks seductively.

I hadn't considered it, but now that she mentions it, I can't stop thinking about the possibilities. My dick swells, instantly ready. Fresh from sleep, it's not a difficult jump to ready and roaring.

"Hell yeah, and those tight-ass pants that sit high on your waist and hug your hips." I allow my free hand to skate down her ribs until my fingertips hit the waistband of my boxers once more.

"You mean these hips?" She wiggles her ass, and that's all the invitation I need. Welp, I think we've delayed this long enough.

I drop my lips to hers, stealing a kiss that she gives away freely when her tongue duels mine in a power struggle that I'd be okay to never win. I tug her shorts over her hips as my lips continue their assault while she manages to kick out of them the rest of the way.

She frees her hands from between the pillow and mattress and breaks our kiss just long enough for me to gasp for air and for her to strip out of her sports bra, leaving us both completely and gloriously naked.

"You were supposed to be bad for me." Daisy sighs when I roll her onto her back and maneuver my body between her thighs. My cock taps her skin and leaves a trail of precum behind as I slide down the bed until my lips hover just over a trimmed patch of dirty blonde curls.

I stare up at the woman I was never meant to fall in love with. I inhale her scent and nearly go dizzy with need the moment it infiltrates my lungs.

"You were off limits." I kiss the inside of her thigh once, then again, allowing my tongue to draw slow languid circles on her skin until she trembles. She pulls up her knees and drops them wider, a silent plea for more.

"You set my life on fire, Tucker." She murmurs, her words slurring with drunken desire as I lean in and run my nose down over her clit, not yet touching, savoring.

Pressing my throbbing cock into the mattress, I send up a silent prayer for patience. I grip her thighs in my hands and spread her open with the pressure of my thumbs. She glistens, and my mouth waters.

I steal a glance up at her shimmering blue eyes. "We were always destined to burn, baby." My mouth drops to her clit. I feel her thighs clench the moment my tongue makes contact with her heated skin.

Using my mouth, I draw out her pants and moans until her words turn from praise to demand. I edge her just to the brink and then pull back, because I know it will piss her off. In the end, it'll be worth it.

Sitting up, I kneel between her thighs.

"Tucker," my name is a warning on her lips that I fully intend to ignore.

Taking my cock in my hand, I stroke myself once. I squeeze the base before letting my hand glide up my swollen shaft and then circle the tip. Dropping my head back but keeping my eyes on her, I repeat the motion. Then again.

I watch her pupils dilate. Swiping with my finger, I use my precum as lube and quicken my pace. I grunt with pleasure and Daisy's hands create knots in the sheets that gather beneath her. Her eyes remain locked onto my every move, and when I stroke myself a fourth time, her hips buck up, and she threatens to take what she wants if I don't hurry.

Reaching down, I grip her hip with my free hand and guide my cock to her entrance, barely nudging inside. She's fucking soaked for me. My cock twitches at the feeling of warmth—*home*. Pleasure floods my system in a wave of contentment I don't deserve. She's always been too good for me.

"You ready, Daisy Mae?" The words rumble up from my chest as I slide in further and relish the way she tightens around me. She's hot and fiery, just like the chemistry that continues to burn between us.

"Make love to me, Tucker." She whispers and her words brand my heart.

Pushing forward the remainder of the way, I don't stop until I'm fully seated. She engulfs me, the feeling no less intense than any other time before. Our bond grows stronger, and with it, my knowledge that this flame that burns between us is one that will never go out.

I try to set our pace, slow and easy. I shoot for sensual and lovey-dovey, but when she demands faster and harder, I lose all control. I plunge into her and let her body consume mine.

The sound of skin slapping skin creates an erotic backdrop of music that I would be happy to listen to on repeat for the rest of my life as my cock pounds into her pussy. Surging her hips forward, she works to meet me stroke for stroke.

Her movements are untamed; wild like the flower she is.

"Daisy Mae. Fuck, baby, come for me," I beg her, unable to stop the orgasm I feel climbing my spine and threatening to take over all coherent thought. I can't fight it, and I don't have the fucking energy to try.

"Tucker!" She screams my name, and the desperation in her voice makes the blood in my veins surge faster. The way my heart beats for this woman…it's love I never knew I had the capacity to feel.

White hot lightning licks at my neck. The world closes in around me, and the only thing I'm aware of is my body fully joined with hers. Stream after stream of hot cum fills her tight pussy. Her body contracts around mine, heightening the intensity of my orgasm.

Together, we come in unison. I give her everything I have. Everything I am belongs to this woman. *Fuck*. I wouldn't want it any other way.

Birth and unwanted status complicated my life. It was never my intention to bring someone else into this chaos. I was content to be solo forever. Content to carry the burden.

Contentment was a life half-lived, and I lived blind, unaware of what I was missing out on.

Fate had other plans.

I ate the fortune cookie before I ate my noodles, and the damn thing still came true, despite Daisy's protests. For as long as I live, I guess I'll grin like a fool up at the moon, and I'll know that this woman has made me the luckiest man on this earth.

I'll know that together we can face a five-alarm fire and come out on the other side, *mostly* unscathed.

Daisy Mae Chandler is the unluckiest lucky charm I've ever had, and she's *all mine.*

# EPILOGUE
# TUCKER

I lean forward, pressing my elbows against the gloss-covered, wooden railing. "It's been seven days, what do you think took them so long?" I whisper to Casey where she sits at a table as counsel to the prosecutor in the trial of our father.

"Trust the process, Yuck." It's all she says before straightening in her seat as the judge enters from her private chambers and takes a seat, commanding the attention of the room.

Daisy sits next to me in the same spot we've occupied during the length of the entire trial. It's been a long process, fraught with uncertainty.

"Will the defendant please rise?" The judge speaks.

Daisy takes my hand in hers, intertwining her fingers with mine. She anchors me to my seat when a mixture of excitement and anxiety makes my stomach turn with nerves. My life's work comes down to this moment.

Everything Casey and I have spent months working toward with the federal legal team.

Every risk we've taken. *Daisy*.

Every person that I've dedicated my life to fighting for. The woman with the rose.

It all comes down to this moment and the opinions of people who never had to live it.

Hilton stands with his counsel at the opposing table. His suit is pressed and his hair, while appearing only slightly grayer, is still slicked to his head and styled with meticulous precision. He's *just* arrogant enough to believe he's convinced them.

"Madam Foreperson, have you reached a verdict?" The judge acknowledges the jury, and my lungs tighten.

An older woman stands in the jury box. Wearing a pair of mustard yellow plaid pants with a visible elastic waistband and a matching plaid jacket, the woman looks like she could be someone's grandmother. She probably is. Her glasses sit perched on the tip of her nose, and her hair is tightly curled into a style I think she has manicured weekly.

"We have, Your Honor." She nods and stares down at a notepad that holds the verdict that I've waited my entire life for. "We, the jury, find the defendant *guilty* on all counts."

"Guilty!" Daisy squeals in my ear. Her hand tightens around mine. Oxygen assaults me as I take my first full breath in…a lifetime. I choke down emotion as Casey glances quickly over her shoulder at us.

The federal prosecutor speaks up loudly in the chaos of the courtroom. "Your Honor, in the case of United

States v. Hilton Stafford, the United States moves for immediate sentencing."

The judge turns to Hilton. "Is the defense ready for sentencing?"

"We are." His counsel answers dryly. I'm certain they're already planning their appeal, but we won. Today, we won.

"I concur. Court will recess. We will return in one hour for sentencing." The sound of the gavel hitting the wooden courtroom bench echoes with finality throughout the room.

Casey turns to me with tears in her eyes. She nods slowly and mouths, "We did it, Tucker." She said my name. Why does that make me feel all warm and mushy inside?

*We did it.*

"You know what this means?" Daisy leans into me, bouncing with excitement.

"My father is going away to a fancy white-collar prison for a very long time?" I kiss the top of her hair and smile. While in my heart I believe he deserves worse, this is the best outcome I think we could have hoped for.

"Oh, Yuck, you have so much to learn, young one." I guess we're back to that. Casey bumps my hip playfully as she comes around the partition that has separated us for the length of this trial. She smiles at me before digging into her bag. Pulling her hand out slowly, she turns her wrist over and opens her palm.

*The puzzle.* The missing piece.

She stares at me expectantly until I extend my hand and she drops the puzzle piece into it.

"You're not half bad for a Stafford, especially a man, you know that?"

"I've heard there's a rogue gene floating around out there somewhere."

"Mhmm, thanks—for everything, big brother." Taking me by surprise, she wraps her arms around my waist and hugs me from the side before quickly releasing me, straightening her suit before anyone notices her outward display of affection…God forbid. After regaining her composure, she spins in the opposite direction and walks to where Tyler, her *person*, stands at the back of the courtroom waiting to celebrate with her. He might also be an attorney, but this was her trial, her closure, and he allowed her ample space to have her moment.

"What do you think that was about? What do I have to learn?" I glance down at Daisy.

"I think she just said that she loves you." She sighs dreamily.

"Not that part, the part where she called me Yuck, again. Is it weird that I'm becoming partial to that nickname?"

"First of all, I think it'd be weird if you weren't. It's good for you to have family. I don't, and I wish I did. I'm glad you have someone that you share blood with that's in your life and mine. As for the other bit, I hate to say this, especially here, but I think she's going to have him," Daisy makes a dramatic motion over her throat with her hand and widens her eyes as if I can't clearly see what she's implying, "Ya know."

"That's not something I'd considered," I think back

to something I remember her saying the day we met at the little coffee shop. "It's not outside the realm of possibility. At this point, I'd rather not know. I will say this, I think she's closer to Special Agents Alex and Emily Straton than you or I realize."

"Okay, but all of that is beside the point. You've got to stop distracting me." Daisy faces me and takes both of my hands in hers drawing my attention away from where Hilton is being handcuffed and escorted from the courtroom. "Do you know what this means now?"

I lean down to meet her eyes and whisper conspiratorially. "You can marry me without fear of death or dismemberment?"

Her mouth pops open in surprise. "*Shut up*, dismemberment was on the table?"

"I'm kidding." I glance around the room to find it mostly empty. "I think."

"Your life is so weird, Tucker Stafford."

"Yeah, but you like weird. Actually, I'd say it's kind of your kink. So, maybe that makes you the weird one and me normal?"

"Now is not the time for riddles. Stay on topic, Tucker." Her hands squeeze mine.

"Fine, please enlighten me. What does this mean? Tell me, so we can get the hell out of here and grab some lunch before the sentencing."

"It means your memoir can officially go to publishing. After Hilton is sentenced, the trial will be over, and this will all be behind us. You can publish your book."

My book. When I handed the manuscript over to my agent, I knew publishing would be put on hold until the trial was completed. I wanted to publish the truth. It was important to me that, for the most part, my work was a factual representation of my life. That meant waiting until the trial ended.

*It's over.*

"Huh, I hadn't considered it, but, I guess, you're right. Also, I didn't miss the part where you ignored my proposal, Daisy Mae."

*"Not listening…"*

-

*What is done in the dark shall one day be brought to light.*
*It's never felt so good to bask in the glow cast by the flame.*

# BONUS EPILOGUE
# DAISY

"I know we discussed handcuffs, but blindfolding is a whole other level of trust, Daisy." Ignoring Tucker's incessant complaints, I pull him along Main Street and fight the laughter that threatens my not-so-innocent lips every time he trips over a crack in the sidewalk and stumbles on his feet.

"Would you hush and keep walking?" My belly tingles with anticipation.

"It's kind of hard to walk when you can't see where you're going. We've been walking for at least a mile. That's excessive, Daisy." I roll my eyes even though I know he can't see me.

Parking downtown is limited, and the guest list for this event just kept growing. For someone who swears he's a total loner, Tucker Stafford sure does know a heck of a lot of people.

I couldn't give away the surprise. Tucker's too smart

and asks too many questions for his own good. I was forced to think outside of the box to pull this off. So, I formulated a plan, and I *may* have gone a touch overboard.

I had an Uber pick us up at his apartment, where I blindfolded him. Then we drove around for an extra ten minutes in the wrong direction before being dropped off at my house, where we began walking.

"We're almost there. Just a few more steps." My smile stretches as we approach what was once my second home, my shop. There's nothing there now, just an open, vacant lot with a concrete foundation sitting between a clothing boutique and a real estate office.

On an ordinary day, the lot would be empty, and parking would be readily available at the downtown storefronts. Today isn't an ordinary day, and there isn't a single empty parking space for as far as I can see wrapped around the square.

Tucker's memoir hit national bestseller lists across the United States within a week of its official publication, and it still sits there, two weeks later. That gave me just enough time to plan a celebration of epic proportions.

If anyone deserves to be celebrated for the success of their passion, it's Tucker. His entire life he's hidden in the shadows, stealing moments or worse, being punished for doing what he loves. Today we're going to celebrate the little boy with the broken heart. We're going to celebrate a man that was willing to risk it all just to do the right thing.

"Will you have clothes on when I open my eyes?" He asks, a playful smile on his lips. He's getting off on the blindfold, no surprise there. "Please say no." His voice turns seductive, but this isn't the time nor the place. Maybe later.

"We're outside, Tucker," I retort.

"A man can dream, and I've been in the dark now long enough that I've been forced to conjure images of your naked body to keep my mind alive and active," I swear, the man acts like he's been in a coma and not blindfolded for less than an hour.

We pass my favorite bakery, the one Tucker swindled into baking me cookies the day after he inadvertently burnt my shop down. They're catering the desserts for tonight's event, and I made sure to order enough of Tucker's favorite red velvet cupcakes that we'll have a couple left over to take home.

"You're gonna regret being hard in about thirty seconds, so you might want to dial back the imagery a notch." Turning the final corner my smile widens, holy smack. The whole town's here.

I slow our steps until we come to a stop at the same exact spot I stole a kiss from Tucker's lips on one of the worst days of my life.

Bessy, as I've so appropriately named my ice cream truck turned mobile office, sits two parking spots over from the sidewalk where we stand. She's so much prettier than that damn cow. Well, she is now that she's been totally remodeled by *the* Holly Chapman.

I'm still fangirling over the fact that Emily Straton has a personal connection to one of the most famous interior designers in the country and that she was willing to work with me, small-town Daisy Mae Chandler, to design my entire fleet of mobile floral units. Seriously, what are the chances?

We gave Bessy a little extra attention, she's vintage, and she deserved it after the hell we put her through.

Tonight, we're making hand-picked bouquets on sight for all of the guests in attendance free of charge.

"Anytime now, Daisy Mae." Tucker rocks back on his heels, and I worry for a second that he's going to fall off the side of the sidewalk in front of all of the people who stare back at us expectantly.

Casey stands next to Tyler, the center in front of the crowd of people smiling back at me. Even Casey smiles, despite her constant denials of love for the man standing next to me. A man that she still refuses to call by his real name.

Ryan Walsh, the investor I never realized I needed, who has truly become a business mentor to me, talks to Special Agent Alex Straton as if they're longtime friends, which is kind of weird and slightly unnerving.

I even spy my neighbor Nelly hovering in the back corner, next to Dale, her wrinkled hand holding his. Turns out Tucker was right about those two. They were canoodling, and not at all concerned with the safety of our neighborhood. It's a good thing Tucker's made it his personal mission to ensure that our front door is locked before bed every night.

I reach up and grip the black, silk blindfold in my fingers. My hands tremble with nervous energy. "I'm going to count to ten." I lift onto my toes and whisper in his ear.

"Five or I'm removing it myself." He counters

impatiently.

Pausing my fingers where they are, I don't release him, yet. "Argumentative much?"

"Four." He counts backward ignoring me. This is my game.

"You're ruining the surprise."

"Three." He continues, complete disregard for my annoyance with him.

"Stop it!" I growl in his ear and hope the people staring back at us don't see the frustration written all over my face.

The blindfold droops where I've loosened it. "Two, is this a party, Daisy?" A boyish grin spreads across his face, and I can't help but be marginally less annoyed at his inability to let me have this moment. It's his moment. He deserves it.

I finish ripping the blindfold off before he can say one, and everyone around us yells at once, "Surprise!"

-o-
## TUCKER

Daisy sits with her legs crossed over her lap on the edge of our bed. She wears one of my sweatshirts that swallows her torso and teases her thighs but hides everything else. The fact that I know she's not wearing anything underneath brings me immense joy.

"We're going to play a game." I saunter over to her and brush her hair behind her shoulders. Pulling out the black silk blindfold she used to throw me a surprise release party from the pocket of my sweatpants, I hold the material out in front of her and wait for her reaction.

"I thought you said we were done with the blindfold." She stares up at me with a curious smile.

"No, I'm done with the blindfold. This is your punishment." I tempt her, knowing she secretly loves it when I pretend to be the bad guy. Mostly because she knows I'm not. My shins bump the bed frame as I try to pull the blindfold over her eyes, but she swats me away.

She crosses her arms over her chest, and it causes her scent to waft up in a wave of lavender and honey that mixed together are specifically hers, and it makes my heart dizzy. "For what? Throwing you the most epic party of all time?" She argues.

I place my finger beneath her jaw and pull her defiant blue eyes up to meet mine. "No, for making me walk over a mile in the dark. I know you were snickering under your breath every time I tripped over my own feet. I didn't much appreciate it."

"Please, I made up for that with red velvet cupcakes, and you know it."

Those damn cupcakes. My stomach smiles at the memory. *So good.* But not as good as I know the woman that sits in front of me is going to taste if she'll just play along.

"Just put the blindfold on, Daisy. This will be fun, I promise." Infuriating woman.

"Whose definition of fun are we talking about here?" It can never be fucking easy. I might complain, but I kind of love that about her. Keeps things interesting.

"Fine, I, Tucker Stafford, promise that if you allow me to blindfold you, it will be a mutually beneficial fun time."

A smile teases my lips. Anticipation thrums in my veins.

An idea came to me when I was blindfolded and being led halfway across the county on foot. I've been waiting to test it out. No better time than the present.

"Fine, blindfold me, but I'm not walking anywhere with you." She elongates her spine and stiffens her shoulders.

"Good, I didn't ask you to. Actually, I want you to stay here." I finish tying off the knot and then turn to leave. The floors of the cottage we now share shift and groan beneath my weight as I walk away. I leave her on the bed and trust she won't rip off the blindfold and ruin the surprise before I can get back. It's a 50/50 gamble.

"Wait, Tucker…you can't just leave me in here in the dark." My smile widens, but I keep walking. "Tucker?" She calls out louder, but I'm on a mission. Walking to the kitchen, I approach the organized chaos she left while preparing a vase arrangement earlier.

This one isn't for an order, this is hers. I've noticed that about Daisy. Her love for flowers extends far beyond creating orders for people. It's not just about the relationships, as she would have people believe. It's her calm. It's her connection to those she's lost. It's her home. It simply is a part of her.

She's left various stems abandoned on the countertop that I steal. Pulling one final stem from my leather bag I left discarded on the living room floor; I carry them back to the bedroom.

Taking one in my hand, an easy one, I hold it just under her nose.

"What do you smell?" I ask and wait.

"Don't be gross, Tucker." She pulls back quickly, unsure of what I've shoved in her face, and refusing any part of it before taking a breath. That's fair.

"I'm not. Focus, take a sniff. What do you smell?" I ask again, and this time she crinkles her nose up and visibly breathes in.

"Is that Jasmine?" She tilts her head to the side, curious I'm sure as to why I'm having her smell her own flowers.

"It is."

I drop the stem onto the bed beside her and pick up another.

"And this one. What is it?" The beautiful purple flower dangles just beneath her nose.

"Lavender." She answers without hesitation.

"She's a genius, people. Give her a round of applause." Clapping lightly, I tease her before grabbing another. "How about this one?"

"Umm…" She hesitates, and cute little wrinkles form on her forehead. "Gardenia." She answers finally.

"Right again." I drop the gardenia and am only left with one final stem. This one wasn't with the others. This one is special. I picked this one just for her.

"Okay, you get this one right, and I'll give you whatever you want." I trace my finger over the neckline of my sweatshirt that sits nestled against her collarbone.

"Anything? Seriously?" She drops her hands onto her lap. Her lips twist to the side, contemplating where I'm going with this no doubt.

"Anything at all." My heart trips. If she gets this right, I don't have another plan.

"And what if I get it wrong?" That's what I'm counting on, but I don't say that aloud.

Instead, I say, "I'm only asking for the same in return."

"I'll take that bet." She answers enthusiastically, her confidence in her skills solidified from her previous correct guesses.

"I thought you would." I hold out the final flower.

She sniffs. Her face twists in frustration, and then she sniffs again.

"Are you messing with me, Tucker?" She wiggles her lip, edging closer to the flower in question.

"No, I'm not. Swear it."

"I feel like you're cheating." I wouldn't call it *cheating*.

"One guess." My fingers create a trail up her neck.

"I…I don't know. I give up." She grumbles in defeat. But what she doesn't realize yet is that we both win.

Tugging the blindfold off, I stand in front of her with the final flower in my hand. She takes it from me and holds it up to examine it, still frustrated at her loss. I'm not.

"Why this one? Why the wildflower? I don't get it." She mumbles.

My heart swells with love. "You've always been a wildflower in a sea of roses."

"You won. What are you asking for?" She asks.

"Only forever."

Don't miss Nicole Dixon's

*Three Wishes*

Keep reading for a preview…

## CHAPTER FIVE
## CASEY
*Chambliss School of Law – Year Two*

"Casey's milkshake brings all the boys to the yard, and she's like, it's better than yours." Soph sings to her own tune from where she sits on the sofa with her laptop open. Her dark hair is pulled up into a sleek ponytail and her face is completely devoid of makeup. Sophie is naturally beautiful. It's completely unfair.

Sophie is from Tennessee, and girl-next-door is written all over her distinct features. There must be something in that Smoky Mountain water. I mean, look at Dolly.

"What are you singing about, Sophie? Marlie, what she is talking about?" I pause just inside the doorway to our apartment, leaving the door slightly ajar at my back.

Marlie proceeds to stare at her tablet and completely ignore me. Lovely.

"Your beau, obviously. We saw him drop you off last night." Sophie explains like she knows what she's talking about. She doesn't. I swear, she wants so badly for one of us to find love. Why does it have to be me? Why can't it be her? Damn.

"Shove it, Sophie. I do not have a…whatever it was that you called it." I drop my backpack down on the counter in our shared kitchen and prop my tired bones up on the tile countertop. Whoever thought tile countertops were a good idea should be strung up by their shoelaces over a lagoon of crocodiles.

Okay, maybe that's a little extreme. Falling asleep watching Nat Geo last night was probably a poor choice. This is why I stick to Hallmark movies.

I'm fully aware of my anger issues. I repeat. I am fully aware of my anger issues.

Whew, my therapist was right, that totally helps.

"Beau. I believe it's Tennessee for man. Also, survey says, you're lying. We both saw him. He's a stud." Marlie finally acknowledges me. She stretches out with a yawn on the couch across from Sophie. Her chocolate brown curls bounce over her shoulders with her movement.

That poor couch, it's so hideous that it's almost comical. I left Mr. Woo all of the furniture in my old apartment. I didn't have the heart to take anything with me when I had a feeling he might need it. It was just the two of us there at the end, and although neither one of us ever admitted it out loud, we had become a family. I miss the old man. I even kind of miss that damn cat, Hissy.

So, instead, I picked these up from the side of the road

about a week after we moved in – my contribution to our communal living space. I told the girls a little white lie about them being vintage—my great aunt's. If I have a great aunt, I don't want to meet her. Nope. My mama is dead, and I have no other family. Period. I'm not searching out a single relative that may or may not be living for the rest of my life. Been there, done that. Almost got abducted by the mafia or some shit. No, thank you.

I didn't want to tell them I went dumpster diving for our furniture. We'd just met! That's definitely not ice-breaker conversation material. I did at least disinfect them. I'm not a total barbarian.

"I am not lying. What is wrong with the two of you?" It's the truth. Steve is my supervisor down at the bar where I flip bottles for extra cash most weekends and a handful of weeknights. Okay, fine, most weeknights. He's good-looking, but he isn't my type. Please, who am I kidding? I don't have a type. There is not a single man on the face of this earth I want anywhere near me. Not a single one.

The truth is, Steve followed me home after my last few shifts. Some creeper's been hanging around, and it's just a precaution for my safety, blah blah blah. It's not the first time, and I'm sure it won't be the last. I can take care of myself, of course, but safety in numbers and all that. I top five feet on a good day. Maybe an extra inch or two in heels. It doesn't matter how well I know how to defend myself when a man twice my size shoves a loaded gun into my hip bone. We're not all trained martial artists, like Soph.

"Seriously?" Sophie looks up from her laptop. She pushes her glasses up her nose with her fingertip and stares at me like I've just grown a second head. What is it with them and this boyfriend thing?

"Yes, seriously. I'm a lawyer, and everyone knows lawyers never lie." I roll my eyes at the ridiculous assumption and try to keep a straight face. Really though, they should know me well enough by now to know this. Ask a stupid question, get a stupid response.

"Ha. Ha. Ha. *You're a law student…not a lawyer.* You think you're so funny. Everyone knows I'm the funny one. You're such a buzz kill. Romance in this apartment is dead." Sophie's head drops back on the couch with a dramatic sigh.

"You've been reading the historical romance novels again haven't you, Soph? Those men aren't real. They don't exist. Period. Move on. Besides, his name is Steve. He is my supervisor. Nothing more." Sweet, Sophie. She just doesn't get it. Romance isn't butterflies and roses, and those men in her books don't exist. They just don't. To even consider that they do is dangerous.

"Speaking of men. We've got a match on the vacant room." Marlie interrupts us.

My ears perk up. My eyes dart to Marlie. We never discussed bringing a man in. I just always assumed we'd select a woman. I thought that went without saying.

Sophie jerks back up so quickly that she nearly gets whiplash from her ponytail. "They're hired! Whoever they are. I'm done looking, and I can't afford this place split three ways much longer."

I keep my mouth shut about the money. I'm not using

that man's dirty money unless I have to. That's why I work for tips. That, and I just need to get out sometimes. If I sit still too long, I start to overthink and overthinking usually takes me to a place I don't need nor do I want to go.

I do use my trust fund to pay for what tuition my grants don't cover. Not because it's necessity, but because there's something satisfying in knowing it's that assholes hush money that's paying for my law degree. The degree that I'm going to use to defend women against self-righteous dickwads just like him.

"Says the woman that's got a shipment sitting on the kitchen counter." Marlie points to where a small brown package sits next to the coffee pot.

"Jalapenos on a tortilla! My glasses are here?" Sophie tosses her laptop off of her lap with lightning speed and hops to her feet, racing to the kitchen counter near where I still stand.

"Marlie, please translate the Tennessee food language." I look to Marlie for help.

Sophie and I come from two totally different worlds. She's country, and I'm, well, anything but country. Marlie is our balance. She's city, but she's also small town. Plus, she seems to have a weird annual obsession with cowboys. I've found it's easier not to ask.

"I think Soph's excited about the frames that probably cost more than her part of the rent," Marlie answers factually.

Sophie rips open the box and pulls out a pair of glasses with hot pink frames. The color is blinding. Pink is not in my color wheel. Actually, I think my entire color wheel is black. Just like my heart. It contrasts well against my white-blonde hair.

Sophie slides her old frames off and promptly replaces them with the pink pair. "Priorities, ladies. Priorities. I will have you know these glasses have been on my wish list for six months! I promised myself that if I nailed my midterms, I would buy them as a celebration gift to myself. Obviously."

Like she wouldn't nail her damn midterms. Soph is arguably the smartest of the three of us, and that's saying a hell of a lot.

"I bet that list was laminated." I can't help but chuckle to myself.

It's funny how the three of us ended up together. We're not a likely trio by any stretch of the imagination. I'll never forget the night I met the two of them. I was working at the bar, per usual. It was karaoke night. I don't typically pay attention to the drunk college kids embarrassing themselves via microphone. It's half torture, half hilarity. I serve the drinks and keep moving.

But that night was different. The moment the beat dropped I paused. Reba blasted from the sound system. *Fancy*. It sounds silly, but it was Mama's favorite song. I might not be country, but my mama…well, she was raised during a different time. And when that chorus hit, I couldn't help but sing along with the brunette with wild curls on stage that had very obviously had too much to drink.

She wasn't doing half bad either, but then the strangest thing happened. She started to cry. Out of nowhere. Tears. Big ugly ones. It was Marlie. The date was August thirteenth. That's when I saw Sophie. She hopped onto the stage with her out-of-place pencil skirt and glasses and hauled Marlie up onto her shoulder in one swift move.

I don't know what made me do it. I never get involved with customers, but I left the bar and walked over to where Sophie was comforting an inebriated and still crying Marlie. Hell if I know what drew me to them. But there I was, telling a total stranger to get her shit together while simultaneously pulling her hair back out of her face to keep the snot out of it.

At that moment I made my very first friends. *Ever*.

Sure, I might give them a hard time, but they're all I have. We're a trio. The very best trio. They are quite possibly the only humans restoring my faith in humanity. Other than Mr. Woo, obviously.

This place has four bedrooms. We've had a few roommates fill that extra room, but not a single one has stuck it out for longer than a month or two. The last girl was the longest. She made it an entire three months. But then she graduated over the summer and just as quickly moved out. We just can't seem to find the right fit.

We've trashed more applications than I can count. I sure as hell don't see how these two think a man is going to fit in with the three of us. Gross.

"That was snarky, Casey. Apologize." Marlie gives me the look, the one that says I'm being the asshole and need to check myself. Marlie's right. Sophie is sensitive to emotions, she's an empath. I – am – not.

"I'm sorry, Soph. It was a long day, okay?" We're barely into the first semester of our second year, and I'm already overwhelmed. The work's not difficult, it's just a lot. Throw in the hours I put in at the bar just to get out of my own head and I'm exhausted. But, what's new?

"You're forgiven, cupcake. Besides, the list really was laminated. How cute am I in these glasses?" Sophie props her hands up under her chin and bats her eyelashes up at me in exaggeration. I love these women; which is exactly why we don't need a man coming in here and messing it all up.

"You're fucking adorable. Makes me want to barf, but in a good way. You know, like rainbows." I smile at her because I know she gets me. She understands my dry humor, and for that I am grateful. Most people just assume I'm a bitch. If we're being honest, I like it that way, it keeps people away. Peopling is hard. Well, it keeps everyone away except the creeps. A fucking grenade wouldn't keep the damn creeps away. They're relentless. Which, I guess, is why they're creeps.

"Better, girls." Marlie draws our attention back to where she scrolls slowly with her finger on her tablet. "Back to the application. What do you think? He's a hockey player. Or, I guess, he was."

"Absolutely not," I answer immediately.

"Why not?" Marlie raises her eyebrows but doesn't look up from where she's reading on her screen.

"He's a man. He's an athlete. Need I say more? Hell no." I can't understand why this is so difficult to understand. We're three very educated women. We're independent. We do not need to bring a penis into this. Our dynamic works. End of story.

"You're not wrong about the man thing. He is

definitely all man. He *was* an athlete. Was being the operative word here." Marlie chews on her lip, very clearly debating something that is not up for debate.

"What? Did he submit pictures with the damn application? Tell me he didn't send you a dick pic. This is too much. Even for me." I drop my face into my hands. What is it that compels men to send pics of their genitals? Like, why? Just say no.

"Shut up, he did not send you a dick pic. Did he?" My eyes bore into Sophie as she speaks. I need someone on my side here, and she's not helping the situation. I'm so disappointed in these two right now.

A muscle in my face moves involuntarily. I think I'm getting an eye twitch.

"Is he cute?" Sophie asks and decides now is the moment she wants to test our friendship.

I'm done. Is this a joke? There's got to be a camera hidden in here somewhere.

"Are the two of you insane? That's all we need. Some testosterone-driven frat boy to bring his stinky man pants-wearing, hair gel-using, muscles in here and ruin everything. He'll manipulate our relationships and destroy our friendships. May as well go ahead and flush our law degrees right on down the toilet too while we're at it."

I'm being dramatic. I know I'm being dramatic, but I can't stop it. If we're being honest, I'm scared, okay. I'm fucking terrified. Who is this man? What do we know about him?

"Well, someone needs to schedule an appointment with their therapist. Do you feel better now that you've released that, Casey?" Sophie walks over to where I'm still propped against the counter and throws her arm around me. Always the touchy one.

"No. Maybe. Yes. Whatever. You're seriously considering this, aren't you?" I look from Sophie to Marlie in disbelief. This can't be happening.

"I've already drafted a lease." Marlie barely speaks above a whisper.

She's nervous. Why is she so nervous? Her nervous is making me nervous.

Pieces of the puzzle in front of me begin to click together slowly. Oh, God.

"Tell me you didn't send it to him. Tell me the truth, Marlie Quinn. Do not perjure yourself in this apartment while sitting on the sacred furniture." I shrug out from beneath Sophie's arm. I can't handle the touching at a time like this. This is a no-touch situation.

"I…" Marlie starts to speak but is interrupted when the door to the apartment begins to move. What idiot left the door standing wide open? Me. It was me. I'm the idiot.

Marlie sits straight up on the couch. Sophie pulls her hands up like she's preparing to throw down with our intruder while wearing her brand-new hot pink glasses.

And I freeze.

I'm frozen in the moment, unsure of what to do next. Great, I'm getting murdered first.

"Knock, knock. I'm looking for a Marlie ummm…Quinn? I think that's what the email said." I hear his voice before I see him. It's rough and masculine. It sounds nothing at all like it should. He should sound like a frat boy, or like some surfer kid. But he doesn't, not at all. He sounds like a *man*.

The door swings open wider, and I choke on my own saliva.

"Fuck." The word squeaks out from the depths of my throat at a level ten awkward on the Richter scale.

"Uh huh, on a biscuit." Sophie drops her hands down to her sides and straightens to her full height next to me, effectively dwarfing me next to her long legs.

"Don't make this about food, Soph. It's weird." I try to recover, but I can't divert my eyes from the man that stands in front of us. It's embarrassing. I'm an embarrassment to myself, but I can't look away.

He's tall, and hard in all the right places. And broad. He looks sturdy. Jesus, it's like I'm describing a fucking oak tree.

The t-shirt he wears is doing nothing at all to contain the muscles I can see from where I stand. Why do I care about man muscles all of a sudden? I've never cared about man muscles before.

He carries a stack of boxes like they weigh nothing. Maybe they don't. Maybe they're empty, but I doubt it. I wouldn't be that lucky. Nah, this man is ripped. But not in that obnoxious *I take steroids and have a tiny dick* way. His hands span the entire bottom of the stack of boxes. And the veins in his arms, they're his own personal interstate of sin. His skin is a warm toasty brown. Like hot chocolate when it's snowing outside. He looks cozy. If a man can look cozy. Can men look cozy? A cozy tree. Why am I thinking about cuddling a total stranger? I'm a tree hugger. What in the living hell is happening?

Caught. He sees me staring and smiles. Or is he laughing at me? Am I drooling? I'm drooling, aren't I? No, I can't be drooling, I choked on my saliva, it went the opposite direction.

He wears a worn baseball cap, but it doesn't hide the caramel color of his eyes. Eyes that are smiling. His eyes are fucking smiling at me. He's beautiful.

I've never seen a beautiful man. This is not good. Not good at all. I loathe myself right now. Is this like some delayed phase of puberty? There has to be an explanation.

"He's yummy. I mean, um. Hi, I'm Marlie. I believe you were looking for me." Marlie drops her tablet down on the couch without a second thought and stands to greet this total stranger.

Reality begins to settle in. In the midst of the beauty that is the man that juggles boxes in front of me in an attempt to shake Marlie's hand like a gentleman, I realize something. I was right. He's going to ruin everything.

"We need a contract. I'll be in my room. He doesn't unpack a single item into this apartment until we all sign. Understood?" I snatch my backpack up off of the counter and hurry toward my room.

"Uh-huh. Sure. Whatever you say." Marlie brushes me off as she helps the new guy in with his things.

They don't get it. Neither one of them get it. They're not listening to me. I grumble to myself as I slam my door behind me and pray to God that he doesn't start unpacking his tidy whities in the room that shares a wall with mine.

We need something in writing that will protect us.

I need something that will protect me.

# CHAPTER SIX
# TYLER

What in the sea of estrogen have I gotten myself into?

I deserve this. This is my punishment. I need to buck up and take it like a man.

But hot damn.

Academic probation wasn't enough.

Being banned from the league I've devoted my life to? Not enough.

Completely obliterating any chance I might have ever had of reconciling my relationship with my sister and best friend. Apparently, still not fucking enough.

I was kicked out of the on-campus housing within twenty-four hours of being discharged from the hospital. Twenty-four fucking hours.

Gia refused to see me. But what was worse? She wouldn't let me fucking near Damien. She had the entire floor locked down.

I didn't do it on purpose. It was an accident. The

whole thing was an accident. That's exactly what I tried to tell the panel when I appealed their decision, but no.

I moved first. I lost control. My fault. No excuses.

According to Coach, I was lucky they didn't press charges. The thought that pressing charges was even a consideration makes me sick to my stomach.

My memory of what happened that night is fragmented into small sections at best. A therapist might say I'm repressing the trauma. I still haven't been able to bring myself to watch the tape. I'm not sure I ever will. I know how serious Damien's injuries that night were…and the blood. There was so much blood, and it was my fucking fault.

I was essentially homeless for two weeks. I was surfing couches, but I couldn't keep bumming off of my former teammates. I couldn't watch them dress for practices and games that I will never be a part of. I had to move on from that life.

I can't dwell on what did or didn't happen.

This is the hand I've been dealt, and that's something only I can come to terms with.

I haven't. I haven't come to terms with a damn thing. I just keep making the next best decision and compartmentalizing everything else. It's a survival technique at best, but it's working.

I found a place to live. But the hits just keep coming because my new roommates are none other than three strong-willed, highly opinionated *females*.

Marlie, the brunette with wild curly hair. I can already tell she thinks she's in charge of the entire apartment and everyone that lives in it. She talks when she's nervous, like, a whole hell of a lot. She's glued to her Kindle when she's not studying. I've learned that her dad is a cop, and her mom is also an attorney in the small town she grew up in.

Oddly enough, I'm pretty sure she has her own personal PI firm following her around. I don't know what kind of witness protection deal her mom has her wrapped up in. All I know is that a couple of investigators reached out to me within minutes of submitting the interest form for the apartment. I had to sign a shit ton of paperwork and complete a background check. I was even required to go to some clinic and piss in a cup. The evaluation was more extensive than the testing they did for the hockey team for the University. If I wasn't so damn desperate, I would have walked, but it's the middle of the first semester. There's nothing available. Trust me, I've looked.

Then, there's Sophie. She's the eccentric one. She spends most of her time in the library. I think she must have some sort of work-study position. She always has a book in her hands. She themes her outfits to match her eyewear, which is…odd. She's so Southern I'm certain sweet tea runs through her veins. The woman makes me put a quarter in a swear jar every time I cuss in the common area, which is a lot. She's the mother of the group, passive-aggressively reminding us to clean up after ourselves daily. And she's always staring at me because she's trying to sort out my aura. Whatever the hell an aura is.

Last but most definitely not least, is my nemesis. The absolute thorn in my side and the reason I now stand in the hallway of our apartment at one in the morning with a roll of fucking toilet paper because who really buys fancy tissues in the box besides teachers?

Is every other person in this apartment oblivious to the crying?

To be so damn mean, her sniffles are fucking adorable, and I just…I need it to stop. I can't take it anymore.

I moved into this apartment three weeks ago tomorrow to be exact, and I haven't had one decent night's sleep yet. I'm on academic probation for the remainder of the year. I need sleep to function. I can't afford to slip up. My degree is the only thing I have left.

This woman. She's infuriating. She's a stick of dynamite with long, shiny blonde hair that I have an odd fascination with daydreaming about running my fingers through. I haven't touched though, I do have some dignity left.

She needs a step stool to reach the top cabinet in our shared bathroom. Oh, I didn't mention we share a bathroom? Yeah, that's fun. My dick gets hard now every time I hear running water, which is extremely inconvenient.

But the shower isn't what is keeping me up at night. The way she blasts Taylor Swift at five in the fucking morning isn't what is keeping me up at night. I mean, when does the woman sleep?

Nope. It's the crying. On the nights she works down at the local bar, which I do not condone for any woman, let alone a woman that looks so…whatever it is she looks like, she comes in and showers – cue uncomfortable dick, and instead of going to sleep like a normal human being she heads back out into the common area. She thinks she's the only one awake, but she's not.

I am wide ass awake, staring at the ceiling with a hard dick and my newly developed supersonic hearing listening to her watch whatever chick stuff I know she's watching in the middle of the night and then the crying begins.

And that is how I have ended up in the predicament that I currently find myself in. Last night I made it to my bedroom door to confront her before I chickened out like a pansy. I've never been scared of a woman before. Let alone a woman half my size, but this woman is different. She isn't just any woman. She's a hard ass, and maybe I know her routines and her schedules by now, but her moods are completely unpredictable. There's something about not knowing what she's going to say next. It makes me want to stick around for more and run for cover all at the same time.

So, I stand here, shrouded in the darkness of the hallway, and debate the merits of going back to bed or actually walking over and offering her the roll of toilet paper I stole from the bathroom to dry her tears. It's the good stuff, so, her nose won't turn pink. Then maybe the sniffles will stop and we can all get some sleep. Or maybe she'll shank me with the remote. Damn the unpredictability.

"Leave now and we never have to mention this." She speaks.

I freeze. My hand tightens around the roll of toilet paper.

"Casey?" I take a couple of steps into our living space, but I still can't see her where I know she's hiding on the couch closest to where I stand.

"I said leave. Go back to your room and pretend like you never saw me." She tries to keep her voice even, but I hear the strain in the way she whispers. She's trying to act tough. She's oblivious to the fact that I've already figured out her little secret. Interesting.

"That's the problem, I can't." I walk the rest of the way in and stop in front of the only light in the room, the television.

"And why the hell not?" She sits up on the couch and I try to hide my smile. Now isn't the time for smiles, but she's so fucking cute I can't help it.

"You're crying." I lift my hand toward her to point out the obvious.

"That's none of your fucking business." She crosses her arms over her chest. She holds the remote in one hand. Her eyes are red and puffy, but it's nearly impossible to take her seriously right now.

"It became my business when it interrupted my sleep pattern." I step toward her.

Her eyes dart to my hand. The hand that I've forgotten holds a roll of toilet paper.

"Why are you holding *Charmin*, Tyler? This just got really awkward." She giggles and a single snort escapes from her nose. It's a welcomed sound after knowing that she's been out here upset by herself.

"Says the woman wearing…what exactly are you wearing?" I take a second to really look her over now that I can see her. All four-feet-something of her. She might claim five feet, but it's a lie.

We surpassed awkward a long time ago.

She's covered from head to toe in a black contraption that zips up the front. Her blonde hair is tied up inside a hood that has…ears. Just when I think I've seen it all, an actual fluffy black tail falls over the side of the couch next to her.

Her face pales when she realizes what she's wearing, but she recovers quickly. "It's a onesie, thank you very much. They're all the rage right now."

A onesie? Like, a one-piece unit for sleeping?

"With what? The five and under crowd? It has feet. Did you buy it in the children's section?" I glance to where her feet are also covered by the same black fabric. There are hints of white scattered across the material, and a little pink up around the ears.

"For your information, this is one size fits all, and I don't even have to wear socks." She shrugs.

There is no way that getup is one size fits all.

"And a tail?"

She shifts on the couch and that's when it hits me.

"Are you wearing a skunk onesie, Casey?" I double over placing my hands on my knees. I try to keep my laughter quiet, but I can't believe what I'm seeing.

"It was the only black one they had on Amazon, and it's soft. I don't have to use a blanket, and it has pockets for snacks. Leave. It. Alone." I swear steam billows from her cute little skunk ears.

I stifle my laughter and straighten back to my full height. I walk over to where she sits. My shins touch the old, worn-looking brown couch. This thing has seen its better days, but the afternoon naps on these busted springs are surprisingly enjoyable.

"You're mighty feisty for a woman crying on the couch in a skunk costume." I bend down and touch the tip of her nose with my finger. She scrunches her nose in distaste. Her bright blue eyes sparkle even in the darkness.

"It is sleepwear, Tyler, and I am not crying. I told you already, it's none of your business." She shakes her head to rid her nose of my finger and I pull back my hand. I won't touch without permission. Even if my finger is doing some weird tingly thing after touching her skin.

"What are you watching?" I look back to where the television is paused.

Despite the late hour, I'm wide awake now.

I'm nearly knocked off my feet when Casey twists my t-shirt in her small hand and pulls me back down to meet her at her level with a strength that is surprising. Nothing should surprise me with this woman at this point. I mean, she's wearing a skunk onesie.

"Don't try to change the subject. We will never speak of this. It goes against the contract." *The contract.*

Women, they think that just because a man has a dick someone is getting fucked. Literally and figuratively. The day I moved in Casey drew up a ridiculously in-depth contract and made every person living in the apartment sign it. In short, there is no fucking in the apartment. Fine by me. I don't need the drama or distractions.

Doesn't mean I can't bite back when I'm being snapped at. Casey likes to push. I don't like to budge, and I'm too petty to let it slide. We aren't in violation of anything right now. I call bullshit.

She clutches the thin fabric of my shirt in her fist. I lean into her hold until my face is just inches from hers. My chocolate eyes bore into her blue. So distinctly different. She sucks in a breath, and I relish the effect I'm having on her. One she will die before admitting to.

"My lips are sealed, Princess," I speak slowly, not daring to look away from her. I refuse to give her the satisfaction of dropping eye contact first. I feel her grip tighten against my abdominal muscles with every word that leaves my mouth. I smirk to myself, and it doesn't go unnoticed, judging by her quick intake of breath. The air in the room surrounding us is charged with a heightened electricity. One that I feel humming beneath my skin with her proximity. This is going to be fun.

"Don't call me that." The words come out in one swift breath. She's soaked. I'd bet money on it. And dammit if that doesn't make my dick hard again.

"As you wish." I smile, and she drops her hand like my shirt caught fire.

Gia always loved the *Princess Bride*. It was one of her favorite movies growing up. Sadness washes over me for a moment, but then it's gone just as quickly. I can't afford to think about things I no longer have control over.

"This isn't that kind of movie."

I straighten back up, but instead of looking at me as she speaks, Casey looks at the frozen screen of this television. She refuses to look at me. She feels the electricity too.

"Then what kind of movie are we watching?" I ask again.

I'm genuinely curious. Is it the movie that makes her cry, or is she crying, and the movie is comforting her?

"Hallmark Christmas." She answers.

Christmas? Christmas is still months away.

"Never heard of it. It's a little too early for Christmas, don't you think?" I run my hand up behind my neck. I can't figure her out. She seems like the Halloween type. I didn't peg her for tinsel and mistletoe.

"It's a thing, okay? Sit down and shut up if you want to stay." She presses play and goes back to watching her movie as if I'm not still standing in the room right next to her like a fifteen-year-old that was just invited to seven minutes in heaven in the basement closet of a dance party. She told me to sit. She invited me into her private space.

Something about this moment feels important. I need to make the next best decision. But what is it? Do I go back to bed with my hard dick and toss and turn until daylight? Or do I stay and see what it is about these movies that captivate this woman? A woman I'm not allowed to touch. A woman that hates my guts but breathes harder when she's close to me.

She tucks her fabric-covered feet into the cushion of the couch. The action is so normal, and yet something about it makes me feel warm inside. I don't remember the last time I felt warm.

I flex my hands by my side. I want to stay. I shouldn't, but she's not crying now that I'm here. Maybe, if I stay, we can both get some sleep on the couch without the crying. Decision made.

I eye the spot next to where Casey is snuggled up on

the couch. Her eyes dart up at me, and then over to the couch on the opposite side of the common area.

"Over there. This couch is mine."

Fine. Looks like it's Christmas in October, and I have a very distinct feeling my thoughts about this woman are going to land me directly on the naughty list.

Five Alarm Fire

## **Carlton Harbor**

Book 1 – Mirror Image

Book 2 – Surprise Reflections

Book 3 – For Always

Book 4 – Starting Over

## **Silent Hero**

Book 1 – Devil You Know

Book 2 – Until Death

## **Paint by Numbers**

Book 1 – One Night

Book 2 – Two Strangers

Book 3 – Three Wishes

Book 4 – Four Score

Book 5 – Five Alarm Fire

## ABOUT THE AUTHOR

Nicole Dixon is a forensic accountant with an affinity for writing sexy novels. She loves data, coffee, travel, and making sure all the voices in her head get the happily ever after they deserve. She made the decision to begin publishing her work in an effort to teach her children to never give up on their dreams, nothing is impossible.

Made in the USA
Columbia, SC
10 January 2025